# Married to the

# Devil

**By**

## H. H. Fowler

Print Edition

ISBN: 9781790384518

*The devil can cite Scripture for his purpose. An evil soul producing holy witness is like a villain with a smiling cheek. A goodly apple rotten at the heart. O, what a goodly outside falsehood hath!*

**– William Shakespeare**

# TABLE OF CONTENTS

# PROLOGUE

*Six Months Prior – 2:33 a.m.*

postle Magnus Winthrop did not trust his wife. At all. Especially when it came down to the mysterious, urbane twenty-two year old Dean Ripley. For a man of the cloth who'd been married to the same woman for over twenty-two years and who'd outwardly displayed no blatant signs of infidelity, it was an extremely cynical position to take. But if he took into account the years he'd allowed that boy to be in and out of his home, and the countless hours his wife had spent supposedly grooming the boy into an astute businessman, Magnus' suspicions were not unfounded.

There were subtle giveaways, the main indicators being the decline in communication and the loss of his wife's monstrous sex drive, that revealed she'd transferred her affections to another male. It didn't matter how nobly she tried to explain that her relationship to Dean was purely platonic, it didn't change Magnus' perception of that ungodly connection between them for what it truly was. Erica Winthrop was obsessed with the boy and he was about to settle his suspicion once and for all. He reached over his sleeping wife and swiped her cell phone from her side of the dresser.

Easing down off of the mattress, he hastened to the en suite and locked himself inside. He did not waste any time going through her phone, looking for clues that would incriminate his wife. He checked her WhatsApp and Facebook messages, her phone texts and all of her notepads. When nothing surfaced with Dean's name attached to it, he began checking her contacts and the calls made – inbound and outbound. Still, there was nothing significant to be revealed. But Magnus was not one to throw in the towel at the first sign of discouragement. It was how he got the nickname, 'Bulldog' from his gambling cronies.

He slowed his search and began to think like his wife would think. *Where would Erica hide something she didn't want me to see?* She didn't use passwords for many of her apps, so wherever she hid anything, it would be in plain sight. Magnus' gaze soon zeroed in on one particular app, which was simply titled, *Memoire*. He clicked on it and to his surprise, there was a password attached to it. *Aha,* he thought to himself. Uncharacteristic of Erica. He had struck gold and he was not leaving that bathroom until he cracked the code.

About twenty minutes later, Magnus emerged with a satisfied smile on his face. The code turned out to be ten characters in length: *deanripley*. How could he have almost overlooked the obvious? The discovery alone further substantiated his suspicion that his wife was not the virtuous first lady she purported to be. She may have faults and failures like everyone else, and probably it was duplicitous of him to hold them against her, but he had given her sufficient time to come clean to him. In fact, her position as the first lady demanded that she be transparent – if not to the congregation, at least to him.

With disgust, Magnus stared down at the contents in Erica's diary before copying and sending the data to his email. It was only a matter of time before Erica's secret inordinate affections toward Dean evolved into a huge problem for him. No one could convince Magnus at this point that his wife wasn't planning to divorce him. The signs were there in plain sight and he would be a fool not to stifle the life out of his wife's plans by using her own weakness against her. She would do the same to him if she had the power to do so.

He returned Erica's phone to the dresser, grabbed his own and then walked out of their bedroom and into another room. If Magnus hadn't an agenda to destroy his wife once and for all, he would have punched her out of her sleep and made her confess to her dirty mind. Instead, he punched in some numbers and listened as the call went through. Shortly thereafter, a male voice answered.

"I finally have what we need to bury that heifer in her own lust," Magnus said into the receiver. He fell back onto the bed, sighing with relief. "Her family's inheritance and her influence in this community will be mine at last."

"That's only if your wife doesn't catch on to your plan before it's executed," the voice said. "I perceive she's not a stupid woman."

"In my book, she *is* a stupid woman. Who leaves their secrets lying around for anyone to find?"

"I doubt she left them lying around; you went sniffing them out like a dog in heat."

Magnus laughed. He loved the analogy. "You're still sweet on my wife, I see."

The voice insisted, "It's not that. I just don't think you give your wife enough credit."

"I assure you," Magnus said with finality in his tone, "Dean Ripley will be her downfall."

"Whatever you say, boss. I'm only being paid to follow your instructions."

"And don't you forget that. Check your email in a few minutes. I'm sending you some information I'm sure will expedite our game plan."

# CHAPTER ONE

*Present Day*

A black Mercedes snaked in and out of the wrong lane, clocking sixty miles an hour on a busy two-way strip. The driver, the motorists feared, was under the influence of alcohol, and they swerved on instinct to avoid a head-on collision. No matter how they blew the horns, which were escorted by a strong dose of profanity, the Mercedes stayed on its trajectory of destruction.

Inside of the Mercedes the occupants were drunk alright – drunk with horrendous rage and violence. First Lady Erica Winthrop shielded her face with her rhinestone-studded purse as her husband, Apostle Magnus Winthrop pummeled his right fist into the unprotected areas on her body. Stomach, thigh, arms – he didn't care. As long as his blows were inflicting pain. At one point he let go of the steering wheel, grabbed her long thick braids and yanked her toward him, endeavoring to pin her head down between his legs.

"Don't lie to me!" Magnus' wide nose was flaring, and his fair complexion had turned a fiery red. "I caught you drooling over him. He's just a boy – the same age as our son!"

"You saw what your twisted mind wanted to see!"

"You're nothing but a two-faced whore!" Magnus pulled down on Erica's braids with his right hand while he used the left to grab the steering wheel. "One way or the other, I'm gonna beat this whoring demon out of you if it's the last thing I do."

Not a stranger to fighting back, Erica swung her purse upward and connected it against her husband's forehead as hard as she could. She then sank her teeth into one of his meaty thighs. She kept the assault going until he released her locks. It was all she could do to prevent him from peeling the hair off her scalp. Somehow, they made it to the church without crashing to their deaths.

"You had better put a smile on your face," he yelled at her. "And act like the woman I trained you to be. Because I will finish you off when I'm done preaching."

"That's if I go back home with you," Erica spat.

Magnus squeezed her cheeks so hard her teeth punctured the inside of her bottom lip. He then pushed her until her head slammed against the passenger door. "Try your luck, threatening me with that garbage. I own you, and everything that you have belongs to me. You ought to be ashamed of yourself, lusting after a boy half your age."

Erica swiped the tears from her face and noticed that they had amalgamated with specks of blood oozing from her bottom lip. When her husband switched into these violent mood swings he did not stop hitting her until he saw blood or until she was in too much pain to move. Initially, Erica thought the abuse stemmed from his jealous rage over her motherly concern for a twenty-two-year-old boy. But now as the months wore on, Erica felt her husband was purposely attacking her out of pure hatred. He despised her, and she realized if she didn't make a drastic move to get away from him, she would not make it to celebrate her forty-third birthday.

The boy in question was Dean Ripley, the son of Freda Ripley – the church's sole janitress. Dean's cosmopolitan charm and his effortless ability to draw people in by his warm smile had always gotten under Magnus' skin. And very few, if any, would protest that Dean was an incredibly handsome young man, with chiseled looks that could stop women in their tracks but could turn men like Magnus into green-eyed monsters.

Despite her husband's warped perception, Erica insisted that Dean was like a son to her and even if there was an attraction toward Dean, she would never overstep her boundaries and invite trouble into her marriage, especially being in the position she was in as the first lady of First Family Worship Center. Her husband had caught her staring at a Facebook photo of Dean and Dean's fiancée. She loved the warmth and unity she felt from the photo (something she didn't have with Magnus), but that was all there was to it. She assumed her listless smile had ticked off Magnus and sent him over the edge. Before she knew it, Magnus' fists were coming at her with vengeance.

Both she and her husband took some time in the rearview mirror, fixing their rumpled exterior before getting out of the Mercedes. Erica had a small laceration at the corner of her lips, but it disappeared with a blush of powder and lip outliner. Magnus was always careful not to bloody her face because he knew she would have a lot of explaining to do. Not only to her family and friends, but to the congregation, who esteemed them highly as one of the island's power couples.

But if only the walls could talk and reveal the horror she'd had to live through, especially within the last ten years of her twenty-two-year marriage. At least she'd put up a good enough fight that would remind Magnus she would be ready for the next attack. She watched as he pulled his briefcase from the back seat, and checked his appearance in the mirror one last time before he exited out of the driver side of the Mercedes.

He then walked around to the passenger side and opened it for her. She stepped out, doing as she'd been trained by planting a kiss on Magnus' cheek for the outside cameras – though deep down she wanted nothing more than to sink her teeth into his thick lips.

# CHAPTER TWO

F irst Family Worship Center, a.k.a, FFWC was known as the church on the beach. A two-story, glass-encased building, it showcased the pristine Caribbean waters from every angle of the Barracuda Cove. The name of the island itself was derived from the early settlers of the1800s, who had been enamored with the fearsome appearance and the ferocious behavior of the ray-finned fish. They were relentlessly hunted as game and by the mid-1950s, the species began to die out. However, the name of the island stuck, and its modern dwellers ensured the history of how the island came to be was passed on in each successive generation.

Freda Ripley's deceased husband, John Ripley had been a descendant of the first group of settlers who'd migrated from the U.S. in search of new territory. Many of the wealthy white men took a keen interest in Black and Indian women, who they'd brought along as wives and concubines to add 'flavor' to the developing community. In fact, the first Premier of the island encouraged diversity. It was very easy for expats to become citizens. The offspring of such wealthy unions eventually gained great economic power. Thus, Barracuda Cove had been colonized with a mixed race of privileged people.

Freda had certainly married into a wealthy family, but her husband was a compulsive gambler, betting on anything from horse races to cockfights. And while he was able to recoup some of his winnings, he lost a considerable amount of it and dug himself deeper into debts that were too high to be remunerated. By the time Freda's only child, Dean Ripley had turned eleven years old, the family was living on government assistance programs. When that door closed, Freda got a job at the only church on the island as a janitress to help keep the family afloat.

Unfortunately, her husband continued to indulge in his gambling habits, angering the locals he owed monies to. Five months shy of her new job, he was ambushed at one of the more popular number houses, which ended in a deadly massacre. Her husband, along with five other men had been shot multiple times from a Smith and Wesson semi-automatic. Freda knew what type of weapon it was because it was her own husband's weapon that had killed him that warm July evening. He had been accosted and robbed of it during the ambush, which was rumored to have been planned for months. Her husband lived deceptively, and Freda was convinced it had finally caught up with him.

She quieted her thoughts when she saw Apostle and First Lady Winthrop enter the building. At first glance, it would seem as if the power couple was excited to get into the sanctuary the way they trotted quickly across the porcelain tiles. But Freda knew better. She was quite acquainted with their marital masquerade. An outward show to protect their public image. No one needed to tell Freda that the Winthrops had just emerged from another one of their nasty fights. She was willing to stake her life on it. The way the apostle limped while he forcibly pushed his wife ahead of him was a clear confirmation of her suspicion.

The church itself was only about twelve years old, but it was very successfully run. And it wasn't the fact that the membership was huge, fifteen hundred people at best. Notwithstanding it being the only church on the island, it was organized in such a way that it attracted the elite from every sector of the community. The lower classes attended too, but they were treated as though they were – never given first preference to the ecclesiastical perks. The atmosphere was more businesslike rather than the blessed sacredness one felt when entering the temple of the Lord.

But in terms of recreation and entertainment, FFWC was an ideal place for the entire family to come. It seemed as if the fun never stopped with one youth activity after another. Leadership rallies, community extravaganzas, children's shows – the likes of which Freda had grown weary over through the years. She was not perfect in her service to God, but she longed to encounter a true worship experience at FFWC. The leaders were too carnal in their dealings and not spiritually acclimated to cater to such needs of the people. And to Freda, most of the people didn't know that they lacked this important aspect of Christian development because they were so used to being fed the insatiable rhetoric of the world.

"Mrs. Ripley, I hope you will be joining your son and me in service this morning."

Freda spun around to the voice of Lily Rose, her son's Canadian-bred fiancée who'd moved to the island from Canada about eighteen months ago. An innocuous, wide-eyed romantic who had won her son's heart.

"Good morning, Lily." Freda rested the mop aside and dried her hands on her uniform. She gave Lily a smile that didn't quite illuminated her expression. It was a sign of exhaustion. "I will be in shortly, my dear. Let me finish these floors and I'll go change into my Sunday best."

"Please do, Mrs. Ripley. You shouldn't be working so hard, especially on a day like today."

Freda blinked her full eyes at Lily a couple of times. The grey hairs at her temples gave her a graceful look. "What is so special about today?"

"Dean didn't tell you?"

"Tell me what?"

"I guess he wanted to surprise you...ah, well, you didn't hear this from me." Lily beamed. "Two extremely wealthy businessmen are visiting this morning from Orland, Florida. Dean had been communicating with them for months, bragging about the church and how the church might be interested in forming business connections in the U.S. Dean had sent photos of his woodwork to them and they were so impressed. There were talks about signing a contract to get Dean's work into stores and having him featured in one of their entrepreneurial magazines.

Freda took the news in stride. Her son was a gifted craftsman who could fashion masterpieces out of wood, conch shells and other materials that appeared unsalable. He had an eye for detail and a brain for business. Actually, Freda was surprised that her twenty-two-year-old son wasn't a millionaire yet. He would have been if his father hadn't gambled away the family's inheritance. Seed money Dean could have used to launch his business ideas. That being said, Freda was concerned that her son's trusting nature would continue to impair his chances of success.

Each time he got close to seizing those once-in-a-lifetime opportunities, something happened that caused things to go south. Freda knew why Dean hadn't told her about these men who were coming in from Orlando because he knew she would have given him a long lecture about being too quick about expressing his aspirations. This was a dog-eat-dog world where greed and selfishness reigned supreme. People stole ideas all of the time. Freda had been trying to get Dean to learn how to test the waters first before throwing his giftedness to the wind.

"Where is Dean, by the way?" she asked Lily. "I thought he would have been here already, seeing that this was such an important day for him."

"He will be here soon. He's bringing some sample pieces of his work for his special guests."

Freda gritted her teeth. "The passion in that boy reminds me of his father. I pray that all goes well for him – for the both of you."

Lily looked confused. "Why wouldn't they go well? This is Dean's chance to show the world what he has to offer. I'm so terribly proud of him."

"So am I," Freda grumbled beneath her breath. "It's the devil in the details that worries me."

Lily had sprinted away before Freda got to finish her thoughts. Slowly, she bent to pick up the bucket of water, along with the mop and carried them to the cleaning space provided for them. Her navy blue, knee-length dress hung in the closet next to them, along with a pair of three-inch heels and a wide-brimmed hat to match. She retrieved the items and made a beeline for the women's bathroom. She washed her face in the basin and then locked herself into one of the stalls.

As she undid her uniform, she heard the bathroom door swing open with a bang. The noise was followed by loud grunts that reminded Freda of a woman in labor. Next came the ungodly invectives that took Freda by surprise. It was not so much what was being said that surprised her, but who the words were coming from.

"That bastard! I can't deal with this bloody marriage anymore. I've had enough of the embarrassment! I swear, I am going to kill that man if he puts his hands on me one more time!"

Freda peered through the slit in the stall door to confirm that it was indeed First Lady Erica Winthrop. She was not an aggressive woman per se. So for Freda to witness such an expulsion of anger was not the norm. In fact, it greatly concerned Freda. The last time someone had been murdered in Barracuda Cove, it had been the doings of an abused and neglected wife. Freda prayed that that murdering spirit hadn't gotten a hold of the first lady. Because that meant the apostle's days were numbered.

Freda almost pitched out of her skin when Erica rushed into the stall next to hers. She could hear the jingle of Erica's jewelry as she raised up the lid of the toilet. The clicking of her heels echoed within the enclosed space. All grew quiet, but then without warning, Erica erupted into a fit of uncontrollable sobs. Gut-wrenching sobs that tugged at Freda's heart. She suppressed the urge to leave her side of the stall to join Erica's only because she felt she would be overstepping her bounds. She may be acquainted with the Winthrops' little public tiffs and had even visited their home on many occasions, but that didn't mean they took pleasure in her counsel. It was her son that they kept in their inner circle, not her.

Three minutes later, Erica quieted down and then vacated the stall. Freda only left her hiding space when she was sure the first lady had left the bathroom.

✳✳✳

Magnus leaned back in his swivel chair and smiled deceptively at the two white businessmen sitting in front of him. He had invited them into his office for a quick exchange after Dean introduced them to him. Magnus had discerned that the men were genuinely impressed with Dean and he wanted to discourage it before the situation became unmanageable. He despised Dean's ambition, his good looks and his reputable character, even more now that his wife seemed hopelessly smitten with the young buck.

Erica could not fool him, feeding him lies that Dean was simply like a son to her. Such baloney! He saw the way she stared at Dean, as if she was savoring a piece of juicy steak. Magnus had noticed the change in Erica when Dean started coming over to their home as a twelve-year-old lad. Their son, Tavian was eleven at the time and the two boys had hit it off from their first meeting. Erica would always comment on how handsome Dean was and that he could almost pass for Tavian's biological brother.

Several months later when Dean turned thirteen, Erica threw a big birthday bash for him. She invited every other thirteen-year-old boy from the church and then hired a band of entertainment acts suited for the precocious teenagers. Magnus observed his wife the entire afternoon and how she interacted with Dean, even failing at one point to acknowledge their own son. That night they got into a nasty argument about it. Before he knew it, he'd punched his wife in the stomach sending her crumbling to the floor. It was the first time he'd ever laid hands on her in such a way.

"Sir, what do you propose that we do with the contract with Dean Ripley?"

The voice of one of the men jerked Magnus back to reality. His name was Gavin Osprey. He looked to be the younger of the two, about twenty-nine years old in Magnus' estimation.

"I say we do nothing," Magnus answered and then sat forward and steepled his fingers on the desk in front of the men. "I have offered you a more lucrative deal, one I hope you will seriously consider. That boy is not ready for such an elevation. He's capricious, gullible and inexperienced in the world of business. I should know because he practically grew up in my house."

The men looked at each other and then back at Magnus. Clearly, they were taken aback by Magnus' curt review of someone who seemed the total opposite in their view. But who were they to question? They didn't know Dean as well as Dean's pastor appeared to know him.

"What about your wife?" Gavin asked after a moment of contemplation. "She doesn't seem to agree."

"You don't need to worry about my wife," Magnus said. "I know how to handle her."

At those words, Erica walked back into the office. She returned to the seat next to her husband, looking composed and ready to continue the act as the submissive, supportive wife.

"Sorry, gentlemen for my brief disruption," she said. "I had to use the lady's room."

Magnus turned his distrustful gaze on her. His office had been designed with an en suite. So there wasn't a need for Erica to leave. She'd left because he'd told her to shut up about her opinions regarding the contracts that were being negotiated for Dean. As soon as the men were escorted into the sanctuary by two ushers, Magnus turned to his wife and pointed his index finger three inches away from her eyes.

"No more foolishness out of you today," he warned her. "You go in there and perform. Do you hear me?"

Erica kept her gaze parked on her husband, her blood boiling with anger. A little bit more and she would have locked her teeth around his finger and ripped it from its joint. "Whatever you want, Magnus," she said. "This is your church."

# CHAPTER THREE

When Freda entered the sanctuary, the usher took the lead and sat her nearer to the back of the building. The front pews were reserved for the elite and for the ones who gave large tithes and offerings to help furnish the Winthrops' lifestyle. Not that they needed the money. They owned one third of Barracuda Cove, inclusive of a magnificently run bed and breakfast, a limousine service and various rental properties throughout the lush landscape of the island. The church itself was worth some three million dollars in assets with a few other entities that kept money flowing in from multiple revenue streams.

Freda knew this because the apostle was always broadcasting such information on the church's locally-owned radio station. He was a real opportunist, who capitalized not only on the reward of the moment, but on other people's weaknesses to enhance his own greed. It was one of the main reasons why Freda discouraged her son from sharing his dreams with the apostle. He was not a man to trust. But her son was so enamored with the success of the Winthrops that he'd turned a blind eye to their shenanigans that continued to surface through the gossip channels.

Freda's eyes roved through the congregation, looking to locate her son and his fiancée. She spotted them sitting in the elite section. It bothered her immensely because she knew the only reason why Dean and Lily were being recognized was because of the two white men sitting next to them. Otherwise, they would have been shuttled to the back of the church – like she'd been. Unrecognized and forced to be marginalized. What a pity her son couldn't see this ruse for what it was.

The two white faces were often speaking to Dean, appearing to be asking questions about the church and its leaders the way Dean gestured toward the pulpit. Freda assumed they were the businessmen Lily had been going on about. According to her they had come because of Dean's invitation. Freda, however, perceived that things wouldn't go as planned, not that she wasn't praying that they would. But if the apostle's hand got mixed up in it, her son was certain to be disappointed. That man was a predator and it didn't matter how reverent he looked in those black cassocks. She turned her attention to the platform when she heard the first lady speaking into the microphone.

"Hello family!" Erica announced in that sales pitch voice. "I welcome you to partake in this beautiful service of thanksgiving. Give your best, give your all. For God expects nothing less from His people. As we always say here at FFWC, the Lord is in charge!"

The congregation applauded her wildly, as if they hadn't heard her say those same lines a thousand times. The congregation loved her and would not mind if she ruled in her husband's stead. However, Freda sat unmoved, uninspired. It irked her that the congregation could be so blind to this religious charade, but then again, they didn't know any better. They didn't have another voice to challenge the status quo. Freda couldn't help but notice, however, how nervous Erica appeared. In fact, she didn't look as if she wanted to be up there on the platform speaking. But one look at her husband and Freda understood why. That monstrous look in his eyes seemed to say that if Erica messed up their routine, she would be sorry she did.

"This morning," Erica went on, "we have some very special guests visiting us from the United States of America. The Apostle and I spoke briefly to them this morning, but our conversation was enriched with great potential for the foreseeable future. I don't want to speak out of turn, but we are pleased to have considered their offer to expand. Now what all that will entail will be made clear in the coming months. For now, I will say that God is doing great things here at FFWC and He is bringing us into some very powerful and profitable connections. Let the church say amen!"

The congregation whooped and hollered their approval. Freda watched her son squirm in his seat. Erica didn't mention anything about his woodwork, his connections to these white men or the fact they were here in Barracuda Cove because of him. On the surface, it appeared as if Erica was being cautious, as if she didn't want to shove Dean into the limelight so quickly, especially when contracts were still being negotiated. But Freda knew better. It was the subtle work of greed creeping in and Freda sensed that things would only get worse for her dear son.

After another five minutes of going on about the church's advancements into virgin territory, Erica turned the microphone over to Magnus. He stood at the podium with his chest puffed out like a proud peacock. He would have been a handsome man had it not been for his severe receding hairline and those beady eyes that roved suspiciously on each side of his wide nose. His only redeeming feature was that he had a smooth, fair complexion that he'd inherited from his father's multi-racial side of the family. A fifth-generation Winthrop who was by far the most successful of them all.

Indeed, in Magnus' view, there was no one as successful and as astute as he was. The king of his domain and master over those who served his ever-increasing needs. The only thorn in his side, which pained him to even evoke in thoughts, was his and Erica's twenty-one-year-old son, Tavian Winthrop. Magnus could do nothing right once Tavian was around. He always called him out on it and such scrutiny was downright aggravating to Magnus' swag.

It was one of the main reasons why Magnus had shipped Tavian off to Vancouver, Western Canada in hopes that Tavian would immerse himself in pursuing a degree in Marine Engineering and he would not have to put up with his son's pious heart. And though it'd been nearly two years since he'd seen Tavian, Magnus couldn't be happier about that decision. He could do without being constantly reminded of his lengthy dossier of sins.

He zeroed in on the two white businessmen and smiled. He was overcome with exceeding joy for yet another opportunity to magnify his influence. By the time he was done amassing his wealth, he would not only own more than half of Barracuda Cove, but his tentacles would reach far into the affluent spheres of his neighboring cities.

✳✳✳

Dean was not invited to the luncheon that Magnus had prepared for the elites, but to show his 'gratefulness' to Dean for introducing him to the two white businessmen, Magnus sent Dean trays of food, along with a promise to discuss Dean's reward at a more convenient time. In the meantime, Dean's job was to continue to scour the land for other business prospects to aid in Magnus' ever-growing affluence.

Dean may have been okay with that, especially because he trusted Magnus like a father, but Lily, on the other hand, was extremely bothered by the blatant disrespect shown to her man. She was not an outspoken person, and one not to fancy making a scene, but she needed to voice her concerns to someone. And who better to make an alliance with than First Lady Erica Winthrop? She was the closest to Magnus and probably had a better chance of making Magnus see the error of his ways. Moreover, Dean had practically grown up in the Winthrops' home, which should account for something.

When she noticed Erica coming through the main exit of the church, she left Dean's side and accosted her at once. It didn't matter that Erica looked as if she didn't want to be bothered or that she was speed-walking toward her Mercedes with Magnus' two-thousand-dollar Tom Ford briefcase. Lily wanted an audience with her and she was not going to let anything deter her.

"First Lady Winthrop...do you have a minute?"

"No, I don't." Erica eyed Lily briefly as she continued to push her strides ahead. "What do you want?"

"To talk about Dean and the two businessmen he invited to church this morning." Lily could hardly keep up with Erica's brisk pace. "I'm not trying to be a nuisance, but I think he deserves to be recognized for his contribution to FFWC."

Erica stopped her movements and turned her reprimanding gaze in Lily's direction. "How dare you approach me with this snippy little attitude of yours? I know Dean better than most."

Lily's white cheeks turned beet red. "I'm sorry, Lady Winthrop; I didn't mean to come off as rude or disrespectful. I respect you and your husband highly and so does Dean. It's just that I think Dean has so much potential and so much to offer, but he is too humble to –"

"You have every right to be concerned," Erica cut back in, softening her features and her tone. "Both Magnus and I were wrong to take credit for something we did not work for. Dean should have been recognized during my greeting and he should have been a part of that luncheon. After all, it was because of him those two white men are interested in expanding our brand in the U.S. I can talk to Magnus, but I can't promise you that anything will come out of it."

Lily was shell-shocked by Erica's candid admission, which seemed genuine enough to garner a new level of admiration. The mere fact that Erica was addressing her husband by his first name and not by his designated title, suggested to Lily that Erica saw Lily as her equal. Well, maybe not her equal. But someone she could be herself with.

"You're staring at me," Erica said to Lily. "Did I say something wrong?"

"I don't mean to, but I didn't expect you to be so transparent."

"That's because everyone thinks that I am a prude."

"I don't think that."

"Sure you do, and I don't blame you. I can be a prude."

Erica shifted her gaze from Lily toward Dean, who was standing near his 2007 Honda Civic with his hands in his pockets. From when he was a prepubescent, she had always admired his chiseled looks: thick brows set against a flawless complexion, bedroom eyes and sensual lips. However, it was his inner qualities that preceded his good looks. A real, humble chap with a heart big enough to love the whole world. He put her in the mind of the actor, Omari Hardwick. Maybe not as buffed as the actor, but Dean was an alpha male in his own right. Erica's admiration would have stopped there, but there was something different stirring in her heart when she looked at him now.

Maybe it was Magnus' persistent accusations of her lusting for younger flesh that had opened the door to such thoughts or maybe it was the custom khaki pants and plaid blazer he wore. Whatever it was, Dean seemed more appealing than she was willing to accept. She'd known him from when he was twelve years old when he and Freda became members of FFWC some ten years ago. In fact, he and her son, Tavian had been teammates on the Boy's Brigade and had spent many occasions at her home playing video games.

Such unholy thoughts of Dean, however transient they may be, were very unwelcome. Actually, she was appalled by them and appalled that Magnus would even try to inject such an abominable idea into her sanctified mind. Her marriage to Magnus may not have been loving or respectful. In fact, it was like sleeping in bed with the devil. She could do nothing without being brutally insulted and emotionally castigated to the point of wanting to kill herself. But she would never compromise her integrity, especially with a boy who could be her son. However, as Erica approached Dean, his hypnotic gaze zeroed in on her, causing her to balk at her emotions. It was the look of a man who loved what he saw. Erica's throat was suddenly parched. *Lord, what in the world is going on with me today? But Dean knows better than to be so obvious.*

"I will do my best to do right by you," she told him, reaching out to shake his hand. "You and your mother have been loyal to the ministry and loyal to my husband and me. Not to mention that you and my son have had a wonderful childhood together. What happened today shouldn't have happened. Take heart; I will take the fall for it and ensure that you get those contracts."

Dean gave Lily a disapproving look before he returned his gaze to Erica. "Just so you know," he said, "I did not put Lily up to do this."

"No need to explain," Erica said. "It's obvious Lily was motivated by love. I don't hold her accountable for wanting the best for you, which I think you deserve."

"Thank you, but I still think Lily shouldn't have made an issue out of it. I would have simply waited for the apostle to rearrange a meeting between us..." He cracked a lopsided smile, which caused Erica's heart to leap. "I have faith that he will do right by me."

*That's a lie and you know it,* Erica mumbled beneath her breath. *But of course, you have to pretend in front of Lily...* "I'm sure he will," she said. "I'm happy that Lily was courageous enough to call me out on the error of my ways. It will cause me to be more careful about my behavior."

Lily was smirking. She couldn't care less about how upset Dean was at her at the moment. He would soon get over it and realize that having the first lady on their team was the wisest move they could have made. Erica Winthrop was a powerful, influential woman with enough clout to push Dean into a glorious future. Lily only wished she'd thought of the idea much sooner. She held her hand out to Erica for a handshake.

"Thank you so much, Lady Winthrop." She beamed as she clutched her fiancé's arm. "You have no idea how happy you've made us."

"It is the least I can do."

When Erica turned around to go back to the Mercedes, her gaze collided with Magnus, who was leaning against the car with his arms folded. Rage engulfed him, though the average onlooker wouldn't have been able to tell. But Erica knew the signs. The tight jawline, the reddening of his fair complexion. The fact that his arms were folded was simply a cover to hide his huge fists. The fists he used to inflict physical pain. She took in a deep breath and proceeded forward. She, however, walked with defiance.

Her tolerance level of the abuse had reached an apogee and she was not going to continue to allow Magnus to get away with what he'd been getting away with. The time had come to fight for her freedom.

# CHAPTER FOUR

Magnus spat to Erica, "Do I look like a blithering chauffeur to you? Get your disrespectful behind in the front seat!"

"I don't think so. I'm gonna sit right here and stare at your meaty neck."

Magnus reached behind him and tried to snatch Erica's braids like he'd done earlier that morning. But she cowered away, barely escaping two right hooks he fired in her direction.

"You whore! I will deal with you when we get home," he threatened. "Don't you forget I –"

"Go to hell, Magnus! Only spineless cowards enjoy beating up on women! I've had enough of you and this loveless marriage!" The words flew out of Erica's mouth before she could stop them. But she didn't care; it felt good to finally explode. Whatever the repercussions that followed, she was ready to fight back. When it looked as if Magnus was still reeling from shock, she drove the point home with a threat of her own. "Hit me one more time and you will see another side of me! I've been a fool for far too long. The hell I look like to you? A punching bag?"

Though shaken by Erica's words, Magnus held on to his authority. "Keep mouthing off like that and I will kill you!"

"I give you permission. In fact, death sounds like heaven to me. At least I'll find some peace away from you."

Magnus slammed the steering wheel with brute force – more so taken aback by this new brashness in his wife. He wondered what caused this sudden burst of energy in her resolve. "I will not stand for this impertinence of yours," he spat at her. "You're nothing without your money. I made you into the respectable first lady you are today. Without my name, you would have been virtually undiscoverable. Your skin is too dark, and your personality is too aloof."

Tears stung Erica's eyes at the way Magnus crushed her self-esteem, but she valiantly kept her composure as she tried to steer the conversation to what was really bothering her. She was not going to take both his abuse and his insults against her business intellect when she was the brains behind everything they possessed. He needed her more than she needed him.

"Was it necessary for you to embarrass me in front of those white men like that?" she tossed at him. "My track record in making sensible business decisions is virtually impeccable."

"I didn't ask for your bloody opinion."

"Then why the hell am I still married to you? An even better question is, why not get a divorce and save us both the stress of having to pretend as if this marriage is a match made in heaven? You can keep your church. I'll leave the island and start over somewhere else."

Those words fueled the flames of Magnus' rage even more, but he wisely tamped it down because at this point in the game, he needed Erica to keep her cool, at least until his plan to destroy her took effect. After all, she was right. She was the one who possessed the higher acumen for business, upon whom he depended to keep their businesses afloat. It was her money he'd married into, and although he hadn't signed a prenuptial agreement and had pilfered a lot of it to amass his own little egg nest, Erica could still find favor in the eyes of a chauvinistic judge who could rule that she walk away with everything. All the prep work he'd put into their twenty-two-year marriage would suddenly go to nothing.

In essence, she was saying to him that he needed her more than she needed him. But there would be a snowstorm in hell before Magnus allowed any woman to control the outcome of his future. Dean Ripley was his wild card and he was going to play his hand with such swiftness and such precision, Erica wouldn't know what hit her upside the head.

"I specifically told you to keep your hands off of this deal," he said in a more composed tone, as he slowed the Mercedes to a red traffic light. "Yet you went behind my back and undermined my authority. That's the reason why I am so upset with you."

*What a crock of lies; you hate the fact that I have the power to mess up your reputation,* Erica wanted say, but she chose a dismissive approach instead. "As usual, I have no idea what the hell you're talking about."

"Don't play crazy; I saw you talking to Dean."

"So? I could have been congratulating him on his engagement to Lily, something you should have done from the pulpit a long while ago. Especially considering Dean looks up to you like a father, which is so ironic, since you can't stand him. But I could have been talking about a number of unrelated topics that don't revolve around you."

Magnus eyed Erica in the rearview mirror, eyes that were filled with suppressed rage. "I am concerned that that boy toy of yours will be the death of you."

Erica viciously ran her gaze up and down the back of her husband's head, not deceived by his Jekyll and Hyde personality. His feigned concern was born out of complete jealousy.

"First of all, Dean is not my boy toy," she clarified. "I have already explained that to you in the clearest of terms."

"Sure you did," Magnus spat sarcastically. "I see the way you look at him."

"You are so insecure, or maybe you're just trying to deflect from your conscience. Because you know as well as I do that Dean should have been given credit for his hard work. He and his mother have been loyal to us and to the ministry all these years. The least you could have done was allow those men to honor their contracts with him, instead of talking them out of it."

"The loyalty you speak of has nothing to do with how the economy is run in Barracuda Cove," Magnus answered. "It is not a commonwealth where the wealth is shared equally among the residents. Two sets of classes reside here: The privileged and the not so privileged. It has always been that way and it will not change anytime soon. Who are we to tamper with it?"

"This drivel of yours has gone on long enough. Do you truly believe that only people like 'us' are worthy to sit at the table of the elite? It was Dean's hard work that drew those white businessmen to this island and I think he should be compensated."

"Of course, Dean will be compensated, but he will never sit at the table of the elite, as you put it. It's just the way it is, and you need to accept that. You go changing the dynamics of the economy and we will incur massive chaos. Everyone will be looking for a hand-out, a piece of the pie —"

"I disagree with that garbage. You just need to admit that you're a greedy dog who wants everything for himself."

"Contrary to what you think, not everyone has the aptitude to understand money like we can. They will squander it, misuse it and allow it to get in the way of making sound financial decisions not only in their lives, but for this island and its future."

"Your greed has blinded you," Erica rejoined bitterly. "But I will not let it ruin this young man's hope of a better life."

"I'm warning you one last time," Magnus said, the coldness immediately returning to his tone. "Stay away from this deal or you will regret it."

Erica kissed her teeth before turning toward the window in silence. If the truth be told, she may have been putting on a strong front, hoping to save herself from another beat down, but inwardly, she was still terrified of Magnus. Over the years, she had witnessed just how beastly and vindictive he could be. He would find a way to get back at her, no matter how long it took. He'd taken retribution on Dean's father and on every other person who'd had the nerve to cross him. A cold, calculating man who hid behind his apostolic designation.

In Erica's mind, her freedom suddenly seemed like a transient thought that would never become a reality. The only solution, she contemplated as Magnus eased the Mercedes into the driveway of their two-story home, was to have Magnus killed.

**\*\*\***

### Vancouver, Canada – Same Time

One of Tavian's favorite hangout spots was a coffee and donut shop on 2902 Main Street where he spent quality time studying the word of God. It was ironic that such a busy place could provide such a sacred atmosphere. But it was at this place where Tavian received the revelation that God was pushing him toward a higher calling of service. At the time, it had seemed like a casual conversation with a single mother of four small children, but her words lingered with him for days...

*"What degree was it that you said you were pursuing?" she'd asked him.*

*"Marine Engineering, at the University of British Columbia."*

*"I'm just going to be blunt with you, okay? I think you're driving down the wrong lane. You should become a pastor."*

*Tavian's pink lips softened into a smirk before he burst into laughter. "You've got to be kidding. A pastor? No way!"*

*"What is wrong with being a pastor?"*

*"Well, there's nothing wrong with it, if that's what you've been truly called to do. In fact, I'm a PK."*

*"A PK?"*

*"Sorry...it stands for preacher's kid. My father pastors a church back home in Barracuda Cove, along with my mother. My father would have my head if he even imagined I was*

*having this conversation with you. The university I'm attending is considered to be in the top 50 in the world."*

*"Good to know, but I still say you can't run from your true calling."*

*"I wouldn't say that I'm running. I just don't think pastoring a church is what I'm cut out for."*

*"Think again, my friend. The way you've ministered to me today reached deep into my heart..." The woman's voice cracked into tears. "If I hadn't talked to you today, the outcome of my life and the lives of my children would have been different."*

*Tavian stared at her, waiting for her to elucidate, which caused her to hang her head in shame.*

*"I was going to drown my kids in a tub of water," she said. "And then I was going to take my life afterwards. I felt like I hadn't anyone to turn to for help." She moved her gaze from the floor back to Tavian's, who donned a stunned expression. "There is something different about you. You carry a great light, that shines through everything you say. Please consider my words...people are waiting – the world is waiting on a young man like you to show them the way..."*

That conversation had happened well over a year ago and the effects of it had driven Tavian to make some drastic moves concerning his career. Four months later, he walked away from one of the most prestigious universities in the world and enrolled into a theological program at World Embassy International Church. A church he'd been attending for the last eight months. Amazingly, in that short space of time, Tavian's knowledge of God had accelerated and catapulted him into the limelight. He was frequently called upon to teach Bible Study and lead the young men into prayer and fasting.

His mentoring relationship with the pastor of the church was only further proof that God was preparing him for an unusual assignment. Certainly, Magnus would be filled with rage over Tavian's decision and would promptly pull his financial support from his son. He then would pressure Erica to follow suit. And although Erica was Tavian's staunchest supporter, her response would be predicated on her level of fear of Magnus. So, it was one of the main reasons why Tavian didn't share this part of his life with his parents, because he simply didn't know how to break it to them. But for a twenty-one year old, it was a lot to give up for the Lord, also a heavy cross to bear. However, Tavian always found comfort in the words of Jesus found in Mark 10:29:

"Assuredly, I say to you, there is no one who has left house or brothers or sisters or father or mother or wife or children or lands for My sake and the gospel's who shall not receive a hundredfold now in this time...and in the age to come, eternal life."

That meant his sacrifice would not go unnoticed by God. Not that he was actively looking forward to being rewarded for his service, but Tavian did have a desire to be married and have children one day. And of course, he wanted some of the comforts that life afforded. He knew by heart the scripture that said, "seek ye first the kingdom of heaven and His righteousness; and all these things shall be added unto you," which gave him confidence that God was a God of His word. For now, his focus was on following the voice of God, and preparing himself for the journey that was ahead of him.

That journey would take him back to Barracuda Cove, and even though Tavian hadn't any indication when that time would be, going back to Barracuda Cove meant that he would have to confront the spirits of religion and deception. The same spirits that controlled his father and the people who sat under his tutelage. It was not an assignment to be taken lightly, but he sensed in his heart that this was the path where the Lord was leading him. To take back the spiritual reins of his native land and propel the residents toward the highway of holiness.

He stood to leave the coffee shop and in doing so, he caught an image of himself in one of the mirrors on the wall. Several people, even his own mother had told him that he bore similar physical features to Dean. Thick brows, kissable lips and a flawless complexion, to name a few. However, Tavian didn't fully agree. In fact, he didn't like being compared to Dean because there was a world of difference between them when it came to their character and their personality. For example, Dean was gullible, laidback and more susceptible to give in to temptation; whereas, Tavian was discerning, reserved and very careful in how he went about making decisions – especially regarding temptation.

Tavian smiled listlessly at the thoughts in his head. He didn't know why he was thinking about Dean all of a sudden. Maybe it was because they'd been such good friends at one time that it was hard to believe they hardly spoke to each other now. In that moment, Tavian realized that going back to Barracuda Cove not only meant he would have to confront the evils of his father, but also his strained relationship with Dean. The thought left a bitter taste in his mouth as he exited through the glass door.

# CHAPTER FIVE

Wednesday night Bible Study was scheduled to begin at 7 p.m. but Magnus left home two hours earlier under the ruse that he was going to the church office to prepare for his teaching series. But if Erica had had Magnus followed, he would have been found in one of the island's exclusive hotels on the fifth floor. The infamous Bristol Reef that had become a spot where major hedonism was practiced. Two other persons were with him: A female, who lay naked on a blue and white duvet, while a scantily-clad male sat with Magnus around a small coffee table. It had not been more than a few minutes since they'd indulged in a dangerously-attempted threesome that left Magnus' forty-five-year-old heart pounding out of his chest.

He sat with his hairy legs extended in front of him, trying to recalibrate his mind, so that he would be able to carry on with bible study in thirty minutes. But he couldn't focus on anything that had to do with God or His Word. Constantly gratifying the impulses of his flesh had made him an expert at ignoring his conscience and had driven the spirit of conviction far out of his reach. Gone were the days he once believed sex was a gift reserved for his wife, who no longer pleased him in the least. A lying, deceptive heifer who refused to admit that she was in love with a boy half her age. It was her fault he had become the abuser he'd turned out to be.

Magnus silenced his mental diatribe and focused on the issue at hand. He did not convene with his sex partners just to have sex but also to discuss the dishonorable demise of his wife. They were trying to determine how best to go about using the information Magnus had found on Erica's electronic diary.

"Let's get this straight," the male said to Magnus. He took a few drags from a cigar and then dropped it in an ashtray. He noticed Magnus' lingering gaze and readily detected that Magnus had a homo issue going on, especially the way Magnus tried to touch him in inappropriate places when they were making out with the woman. But he paid it no mind...for now. "You're not concerned that your wife will figure out we have intercepted her email? She's a smart woman. I get to observe –"

"...her every day and see how perceptive she is...yada, yada, yada," Magnus finished for him. "So you keep saying."

"I'm trying to get you to see that it won't take her long to realize that she and Dean have been set up."

"I'm counting on it," Magnus replied tersely. "Their lust for each other is too strong to be deterred by either of us. Our job, or rather your job is to simply catch them in the act."

The male stared hard at Magnus. "Why do you hate your wife so much?"

"Hate is not the issue," Magnus said. "If I don't make the first move against her, she will destroy me. Her influence over our businesses and over the church must be taken away and the only way to do that is to get some visual feed of her having sex with

Dean Ripley. I'm convinced they have done it before, maybe dozens of times, but so far I've failed to uncover this unfortunate truth. This time, though, I will not fail."

"Even if what you're saying has any truth to it, she hasn't made any decisive moves toward Dean. She knows what is at stake and I don't think she is willing to take the risk. Especially with her role as first lady."

Magnus sniggered derisively. "You don't know my wife. She is patient, calculating and very subtle with her actions. She's lashing out at me now, which shows she is becoming increasingly exasperated with me as the days go by. When the time is right, she will go to Dean for comfort. That is why I need to be one step ahead of her. The divorce court will rule in my favor if I can prove infidelity in our marriage. Then everything that heifer owns will be mine."

"That's either your greed or your paranoia talkin," the female chimed in. She scooted to the edge of the bed, allowing her feet to touch the floor. "But I'm not complaining. As long I receive my share of the booty, I'm cool with whatever the hell you wanna do. What do you need me to work on from my end?"

"Keep doing what you're doing," Magnus said. "Sexualize Dean and everything he does. Turn every conversation into an opportunity for my wife to feast upon her lust."

✳✳✳

Magnus balanced to his feet and began to put his clothes back on. "I have to leave for another meeting before I head to the church for Bible Study."

Magnus had ten minutes to work, which was more than enough time to do what he had to do. The meeting wasn't far at all. In fact, it was in the night lounge of the same hotel he was presently in. He stepped off the elevator, turned left and made a diagonal line across the foyer. He greeted the bouncer at the door, whom he was well-acquainted with. It was because of Magnus' convincing recommendation that the bouncer landed the job at such a clandestine place as the Bristol Reef. So, he was always quick to assist Magnus in whatever he needed, including keeping all of Magnus' secret meetings under the radar.

"Is he here?" Magnus asked him.

The bouncer gestured toward the general direction of the dance floor. "Yes, sitting over there by the bar. He and another dude. They've been waiting here over an hour."

"Desperate people will do desperate things," Magnus said. "Waiting will be the least of their worries."

"So I have noticed. I tried to secure the private room, but it is occupied at the moment."

"Don't bother; I will not be long at all." Magnus pulled out a crisp one-hundred-dollar bill and pushed it into the bouncer's shirt pocket. "Thank you."

"No problem, sir."

Magnus picked up his steps, moving swiftly toward the bar. He slipped onto the stool that was next to the young man he had made the appointment with.

"Mr. Derek Atkins?"

The young man rested his cocktail down and turned his body to face Magnus. "Yes, sir."

"I was expecting you to be alone," Magnus said. "You wasted no time recruiting."

"Yes, sir. I hope you're not upset. But when you asked me if I knew anyone else willing to make some quick change, I thought of Tibo."

Magnus moved his gaze between both men. Derek was short in stature and skinny, and Tibo was tall and imposing in size. Both Derek and Tibo worked at the B&B, which was one of the requirements Magnus needed to move his plan along in the right direction. If he ever hoped to bring his wife to open shame, he needed to select the right man for the job who would be able to monitor Erica's every move while she was at work. Dean's kiosk was literally footsteps away from the B&B, giving Erica tons of opportunities to express her prurient desires. All Magnus needed was one photo or one video clip of them together in a compromising position. This he had already explained to Derek during their first encounter.

"Alright, let's see what the two of you are good for," Magnus said to the young men.

Derek lifted his cell phone from the wooden countertop and tapped into his photo gallery. He showed Magnus several pics with Erica staring out of the window of the B&B and a few of them with her on a deck, appearing as if she was looking out toward the ocean.

"What the hell are those?" Magnus asked.

"Pics of your wife staring out the window at Dean. I caught this one of her when I came into the foyer to collect some travel information for a guest –"

"Do you understand what compromising position means?" Magnus cut back in. "How do I even know what the hell she was staring at? Dean isn't anywhere in these photos."

Derek apologized profusely. "I will do better, sir, but it's hard to catch them alone. She only stares at him and never goes out to the beach to visit him."

He pulled out an envelope containing one thousand dollars. Resting it between the men, he said, "This will be your final payment if you don't come up with something I can actually use."

Derek reached for the envelope. "Trust me, sir, I will do better next time. How much time have I got?"

"If you have to ask that question," Magnus spat, "then you are already starting off on the wrong foot. Make it happen or forget you ever met me."

Magnus stood, his gaze lingering on Tibo. Tibo never said a word, but Magnus could tell he was sizing up the situation, seeing whether or not it was worth his involvement. Magnus liked that, because it showed Tibo had an analytical mind. Such minds were needed for an operation as complex as this. Derek, on the other hand, appeared too anxious and too stupid. Magnus was not sure if he could trust him yet.

**\*\*\***

The way the Winthrop's bed and breakfast had been built, as with many of the wooden structures on Barracuda Cove, the

44

crystal-clear waters could be seen shimmering in the hot sun. It gave the waves their white beauty as they rolled and dissipated at the shoreline. The bed and breakfast itself was in a prime spot, surrounded by an array of tourist activities, including deep sea fishing and touring the dark caves dug by the first settlers for protection from hurricanes. People from all walks of life visited Barracuda Cove and when they needed somewhere to stay during their visit, Erica was among the first in accommodations to receive their business.

In fact, the B&B was presently operating at a ninety percent occupancy rate and with this time of the year being the Thanksgiving season, Erica presumed that the bed and breakfast would be filled to capacity by the end of the week. There were twelve rooms in total, each outfitted with two king-sized beds, a large en suite, a kitchenette and a quaint sitting area. In addition, the guests could dine for breakfast, lunch and dinner outdoors on the veranda, enjoying the picturesque scenes of the beach. There was a hot tub, two saunas and a tennis court for those wanting to work up a sweat.

There were seven employees in total who worked at the B&B and who helped Erica run a very smooth operation. Justin was considered to be the manager (though he was simply called the team captain), he dutifully worked the front desk and oversaw the entire operation. Especially when Erica was not around. Ian and Sandra worked the front desk along with Justin, as the twenty-four-hour schedule was divided into three shifts. Derek was mainly responsible for concierge services, while Tibo patrolled the grounds as the handyman/pool guy. There was one laundry attendant named Brenda and one cook named Rochelle.

Erica ensured her guests received the ultimate tourist experience because she understood firsthand as a business guru that customer service could either advance or destroy an establishment. Howbeit, observing the wonders of nature and running the family's businesses weren't the only things that kept Erica's attention. There was a secret pastime of hers that was growing in intensity as the days rolled by. And although she would never confess it openly to anyone, Erica knew in her heart of hearts that it was creating a problem and it was not going away by ignoring it. She had to do something about it before it destroyed her.

Whenever there was a lull in her busy hours, she would walk over to the western side of the B&B where the beach vendors set up their kiosks and stealthily watch the way Dean interacted with the tourists. An aficionado at expressing hospitality to strangers. His infectious smile instantly made the tourists feel welcome. He wasn't the only skilled artisan on the beach, but his magnetic personality seemed to trump his competition's. In a matter of minutes Dean could sell several of his masterpieces with little effort while his competition struggled to sell one. And it had been that way ever since she'd helped Dean erect his kiosk four years ago.

An incredibly handsome bloke he was. The kind of handsomeness that would make a married woman burn in her flesh. Similarly, to what she was experiencing right now, despite her trying to suppress such inappropriate feelings. Dean's ripped abs weren't making it any easier on her. Like many of the young men who walked the beach in the glistening sun, Dean's naked body was only covered with a pair of shorts and flip flops. His complexion reminded her of hazelnut, a smooth, velvety texture, so regal-looking that it was impossible for one not to take notice and stare at one of God's greatest masterpieces.

"He's easy on the eyes, isn't he?"

Erica straightened up from her slouched position and leveled her gaze on one of her high school friends, Netty Edmonds. She and Erica were the same age, but Netty looked five years younger. Not that Erica looked her age. In fact, she looked younger than her forty-one years. It was just that Netty was a strong supporter of surgical enhancements. The last time Erica saw her, she'd gotten a nose job, breast enhancement and Botox injections in her lips. Amazingly, her artificial augmentations looked just as real as the women naturally blessed with them. And it provoked a bit of envy in Erica.

"You don't have to admit anything to me," Netty said, as she tailed Erica back to the front desk. "I could see the devil's lust in your eyes."

*You sound just like my husband,* Erica wanted to say, but instead, she pouted and replied correspondingly to what she'd said to Magnus, "The only thing you saw was what your dirty little mind had already concocted. I was looking at how beautiful the ocean appeared this afternoon."

Netty gave Erica a mocking smirk. "Mmmm hmm...And I was born on the moon. Look at me, darling. Does it look as if I could be conned by a cougar? I'm the queen of 'How Stella got her groove back.' The boy is an unforgivingly gorgeous stud who would send any woman tripping out of her mind, and you're no exception. You'd be a fool not to partake of something so beautiful and forbidden."

"Shut up with that nonsense," Erica chided. "I'm a married woman and the first lady of FFWC. I won't be seen with or take advice from an unscrupulous heifer such as yourself."

Netty countered without missing a beat. "You old hag, release that built up tension before you crop out from that sanctimonious demon."

An awkward pause ensued before both women exploded into laughter. They had been well-acquainted with each other's temperament for a while and neither could completely sway the other. Erica, the reserved, all-business type and Netty, the outgoing, riotous she-devil. They were the epitome of the axiom that opposites attract.

"You are a bad influence on me," Erica said, as she curbed her laughter. "I don't know why I entertain you in my presence."

"Because a part of you wishes you could be me."

"Oh, please. You sleep with men half your age and you see that as something to brag about?"

"At my age, it is a compliment. Furthermore, I worked too hard and paid too much money to let this slamming body go to waste. And you shouldn't either, even though you could use a little enhancement." Netty waved her hand in the general direction of the beach. "Look around. This island is swarming with young, hot, heterosexual males, who would drop their pants in a heartbeat for some pocket change."

"Disgusting!" Erica spat. "I don't have the slightest interest...I'm happy with my appearance and therefore, I don't need any enhancements to ensnare anyone. You keep forgetting that I'm off the market as a single woman."

"But are you having good sex?"

"It's irrelevant to make an argument out of whether I'm having sex or not with my husband. I am still married! Do you have any idea what that means?"

"I guess you do have a point," Netty said, pursing her fiery red lips. "But you should consider bleaching your skin. Your complexion is a bit on the dark side."

Erica gasped in mock surprise.

"Don't get me wrong; you're not bad looking. I like the braids and urban bangles you have going on there. Makes you look like an Ethiopian queen."

"Coming from you, I don't know if I should take that as a compliment or a sarcastic remark."

"Take it however you wish. You just need to learn to stop being so uptight and live a little."

Erica shook her head at Netty in a deprecating manner. "So it's just sex for you, huh? What about love? And the sanctity you can only find in marriage?"

Netty returned a similar deprecating smile. "I was trying not to go there, but you pushed me. You're the last person who should be giving advice on love and marriage. Because your marriage to Magnus is nothing to be desired."

Erica stiffened at Netty's words. They may be true but that didn't give her the right to throw what Erica had confided in her in Erica's face. Netty must have seen the disappointment in Erica's eyes because she was quick to mumble an apology.

"I didn't mean it the way it sounded," Netty said.

"Of course, you did, but I won't throw a hissy fit. You're right. Magnus and I are far from being the perfect couple. In fact, we fight so much until I have a great fear that one of us will soon end up killing the other."

Netty squeezed Erica's hand and smiled. "If I didn't know you, I would have called you stupid, but for now, I will say that you've been rather patient. It's about time you got fed up with this situation. If it were me, I would have busted Magnus' eyes out of his head and left his behind a long time ago."

"You can say that because you're not in the situation," Erica rejoined. "I used to think to myself, *The day my husband puts his hands on me, I am walking out my marriage –*"

Erica paused, her attention being drawn to the bustle of tourists on the outside. Well, that was what Netty had initially assumed until she zeroed in on what Erica was truly focusing on. Dean was sitting on a ledge, leaning back on his elbows. His bare chest glistened in the sun, making his skin glow like a halo was surrounding him. The mohawk haircut he donned was fresh and masculine, enhancing his already alluring features. It was quite clear to Netty that Erica was smitten with him.

A short time after, a white girl walked toward the ledge, propping herself onto it. Dean sat up and gave her a kiss on the lips. Within seconds, they were enraptured in a very animated conversation, stimulating Dean's facial muscles into a toothy grin. Only one girl could get Dean to laugh like that and that was Lily Rose – Dean's beloved fiancée. The couple was truly enjoying each other's company. It was to Erica's chagrin that she had to look upon such blissfulness while bemoaning the lack of her own.

"As I was saying," Erica said, as she reverted her attention back to Netty. "Very often our words don't mirror our actions. We say we're gonna do one thing, but end up doing another. I'm ashamed to admit that I'm terrified of Magnus and of what he will do if I walk out of the marriage. Sometimes I think the only solution to get away from him is to have him killed."

Netty's eyes widened with feigned alarm. "Listen, girlfriend, I don't know if I should be privy to such information."

"I didn't mean it –"

"Understand me, clearly...I love you, sweet girl, but I ain't fixing on going to prison for being an accessory to murder."

"Oh, Netty."

"Don't 'oh Netty' me! I ain't going to prison!"

"I may be a prude, but I'm not stupid. I would never follow through with –"

"Killing your husband? It was just a passing thought? Right. We all have thoughts about killing someone at least once in our lives. Sometimes we imagine it's the only way out of a situation and hopefully plan the perfect murder, so we don't get caught. But I know a scorned woman when I see one and you are one scorned woman! What's to stop you from going through with it?"

"For heaven's sake, stop with these crazy insinuations of yours!" Erica spat.

Netty exploded in laughter. "Don't go getting all bent out of shape on me. I was only joking with you."

"You shouldn't joke about something like that."

"Well, it was you who mentioned killing your husband."

"Do you have to keep on saying it? What if someone overhears you?"

"You see, this is what I'm referring to when I say that you're so uptight, taking everything so serious. Live, laugh and enjoy life. Stop sweating the small stuff." She squeezed Erica's hand one last time. "I didn't mean to ruffle your feathers – well, I guess I did."

Erica cut her eyes disapprovingly at Netty.

"What I meant," Netty tried to explain, "is that I agree that you've wasted enough years suffering under Magnus' oppression. It's time that you did something to make you happy. If you want Dean, I say, go after him...if you don't, I will."

Hot air flew out of Erica's nostrils. "Netty...go! In Jesus' name!"

"Okay, I'll take my leave now, but think seriously about what I've said. Dean isn't gonna wait around forever. He's getting married to that white chick in few months, isn't he? Which means your time is even shorter than it has been."

Netty slipped off the stool and was through the exit before Erica could recover from Netty's unscrupulous, devilish suggestions. But if the truth be told, Netty's words weren't too far from the truth. Erica was simply too embarrassed to admit that Netty had unwittingly exposed her wicked thoughts. But didn't everyone have wicked thoughts now and then? It was part of the dilemma existing in a corrupt world run by Satan. However, that didn't mean that people usually follow through with such evil thoughts. This was what she was trying to explain to Netty, but Netty was too cynical of human behavior.

Turning her attention again to the beach, Erica observed through the huge glass windows Lily sporting with Dean. A feeling of envy suddenly overcame her. She didn't hate Lily. In fact, she loved Lily for Dean, but didn't care to be reminded of the misery in her own marriage. In that moment, Dean's eyes seemed to blink in her direction and for a brief second, his handsomeness sent shockwaves coursing through her veins. If she minded her wayward flesh, she could stare at him all day. He just seemed so happy and carefree – qualities she'd long dreamt of experiencing ever since she had sense of her wants and needs. A quick prayer fell languidly from her lips:

*Lord, please guard my heart and don't allow it to lead me down a path that I will regret.*

# CHAPTER SIX

J ustin was Erica's right hand man and he took that position seriously. When he didn't see Ian show up for his shift, he called him immediately to find out what was going on with him. Justin would have let Ian off the hook this one time if Ian's behavior hadn't warranted concern. Ian had always been present and had always been on time for work. Justin never had any problem with him. That was until about six months ago.

Even Ian's demeanor had changed. The once bubbly, witty young man was now withdrawn and sad most of the time. The times Ian did laugh and try to be his old self, Justin could see he was putting on and that there was something serious boiling beneath the masked exterior. Justin's attempts to get Ian to open up about his problem always ended in a dismissive smile. Ian insisted that everything was going well and there was no need for concern. However, Justin was relentless and would not stop until he found a way into Ian's head or whatever it was he was involved in.

"Where are you?" Justin spat into phone.

"I am five minutes away," Ian answered, adding quickly, "My car broke down."

"Again? That has been your excuse basically every day this week, and last week, and the week before that."

"I know...I'm working on getting a new car."

"Why don't you catch the public bus and let Sandra drop you home when your shift ends?"

Justin could hear a prolong pause in Ian's voice. "I never thought about that," he finally said, but didn't belabor the point. Instead he decided it was time to end the conversation. "I'm like literally a minute away now. Please cover for me until I arrive."

"Don't I always?"

Justin hung up the phone just as Erica was coming out of her office. She appeared to be making her way toward him, but instead, her strides rotated in the direction of the eastern window. She stopped several inches away from it and allowed her eyes to take in the picturesque view of the beach. Justin wanted to talk to her about Ian, but he decided not to bother her. Instead, he walked outside toward the valet parking booth. Derek looked as if he had his hands full. There were two sets of guests waiting to have their vehicles parked. In addition, there was a family of four struggling with their luggage moving into the foyer.

"It looks as if you could use some help," Justin said, coming alongside Derek.

Derek breathed a sigh of relief. "Oh man, thank you! I could definitely use the help. I hate November and December."

Justin suppressed a smirk. "So does everyone around here. They may be our busiest months, but they are also our most profitable months."

"Oh really? Maybe for you, but not for me." Derek grabbed the guests' luggage and put it on a cart. He then tossed their car keys to Justin. "Take the car in the front and park it in space 10. I will be right back."

"No problem, buddy. That's what I'm here for."

Justin was smiling, but in the back of his mind he was sensing some friction from Derek. But he didn't read too much into it, thinking that Derek was not good at multitasking. He had expressed a few times that he needed an extra pair of hands, but Erica didn't see the need, especially when there were enough employees on staff to assist each other.

On his way back to the valet parking booth, Justin spotted Tibo, shaping up the hedges that lined the walkway on both sides. He greeted Tibo with a huge smile, but Tibo barely acknowledged him before returning back to the work at hand. Justin shook his head in a confused manner, wondering what the devil has gotten into his coworkers.

***

"I have to get back to work," Lily said. "I've already spent ten minutes over my allotted time."

She pulled Dean in for a tight hug and took in his fresh aquatic scent. It instantly reminded her of that day when she'd walked out on the beach and was immediately accosted by his charm. He'd run up to her to show her a three-foot eagle he'd carved out of oak and told her he would sell it to her for half the price if she bought a pair. In addition, he would personalize the wooden masterpieces with any words of her choice, free of charge.

Though he appeared very unassuming in personality, he was confident enough to impress her with his persuasive skills, which seemed to blend well with his striking features. It was this humble but gregarious combination that added to Dean's appeal. It was her first week in Barracuda Cove and as an expat, she had come to fulfill a six-month contract for an international bank. She had only visited the beach that day to bask in the sun and get acquainted with the tourist attractions of the island, but it turned out to be more than she'd expected. Little did she knew that six months would turn into eighteen months and a strong desire to migrate to Barracuda Cove.

Dean's determination to sell her his work lasted all but three minutes. She bought the wooden pieces, not because she really wanted them, but because she was too enthralled by his presence to turn him down. For a white Canadian girl who hadn't any inclinations toward dating someone outside of her race, she was shocked to discover that she may have experienced love at first sight. That day when she'd left to return to her apartment, she'd asked herself a dozen times how was it possible that she could be smitten with a man she'd only known ten minutes. That first encounter had whetted her appetite, and soon Lily found herself going to the beach every chance she got.

And although it was Lily who initially pursued Dean's attention, they quickly grew fond of each other's company. She would bring him lunch and then help him sell his artifacts to every tourist that walked by his stall. She would even take a few samples of his work to her place of employment, hoping to generate interest in a young man who Lily was so proud to showcase. When she called back home and told her parents that she'd found her soulmate and that it looked as if she would be taking up residence in Barracuda Cove, they brushed it aside as another one of her flights of fancy. But to their surprise, she'd already accepted Dean's marriage proposal without their knowledge.

"I'm not ready for you to leave just yet," Dean told her. He clasped her fingers with his, bringing her creamy knuckles to his lips. "I have something to show you."

Lily smirked, noticing the tiger head bracelet on Dean's wrist. She could see that it was an expensive piece of jewelry. He'd worn it ever since the day she'd met him, which prompted her to ask him about. He was honest enough to tell her that it was a gift given to him when he was sixteen years old, but he wouldn't reveal who'd given it to him. Lily figured it was from a past girlfriend he'd valued very much, but because she didn't want to make it an issue, she decided it was best to pretend as if it didn't bother her. Dean's winning smile was enough to paralyze any negative thought in her mind.

"You're always showing me things...and giving me things..."

"Because you're the only one I want share everything with," he said. "Do you want me to stop?"

"No, silly," Lily giggled. "I just want you to know how much I appreciate you and all of the hard work you take on, just to make something of yourself."

"Well, you're a helluva an inspiration. I feel your support and your unrelenting desire to see me succeed. You went out of your way to get Erica to see my worth."

"So you're not upset that I intervened?"

"Nawh, but I will say that it made me uncomfortable, because you know I don't like forcing anyone's hand to do anything for me."

Lilly took Dean's hands and guided them around her waist, while she locked hers around his neck. "You are so gifted. It bothers me when I see people overlook you or try to swindle you because of your good nature."

"If you're still going on about the incident that happened this past Sunday, I'm over it."

"I knew you would be. Unlike most people, you don't hold grudges." Lily stared in Dean's eyes and was reminded why she loved him so much. He possessed an incredible amount of grace to accommodate the idiosyncrasies of human behavior. "You may disagree with me, but I see Apostle Winthrop as an opportunist who capitalizes on other people's vision."

Dean playfully tapped her on the nose. "Be careful talking about your pastor in such a negative way."

"Technically, he's not my pastor," Lily said. "I'm only attending FFWC out of my love for you. I know that sounds horrible, but it's the truth. If there had been another church on the island, I would have suggested we go there."

"Oh ye of little faith," Dean teased.

"I do have faith, but it's not in Apostle Winthrop, especially after I saw what he did to you on Sunday. He knew you were the reason those businessmen came to Barracuda Cove and yet he intentionally kept you from interacting with them."

"Lily," Dean singsonged. "Let it go. Didn't you get Erica to look into it for us?"

"I did, and we have yet to hear from her."

"It's only been a few days; give her some time."

"Time is of the utmost importance when dealing with a contract of this magnitude...I know you want me to relax and I will, but I need you to answer this one question for me: Did those businessmen try to contact you on their own since you saw them on Sunday?"

Dean's eyes dithered with a hint of disappointment. Mr. Gavin Osprey was the one spearheading the connection and had left a text message on Dean's cell phone, promising to contact him, but he never did.

"That is what I was afraid of, Dean," Lily said after Dean didn't respond. "Apostle Winthrop may have already convinced those men to side with him."

"You don't know that. And even if he did, there will be other opportunities. I will not live my life begging for someone to give me a hand up."

"It's not begging. It's fighting for what rightfully belongs to you."

Dean leaned forward and pressed his lips against Lily's pale pink lips. It immediately softened the fire in her eyes. "I know you want what's best for me," he said. "And I can easily see how that could become one of the controlling factors of our relationship. Because I too want the best for you and would fight to ensure that you have a good life. But I would rather have you by my side than any amount of success my gift could produce. I trust that God will allow things to work in my favor, regardless of how hard the enemy fights."

Lily hadn't any comeback for Dean's sound words. But it was this side of him that inspired her to become the best wife she could possibly be, even when she didn't fully understand Dean's philosophy of life. She didn't come from a family that talked much about God or where much emphasis was placed on godly values. They never attended church, hardly ever read the Bible or found pleasure in hanging with people who were considered uneducated zealots. So being with Dean was both a spiritual and emotional learning adventure. She gave him an apologetic smile.

"I'm sorry for allowing my passion to get the best of me," she said. "I love you so much and I want you to know that I will always be by your side – no matter what we face."

"I believe you." Dean lifted Lily off her feet and spun her around, kissing her on the lips. "But I've kept you long enough. Go before I cause trouble for you on your job."

Lily held on to Dean's arm. "Didn't you say you had something to show me?"

"I do, but we got sidetracked. I will show you at another time."

"You promise?"

Dean leaned in for another kiss. "Go before I change my mind."

His face illuminated as he watched Lily's feet sink in the sand, frustratingly slowing her pace. When she finally made it up the wooden deck and onto the sidewalk, she waved wildly at him before she skipped out of view.

"Are you Dean Ripley?"

Taken aback by the unexpected intrusion, Dean spun around to address the voice. His gaze took in a boy, who could be no more than fifteen years old.

"Who is looking for him?" Dean asked.

"I was told to give him this." The boy handed Dean a folded piece of paper. "See that he gets it."

The boy ran off.

Dean unfolded the piece of paper and read its contents. Puzzled, he refolded it and stuffed it in the back pocket of his shorts. His gaze pierced through one of the huge glass windows of the bed and breakfast, catching Erica staring at him. She immediately backed away, which made Dean all the more suspicious of her actions. He ran a nervous hand back and forth through his mohawk, which he rarely did unless something shook him greatly.

If there was any shred of truth in that letter, he knew he had better keep his distance from Erica Winthrop – as far away as humanly possible. Because he was not going to be the poster boy for the biggest scandal in Barracuda Cove.

# CHAPTER SEVEN

B y the time Erica pulled up to her white palatial home that evening, she was completely spent. Nothing unusual, as she was always tired after working nine full hours, six days out of the week. The atmosphere at the B&B was sedulous, which kept her on her feet all day. However, Erica wished she could say that her energy today had been spent physically on the rigors of the establishment, but rather emotionally. Staring at Dean and fueling inappropriate thoughts about him had driven her to a state of mental whimsicality. She struggled to make sense of her feelings for Dean and the distasteful outcome of allowing herself to fall prey to those feelings. Such vacillation could indeed drain one's cerebral reserves.

But never had she been more embarrassed in her life than when he looked up from the beach and caught her gawking at him. She'd never expected him to do that. It was as if he knew she was watching him. Now, how would she be able to convince Dean that her feelings for him were only platonic? They had to be because if not, everyone would know that she had been denying the truth all along. Magnus, for one, could not handle the truth, even though he insisted he *knew* the truth. He would probably end her life without giving her any more chances to explain herself. If for this reason alone, she had to keep her distance from Dean. What good could come from such a blasphemous relationship anyway?

She shoved those thoughts to the back of her mind as she stepped out of her Mercedes. The first thing she noticed that was out of place was a black limousine parked across the driveway. Her husband's navy blue Land Rover was in its designated spot, which was another strange sign because her husband was never home this early on a Wednesday night. It was set aside for poker, where he and three of his 'ecclesiastical' friends would gamble thousands of dollars late into early morning at an undisclosed location. Of course, this was yet another one of her husband's secrets that allowed him to accumulate quick cash in a safe environment without having his image publicly stained as a preacher.

Erica couldn't care less where her husband and his friends played their games; she simply didn't want them to bring that filth into their home. She'd seen how gambling and alcohol had destroyed both her grandfather and her father. The more losses they incurred, the more they gambled until they began to steal to cover their financial responsibilities. There was a serious gambling spirit hovering over Barracuda Cove, and it had been the unfortunate demise of strong family structures and of several notable men and women who attended FFWC.

When Freda told her that Dean's father had been murdered because of his gambling habits, Erica could identify with the loss. Because she too had lost her father in a similar manner. A few months after the divorce of her parents, her father was robbed and then shot to death after winning a sizeable amount of cash at one of the hundreds of gambling houses that existed on the island. Her grandfather was a gambler too, but had drank himself to death. The alcohol had knocked out both the left and right lobe of his liver and left him swollen like a balloon.

Thank God her mother was wise enough to hide a portion of the family's fortune in a lucrative investment account without her father's knowledge. By the time Erica's mother died ten years later, the money had almost tripled its original amount and Erica's inheritance was secured. That was until she married Magnus without requiring him to sign a pre-nup and now he, too, had been smitten with the spirit of gambling. A lethal combination because now her inheritance was under constant threat of being taken away from her. And although Erica adamantly kept her concerns before Magnus, he persisted in stating his gambling habits had nothing to do with her or their marriage.

Gambling was his way to unwind from the stresses of the church. In fact, he was a skilled gambler, judging by the fact that he rarely lost. Ten thousand dollars in one sitting was not uncommon for Magnus to bring home from his winnings. Anything less was considered a bad night and he would not rest until he recouped whatever loss he had incurred, even if it meant he had to play several nights back to back. It was during these times that the responsibilities of the church rested heavily on Erica as she would have to create an excuse for her husband's absence.

A blast of wind from the sea scattered her braids over her smooth chocolate face as she continued to move across her manicured lawn. High winds were common throughout the year, especially for the residents who lived closer to the water like the Winthrops. She could have walked the ten-minute commute from the bed and breakfast to their home, because everything they owned, including the church was located on one long stretch of land that divided the island right and left. But with the potential danger due to the recent increase in Magnus' backstabbing ways, Erica didn't take the chance in risking her safety. He'd crossed so many people that Erica was surprised her husband was still standing or that someone hadn't tried to bomb one of their business establishments.

When she turned the doorknob and entered their two-story foyer, she was immediately greeted with vulgarity, echoing from the dining room area. Words unbecoming of men who held such holy titles in the church. Right then and there Erica knew for certain that Magnus had brought that gambling spirit into their home, as if what he was already putting her through wasn't enough. But she would not stand for it. She dropped her handbag and keys on the table in the foyer and marched toward the unholy commotion.

Her presence startled the men, one of them jumping up as he rooted for an apology. Erica recognized him as one of the white businessmen that Dean had invited to Barracuda Island. But she looked past him and parked her indomitable gaze on her husband. Their dining table was covered with money from one end to the other and a few empty beer bottles were scattered throughout. Erica didn't think she could become any angrier.

She spat at Magnus, "It's not enough for you to keep your gambling habits confined to wherever you hide to do it; you had to bring it into our home? What is the meaning of all this?"

Magnus, being in the presence of his company and not wanting to appear weak in their eyes, allowed his ego to swell. He whipped Erica with his half-drunk eyes, letting her know he wasn't going to let her humiliate him like that. Slowly he rose from the table, his arrogant strides landing him six inches from Erica's face. He bared his teeth like a Pitbull.

"Apologize to these men for your disrespect," he instructed her.

"I am done being your puppet," Erica lashed back. "It's time you showed me some respect. I do your every bidding, slaving all day at our businesses while you contaminate –"

Magnus backhanded Erica in the mouth so fast, she spun a full one eighty and toppled to the floor.

"Gentlemen, please see yourselves out," he said to them. "My wife and I need to have a talk."

The men stared in shock. They knew if they left, they would be leaving a helpless woman to defend herself against a half-drunk madman. Despite this, they grabbed what they could from the table and made a hasty exit. Who were they to get involved in a private affair between a married couple?

"If you cause me to lose those contracts with those men," Magnus threatened, standing over Erica, "I will beat your insolent behind until you foam at the mouth. This is *my* house and I do as I want in it. You don't question me, you stupid, black heifer! How dare you try to belittle me in front of my guests?"

Magnus reached down and snatched Erica's throat. The pressure he applied caused her to grab, scratch and kick like an obstreperous cat. One of her kicks connected with Magnus' stomach, which sent him flying backwards into the China closet. Too drunk to feel any pain, Magnus was quick to rebound. He grabbed her by her braids and dragged her violently down the hall to their half-bath. Erica's strident screams were loud enough to shatter every glass window in the house, but Magnus refused to be deterred by them. He was going to teach his disrespectful wife a lesson.

"Magnus, don't do this!" Erica pleaded. "I take back my words!"

"Too late for that," Magnus grunted. "I told you if you kept mouthing off at me like that I was gonna kill you. Today is your lucky day!"

"Magnus, please!"

"Shut the hell up! The world will be a better place without you."

He kicked open the toilet and pushed his wife's head into the urine-filled water. After fifteen seconds, he allowed her to come up for air, wheezing and coughing like an asthmatic patient. But just when she had caught her breath, he dunked her head down into the toilet once again, this time for twenty seconds. Choking and nearing complete disorientation, Erica begged for her life, which was ironic because it had only been a few days ago that she'd given Magnus permission to kill her, thinking she would be better off dead than to remain alive in a loveless marriage. Now that she was at the mercy of his rage, death didn't appear as welcoming as she'd imagined. She wanted to live.

He looked as if he was about to put her down for a third dunk, but he grabbed her legs instead and dragged her into the middle of the hallway. She didn't know what made him stop, but she was thanking God that he did because Erica was certain she would have drowned the third time around. There was hardly any breath left in her.

"Next time," Magnus hissed, "I won't stop until I'm sure you're dead. Let this serve as a reminder for every time you think about stepping out of line. I run this joint; not you! Clean this mess up. I have company coming over in the morning."

He clobbered her in the stomach before he staggered away and up the stairs to their master bedroom. Erica did not move for at least an hour, more out of fear of provoking her husband than the physical pain her body was in. Tears rolled down her cheeks as she gathered herself and limped toward the kitchen. She didn't even know why she was limping because she didn't remember injuring her leg. But when she looked down at her right ankle, it was pouring blood. She must have kicked it against something while she was fighting for her life. Seeing the blood made her cry even more.

She pulled a first aid kit from the pantry and as she was tending to her wound, the cordless phone came to life. She ignored it, as the intensity of the pain in her ankle seemed to have doubled in minutes. She prayed to God that it wasn't sprained because it would be another lie she would have to concoct. Like the one she'd concocted a few Sundays ago when Magnus bruised her neck by choking her out of her sleep. She had to explain to the Women's Auxiliary Leader that the abrasions were the result of an acne flare up.

If only she could build the courage to leave Magnus, she would do it in a heartbeat. But fear had her visualizing the worse scenario of what would happen if she did. Apart from killing her, Magnus could come up with a hundred ways to exact revenge. He was that calculating and that evil to ensure he was the one who would succeed. It didn't even matter at this point if she left with just the clothes on her back; she just needed to leave. This charade wasn't working anymore, and Erica felt her fear may drive her to do something drastic.

The voicemail machine soon kicked in, bringing Erica's anxious thoughts to a halt. It was her son, calling from Vancouver, Western Canada. A feeling of comfort washed over her because she could depend on him to leave her spirit encouraged. She balanced to her feet and hobbled as fast as she could to intercept the recording.

"Hey, Tavy. What's up?"

"Hey Mom. Is everything alright?"

"Even if they weren't, they are now. I am so happy you called."

"I hope I didn't wake you; you work harder than any woman I know."

Erica fought hard to suppress the tears in her voice. How could she explain to her son that his father had almost drowned her in a toilet filled with urine? Tavian would probably book a flight out of Vancouver that very night and confront his father. He knew that she and Magnus didn't have the best marriage, and even though Erica had been careful not to reveal the darker side of her relationship with Magnus, she knew Tavian would still stand up for her. In fact, it would kill him to know the amount of physical and emotional abuse she'd had to endure over the years. Many times, she'd been tempted to bare her soul to him, like she was feeling at that moment.

"You know me so well. I haven't too long arrived home from the B&B and I was trying to unwind." Erica winced as she lowered her butt back down on a chair and began firing questions at him. "Is something the matter? Are you okay?"

"Well, it depends on how you perceive it," Tavian said.

"What is it?"

Tavian didn't bother to beat around the bush because he realized if he didn't use this opportunity to tell his parents about the changes in his vocation, he would continue to procrastinate and begin feeling as if he were living a lie.

"I've abandoned marine engineering to study theology," he sputtered. "Please tell me that you're not upset, because I really feel as if this is the path I should be on."

Erica wasn't surprised, and she certainly wasn't upset. Her son had always had a special love for the Lord ever since he was a little boy. She wouldn't dare tell him he'd made a wrong move because she didn't think he had. It was Magnus who'd shipped him off to Vancouver and forced him into something he didn't want to do. In fact, she'd warned Magnus that their son would rebel and then despise him for what he'd done. She would be the one to say she told him so. The news was welcoming because she knew it would be the perfect antidote to strike against Magnus' poisonous venom. Their son was a snare to Magnus' unrighteous soul.

"I am not upset," Erica told her son. "You know I never really wanted you to go to Vancouver in the first place."

"But it's been two years and I never heard you discourage me from pursuing something you knew my heart wasn't into. So naturally, I assumed you accepted what Dad had done."

"I wanted you to come to this decision on your own, without me negatively or positively affecting your judgment. It is important for you to be assured in your own soul that God has spoken to you."

"I guess I can understand that, but you ought to know your support means the world to me. I wouldn't have minded hearing your thoughts on the matter." There was a brief pause on both ends before Tavian spoke again, "Do you think Dad will be upset?"

"You know he will," Erica said. "But it doesn't matter. You're old enough to make your own decisions. He shouldn't have forced you to do something you didn't want to do to begin with. So the blame will be on him; not you."

"But once he finds out what I've done, he will pull his financial backing away from me and I'll be forced to come back home."

"I have money of my own, you know; I have always helped you and I'll do it again. But I thought you wanted to come home. So what does it matter if your father responds in a way to spite you? You can study theology right here in Barracuda Cove."

"It's not that I don't want to come home. I feel as if God wants me to stay here in Vancouver for a little longer for the purpose of spiritual training. I am attending an anointed church and the pastor is very proficient at operating in the gifts of the Holy Spirit."

Erica didn't know what to say to that. The church that she and Magnus pastored was far from spiritual, much less operating in the gifts of the Holy Spirit. Erica doubted Magnus even knew what it was to be a true follower of Christ. Because from the time she married Magnus, he'd lived a carnal, self-absorbed life that revolved around money, lies and deception. Had she known beforehand that Magnus had only married her to cover his backside, she would have thought twice about accepting his proposal.

"Tavy, please come home," Erica said. "I need you now more than ever. I will ensure that you get the spiritual training you need."

"How?"

"You are the legitimate heir of First Family Worship Center. What other way is there for you to learn?"

"If you're alluding to me sharing office space with Dad, it is out of the question. He's not going to allow me to have any say and you know that."

"I will talk to your father −"

"Mom, I don't think you understand. This move has nothing to do with you or Dad. God is in charge and I am inclined to follow Him."

Tavian didn't talk much longer to Erica after that. And even though he'd told her he loved her before disconnecting from the line, Erica could tell that he was bothered by the way she trivialized his point of view. It was not that Erica didn't value her son's decisions, because she was the one who'd said he was old enough to make them.

But having Tavian back home in Barracuda Cove would upset the dynamic of her abusive relationship with Magnus − something that Erica was banking on. Because without Tavian, she could kiss her escape plan good bye − if she ever was to be successful at actually going through with it. Tavian was a true man of God and he was not going to stand for any measure of injustice, especially concerning his mother. But how could she get Tavian to see her point of view without appearing like an opportunist?

She rotated to the freezer behind her and pulled out an icepack. She usually kept them on hand because there was no telling which day of the week Magnus would give her a busted lip or injure some other body part. Nothing to look forward to, but it was the way she'd survived for years. Always living in fear for her life. She hobbled to the living room and eased onto the chaise lounge, so that she could elevate her ankle. After she'd nursed it for about twenty minutes, she drifted off into a lugubrious sleep.

# CHAPTER EIGHT

Freda was baffled to see her son lounging over the kitchen counter at six-thirty in the morning. By this time, he would be on his way through the door to catch the first set of tourists who strolled the beach at 7 a.m. But he was not attired in his work shorts and sandals as she was used to seeing him every morning, which told Freda that her son was really bothered by something. His head was down, staring at a piece of paper.

"Whatever you're reading must be really interesting."

Freda's voice caused Dean to scramble into a straightened position, hiding the piece of paper behind his back. Freda instantly knew there was something in it her son didn't wish for her to see.

"Mom, you really shouldn't be sneaking up on a brother like that."

Freda adjusted her wig, suspicion roving in her eyes. "What are you hiding from me?"

"What's that?"

"Don't deny it because the guilt is all over your face."

Dean walked toward his mother and kissed her on the cheek. "Has anyone ever told you how fabulous you look in your uniform? And love the wig. One day I'm gonna make enough money for all of us and you won't have to go back to that old, dirty job."

"That *old, dirty* job has kept food on the table and the mortgage paid all these years. Thank you very much!"

"But you won't have to struggle much longer, my darling sweetheart. You feel me?"

"You're trying to change the subject and I won't let you." Freda followed her son into the short hall that led to his bedroom. "Does this have anything to do with those white men that visited the church last Sunday?"

Dean feigned a bemused look, which somehow accentuated his easy-going persona. "What are going on about, Mrs. Ripley? You ought to know it's much too early in the morning for all this harassment."

Freda stuck her hands into her sides and gave her son one of those, don't-play-with-me scowls. "I want you to know I know all about your business deal. Lily spoke to me and she told me that you've been sending photos of your work to these men, hoping they'll give you a contract."

Dean didn't bother to refute his mother's claims. "Lily shouldn't have burdened you with this."

"Don't use Lily as a scapegoat. She was under the impression that you had already told me, seeing that I *am* your mother. How many times do have to tell you that you can't trust people so easily? You are a gifted young man and there are many sharks out there who would love to take advantage not only of your gift, but who wouldn't hesitate to crush your good heart."

*If I haven't heard that a thousand times already...*"You don't feel that I can trust Apostle Winthrop?"

Freda paused in her rant as she thought about the question. She didn't trust Magnus as far as she could pitch him over a fence. But she did not want to be known as the one who sowed seeds of distrust in Dean's mind about his spiritual leader. After that treacherous stunt Magnus pulled Sunday past, she was hoping Dean would have come to such revelation on his own. Maybe her son did see the Apostle for who he was, but Dean had a way of making situations appear harmless.

"Why did you single him out?" she asked him. "I wasn't talking about anyone specifically."

"Because he's the only one I've been confiding in recently about my dreams. Those white businessmen offered to come to Barracuda Cove when they saw the work I posted in an entrepreneurial forum. We exchanged contacts information, and they promised to go over some contractual ideas with me when they arrived. Nothing has been made official."

"Then why didn't you explain that to me?" Freda questioned. "Because Lily certainly made it seemed as if the agreement had been settled."

"You know Lily can get overexcited sometimes, but she means well. However, I didn't say anything to you because I knew you would continue to feed your worries into my spirit."

"Is that how you view my concern for you?"

"Is that what you call it?" Dean quipped.

"What else could it be? I've had dreams about your future, just as I've had dreams about your father's. He didn't listen –"

Freda wasn't finish scolding her son, but Dean quieted her by asserting his position as a man and not a twelve-year-old boy. "Mom, no disrespect to you, but I am not my father. I move on my own merit," he told her. "You must let me live my dreams the way I see them. That doesn't mean I won't value your advice. But by the same token, that does mean I need you to respect my decisions. Even when they don't line up with your expectations."

Freda gave her son a disapproving glare. She didn't mind him making his own decisions. It was his heart behind the decisions that concerned her. He was so nonchalant about how the world truly works that Freda feared Dean's gift would never get the recognition it deserved. His father had a similar perspective on life, though far from being honorable in her eyes, at the end of the day, it had destroyed him. John Ripley's impulsive and deceptive gambling habits may have led to his murder, but it was his inability to understand that one couldn't do wrong and get by that had sealed his fate. Had her husband listened to her warnings, he may have still been alive today.

"If that's what you want, I won't bother you anymore," Freda spat. "Obviously, you have outgrown my wisdom."

Dean stared at his mother, detecting a measure of hurt in her inflection. He walked over to her and placed his arms around her.

"That is not what I'm asking of you," he said. "Apart from Lily, you are the only woman who means the world to me. I will never outgrow your wisdom..."

*There is a third woman, Freda said to herself, who I know means more to you than Lily or I ever will. I just pray you don't let the devil fool you into making any crazy moves.*

"...I just need to feel like a man," Dean continued without the slightest clue of what his mother was thinking at the moment. "I'm twenty-two and sometimes I feel as if I'm still a boy, running to his mother's every beck and call."

"Well, I do admit I can be a bit smothering," Freda said. "But that's only because you're all I've got left. When you and Lily are wed and you all move into your own place, I'll be left alone."

"Don't sound so dismal. Lily's apartment is within walking distance of here."

Freda took her son's hand away from her shoulders, shocked by the insinuation of Dean's living arrangement. "You never told me you were moving in with her."

Dean walked over to his bed and propped himself on it. "It will be my apartment too, once we add my name to the lease."

"But it's still her apartment!"

"It will be ours. I will be taking over the monthly payments."

"It's the principle behind the whole matter. Why can't you stay here? It may only be a two-bedroom shack, but it belongs to the Ripleys. It's yours and you shouldn't be ashamed of it."

"Mom, didn't we just have this discussion about three minutes ago? It's my decision to make."

Freda threw her hands up in surrender. "If I continue going back and forth with you like this, I will be late for work."

Freda swirled on her flat heels and marched out of Dean's bedroom. Had she not been so upset, she wouldn't have left without pressuring Dean to reveal the contents of the letter she'd caught him reading. She was certain it had something to do with her son's connection to those white men. But if her son wouldn't tell her, she would find out by some other means. Better yet, she would go on a two-day fast and ask the Lord to send those white men back to Florida if their connection to her son was not divinely assigned.

Dean breathed out a sigh of relief. He couldn't wait for his mother to leave, so that he could have his privacy. He hoped his mother had forgotten about the letter altogether because he would never want her or Lily to ever lay their eyes upon it. It could tarnish Erica's character and their faith in her – no matter if the letter came from Erica or not. He should have gotten rid of it the minute he'd read it, but his incredulity kept Dean skimming the contents, as if trying to determine if it was a hoax:

*What would you do for $50,000? It can go a long way in helping to plan your upcoming wedding. Hopefully it will be enough to fund your business ventures. However, if you need more, you know I'm good for it. I only need you to agree to one thing and I think you know what that is. I have loved you since you were twelve years old. If you're interested, respond to this anonymous email. I suggest you create an anonymous email too, to protect our identity. You know I'm big on confidentiality, which means I won't say anything if you won't.*

The words or the panache of the letter didn't quite fit Erica's personality. At least not the Erica *he* knew. She would never be so brazen with her affections, which means it could be someone trying to frame her. She was a powerful woman with a lot of money, influence and social standing, creating an enticing target for blackmailers. Then again, as Dean set the letter aside and reached back into his memories five years before, he questioned his own assessment of the woman he thought he knew. Because there was a side to her that was both scandalous and mysterious.

And even though she fought valiantly against such unwanted proclivities, or rather deny that they even existed, the fact remained that Erica had secrets. And one of those secrets was that she cared for him more than she was willing to admit. The proof had always been there. She bought him gifts – expensive gifts – whether it was his birthday or not. She would often purchase his wood designs, just so he would have money in his pocket to carry him through the week. And he would get this weird vibe from her whenever she stared at him, as if she was undressing him in her mind. Similar to what he experienced on the beach yesterday when he caught her staring at him from a window.

As Dean recalled, Erica didn't care what her husband or her son thought about her actions or that her actions could be construed as inappropriate (because as far as she was concerned, she was simply committed to his success). For a seventeen-year-old boy at the time with his hormones spiraling out of control, Dean would be the first to admit that he misinterpreted Erica's kindness as unbridled lust. At least, that was what she'd told him that it was – a total misunderstanding. And she would strongly discourage him from even considering that anything could develop between them.

Hence the reason why he'd minimized his conversations with Erica and had refrained from visiting the Winthrops after Tavian left for school. With Tavian gone, he hadn't any real excuse to visit anyway. Furthermore, it would look quite strange for a young man of his age to seem as if he was encouraging such a close-knit relationship with the first lady. People could interpret her overt kindness as unsuitable, not only for a married woman, but as one of the leaders of FFWC. She had also promised to pull back and allow him to operate his kiosk without interfering. Eventually, the gifts ceased, along with the frequents visits to his business.

He owed much to her for her support in the early years of whatever little success he'd had. That was why it was not a surprise to him that she'd sided with Lily to get those contracts into his possession. Like Lily, she was excited about his success. But with such strange memories, and an 'anonymous' letter purporting to be from her, Dean was forced to rethink the intentions she'd displayed back in those days. Was it truly motherly affection or were her feelings for him finally getting the best of her?

Maybe it was his upcoming marriage to Lily that had provoked her to such desperation; maybe she regretted the fact that she may have missed a once-in-a-lifetime opportunity of exploring love with a man half her age. Whatever the reason, Dean knew he could not allow this letter to pull him back into that dark place. A place where his hopes were high only to have them dashed by Erica's fear of a scandal. He was going to marry Lily and spend the rest of his life with her. That was what he should be focusing on right now, not trying to chase after a fleeting dream that would never come to fruition. Erica would make sure that it didn't.

Yet the question lingered. Should he confront her about the letter? If he did, what would he say? That he thought she was being framed? What if the letter had truly come from her? How was he supposed to respond? He hadn't visited the Winthrops' home since Tavian matriculated to Vancouver, nor had he had a heart-to-heart conversation with Erica in years. But Dean wanted to believe that he and Erica were still comfortable enough with each other to discuss something like this. Again, the proposal didn't sound like a wholesome deal, nor like the woman he knew, but Dean had learned a long time ago desperate people did desperate things.

He brought the letter up to his face and read the contents once more. Against his better judgement, he reached for his phone and took a few minutes to create a new email account. He then typed into it the email address given in the letter. If Erica was truly the person behind this proposal, he would know for sure by the answer she gave to his question. An answer only she would know.

# CHAPTER NINE

L ily stepped out of the shower and draped herself with a pink housecoat. She didn't have to be at work for another two hours, so she would use the time wisely. She then sat down in front of her vanity mirror and began her skincare regimen. Her complexion hadn't always been as smooth and creamy as it was now. About a year before she met Dean, she'd suffered with terrible cystic acne, so red and painful that she often shied away from washing her face. Her dermatologist had told her that her breakouts could have been stress-related and advised her to reduce her stress levels if she wanted to see any improvement in her skin.

At the time she was working an eighty-hour week, recovering from the wounds of a cheating ex, and on top of that, dealing with the crazy antics of her parents, who couldn't understand why she was still a virgin. They surmised that that was the reason her boyfriend had been unfaithful to her. The liberal views of her antagonistic parents had always garnered heated arguments between them. According to them, she studied too hard, she worked too much, she wasn't eating enough, she wasn't socializing enough, and the list of cynical remarks continued, even up to the point when she'd migrated from Canada eighteen months ago.

It was why she struggled to tell her parents that she'd gotten engaged to a wonderful young man. She knew they would bombard her with a million questions and none of them would be positive. They would first have to get over the fact that Dean was Afro-Caribbean before they would even remotely share in her happiness. But at this point, it didn't matter what her parents thought. Lily was so relieved and so grateful to have met a man like Dean who she could spend the rest of her life with, that disowning her parents had become a great welcome idea. But Lily knew that Dean would not allow her to do that.

He was big on forgiveness and had told her that if she expected God to pardon her sins, she would need to do the same with those who'd wronged her. So Dean was the reason she'd been calling her parents twice a month, keeping the lines of communication open. They didn't have much to say except for the same dreary questions they'd always shoot at her: *You found a man yet? Are you a lesbian because you don't look like you like men? When are you coming back to Canada? Your father and I could use the help. We need some money to pay these bills.* She dreaded calling them each time, but she'd promised Dean that she would.

Once she'd applied the final step in her skincare regimen, she grabbed a stack of wedding magazines from her dresser and dropped them on her bed. She then walked into the kitchen and fixed herself some coffee. The next hour would be dedicated to organizing her wedding colors, from her bridal party down to the trinkets she and Dean would give away as thank-you gifts. However, as she was about to settle into the task, her cell phone vibrated next to her on the bed. She normally didn't ignore calls except when she really couldn't help it, so she answered without studying who the caller was.

"Hello?"

"Why the hell you sound so chipper this morning?"

Lily sat up straight. "Mom?"

"Sound as if you were expecting someone else."

"Yes, ma'am. I mean...no, ma'am –"

"You were supposed to send me some money. I'm still waiting."

"But I just sent you fifteen hundred dollars last week."

"I told you that your father and I need three thousand dollars, but you got sneaky and only sent half of it. You didn't think we would notice? We have piles and piles of bills to pay."

"And so do I, Mom," Lily rejoined. "If I continue to –"

"What bills do you have? You're making more money than you know what to do with. Half of it is being wasted on those stupid books, anyway. It's all you ever did when your father and I would give you lunch money...you never know when to stop overloading that pea brain of yours. That's the reason why men continue to run away from you, you're too bloody shrewd for your own good. You will never keep a man if you don't loosen up and act like the rest of us."

Lily tried to tune out her mother's voice, but it was hard to ignore the bitterness and the hatred she detected in it. It was like her parents' whole aim in life was to see her fail. But little did they know, it only gave her the motivation to keep pushing. Especially now that she was engaged to a decent, kindhearted man, who didn't berate her or feel inferior because of her intellect. Lily couldn't care less about inviting them to her wedding. In fact, if the decision was left up to her, it would be years before she told them she'd gotten married. She could do without the negative vibes coming between her and Dean.

Lily blew out a long breath after her mother had paused in her vicious rant. "I will send fifteen hundred dollars first thing tomorrow," she said in a resigned tone. "But know that I can't give you anything else for at least a month. Whether you believe it or not, I do have bills and –"

Lily's mother disconnected the line without the courtesy of saying 'goodbye.' It pierced Lily's heart, but she refused to shed a tear over it. Her mother was not going to ruin her mood. She picked up one of the wedding magazines and let it draw her in for the next two hours.

✳✳✳

"We've got a hit!"

"Indeed, we do!" The female accomplice hunkered down next to her male counterpart and clicked into the fake email account Dean had responded to. "That didn't take long, did it?"

"Lust is such a strong magnet; it doesn't care about your status in life."

The female gave a hearty laugh. "We are a prime example of that blessed truth. I'm almost twice your age, but that didn't stop you from pursuing me."

"I didn't pursue you; I happen to be a victim of circumstances. Being constantly locked up with you and Magnus in a sin-charged atmosphere has weakened my resolve."

"Whatever! You loved every minute of it."

"I don't expect you to understand. Once I'm done with this gig, I'm going to the United States. I can barely tolerate observing Erica at the B&B every day, knowing I'm being paid to destroy her."

The female playfully patted the young man on the shoulder. "Good for you; you still have a conscience. Get over it and forward this email on to Erica. And you had better make sure she takes the bait. It'll be the only way we can electronically monitor her WhatsApp messages, her phone calls and texts. I'm certain the use of these will increase significantly once the conversation picks up between her and Dean."

"I have my doubts, but you and Magnus are convinced that this will work."

"It will," the female spat. "Erica is obsessed with Dean and it's only a matter of time before she lets down her guard."

# CHAPTER TEN

T he 7 a.m. jasmine-scented breeze woke Erica and lured her toward the wraparound balcony attached to the master bedroom. She almost collapsed at the threshold of the French doors when her ankle gave way. It was a sharp jolt of reality of the horror Magnus had done to her last evening. The scenes played over and over in her head like a galling scorched record. The hurtful words Magnus had slung at her, calling her a stupid black heifer. She couldn't believe her life had come to this.

Her cheeks were stained with tears as she'd cried herself to sleep; things were never going to get better and she was only deceiving herself into a living a life that could only end in tragedy. Her freedom was crucial and better it be sooner than later. However, her fear of Magnus kept her docile in her attempts to escape. After last night, she wasn't so sure her foolish ruse of putting on an air of defense was having the desired effect. It had backfired big time. In fact, it seemed to have sent Magnus over the edge. Her husband was not going to let her walk away from their marriage without retaliation. Actually, it seemed he would rather kill her first.

Everything they owned and had built was because of her. She was the glue that held everything together and she was of more value to him as a union than a separated entity, working to undermine his efforts. If Magnus could stuff her head into a toilet filled with urine and showed no remorse for what he'd done, it was enough to convince Erica that Magnus would go to any lengths to ensure he kept control over her. An endless cycle of abuse that was suffocating the very essence of who she was. Thoughts of having Magnus killed suddenly resurfaced. It seemed like the most plausible solution; however, it was also the riskiest. All the evidence could point back to her and although she may gain freedom from the marriage, she would lose it behind bars. That didn't seem worth it. She would rather endure the abuse until she figured out an alternative way out of this misery.

She eased into one of the wicker chairs and gently lifted her now slightly swollen ankle onto the table in front of her. The cool breeze whipped at her braids before it attacked the translucent nightgown she was wearing. For some people the breeze would have been too much, but Erica loved it, especially how the scenic views of the ocean surrounded their home. Providing the perfect therapy for a dejected spirit. She'd brought her cell phone with her so that she could call the staff at the B&B and let them know she wouldn't be able to make it in to work today because of personal issues. She would have to fabricate another lie if she did go in to work.

She could remember the first time Magnus struck her, almost ten years ago, after hosting a party for Dean's thirteenth birthday. Of course, Magnus blamed it on her disrespecting his authority, but truly, it was Magnus' jealousy of Dean and the attention she'd shown Dean. But if her husband were to be honest, it would reveal that he was the one who'd derailed the situation when all she wanted to do was teach both Dean and Tavian the skill set needed to become successful entrepreneurs. Her son and Dean displayed great potential for the business world and those two got along so well that Erica assumed including Dean into their family circle was the natural thing to do.

Back then there was nothing romantic about her relationship to Dean, or that was what Erica had forced herself to believe. The young man had only been thirteen years old at the time, which would make her nineteen years his senior. What kind of pervert would she be if she'd allowed such a thing to develop between them? Her husband was sick in the mind to even suggest it. The more she denied it; the angrier he became, and they eventually ended up getting into a physical altercation. How she ached during those times to put his sins on blast to the world and expose him for who he really was. He was always trying to make her look like an unrighteous misfit when he was the one deserving of being tossed into the hottest part of hell.

Her fingers hovered over the keyboard of her phone and as she moved to speed dial the phone number of the B&B, she noticed an email notification sliding down on the screen. She wouldn't have concerned herself with it had the subject matter and who it came from not pulled her attention front and center. The email address, *MrDean_Ripley22@live.com* was supposedly from Dean and the subject of the email simply read, "I have a question for you." It was not an email address Erica readily recognized, but maybe Dean had created a new email. She clicked into it, despite her reservations, and read its contents:

*I pray all is well with you. As the subject matter mentions, I need you to settle my mind because I've been wrestling to figure out where you bought that Gucci bracelet you gave me for my sixteenth birthday? You know, the one with the tiger heads. Do you remember the name of the store? I was hoping to buy a similar gift for Lily and surprise her with it.*

95

Erica pouted her lips at the words. The email was a bit strange to say the least, especially because it was the first one she'd received from Dean in a very long time. An even stranger question was why did Dean want to purchase the same bracelet for Lily? It was her special gift to him she'd had custom-made. There wasn't a need for a replica.

As she contemplated how to respond, Erica cast her gaze on the ocean and watched as the white waves rolled toward the shore. Giving Dean the information he sought wasn't the problem. It was the pang of jealousy stirring in her heart. But Erica would die before she admitted that fact. To her, it was righteous indignation over something she felt Dean had no business asking. She clicked on the reply button and typed:

*What a surprise to see an email from you after such a long time...but how sweet of you, wanting to surprise Lily with such a special gift, though it will cost you a small fortune. However, if you need my help, I'd be more than willing to assist. But knowing how independent you are of receiving 'donations,' as you would call them...lol...you'll probably sell your entire kiosk to secure what you desire for the love of your life (Smile). I ordered the bracelet from an online catalogue called, "The Elite." And you do realize that the bracelet was custom-made, right? Of course, you do. I told you that it was...*

"What the hell are you smiling about this early in the morning?"

Erica jumped at the intrusion of Magnus' voice. It was a groggy version of an inflection fueled by antagonism. Erica subtly pressed 'Send' and closed out her email. Remembering not to provoke her husband to further wrath, she feigned a sad countenance.

"If I don't find something to smile about," she answered evenly, "I will remain in a constant state of depression. Look at how beautiful the ocean is. One of God's masterpieces that brings peace to a troubled mind. Do you agree?"

Magnus' gaze fell to Erica's ankle and noticed that it was wrapped in gauze. The high alcohol level in his system made the details of last night a little fuzzy, so he couldn't recall what really happened. Although he did remember Erica screaming as he pushed her head down in a toilet. Or maybe it was something he dreamed, because he couldn't believe he would do something like that to the woman he'd been married to for twenty-two years. And if he had, Magnus justified, Erica must have driven him to it. If only he could remember the events of last evening.

"What happened to your ankle?" he asked.

Erica shot her husband an incredulous look. "Don't tell me you were too drunk to remember?"

"If I did remember, would I be asking you about it?" Magnus snapped.

Erica sighed away her snippy comeback. "Don't worry about it; I'll be fine," she said. "Just know that I'm taking a few days off until my ankle heals."

"You can't do that –"

"The B&B and the other businesses will not crumble in financial ruin if I take a few days off. I have trained capable people to cover for me when I'm not there."

Erica's answer didn't seem to appease Magnus' concern in the least. "You can't trust anyone, especially when it comes down to these scallywags on this island. How could you effectively monitor anything, sitting on this balcony with your feet up on a table?"

"This paranoia of yours is not healthy. We must learn how to trust people. I could drop down dead at any moment, or something could happen to you unexpectedly. What then?"

"There's a reason why Tavian is considered the beneficiary of our estate. Everything stays within the family and that includes who runs our businesses."

Erica rolled her eyes inwardly. Magnus knew full well that he wouldn't have included Tavian in the will if she hadn't threatened to leave the bulk of her inheritance to Tavian. Magnus was a greedy dog who cared about two things: making money and hording it for himself. He wouldn't have had any need for her without her inheritance or the fact that she was much savvier than him in business.

"When did you last speak to your son?" she tossed at him. "Because you might discover that he may not have any interest in running our businesses."

Magnus eyed Erica suspiciously. "What are you talking about? I sent that boy off to college –"

"To study Marine Engineering," Erica interrupted. "What is Tavian going to do with that degree when he comes back home? And that's only if he does."

"I don't like how you're dropping these bloody innuendoes. I plan to open a marine shop when Tavian returns. So, what do you mean *if* Tavian comes back home?"

"I'm just saying."

"Don't give me that condescending garbage. You two have been discussing plans behind my back and I want to know what they are."

"You know as well as I do that you don't really want Tavian to come back to Barracuda Cove. And if he did, you would want him as far away from you as possible."

Magnus hit the French doors with his fist. "Don't spin this conversation to suit your agenda! Tavian is my son and I will do with him as I see fit!"

Erica grew quiet, simply to keep her composure in check. But it was the hardest thing to do with a miserable, abusive tyrant like Magnus always ready to pounce on her every move. She did not dare tell him that Tavian had abandoned marine engineering to study theology. She was convinced Magnus would move heaven and earth to make Tavian regret it.

"This conversation didn't have to get out of control like this," Erica said in a resigned tone. "All I'm saying is that we keep an open mind because we don't really know where the future will take us."

"You believe that nonsense if you want," Magnus rejoined. "I am in charge of my future and I know exactly where it's headed – with or without you! You won't have the upper hand over me forever." He turned to leave but paused as if he were forgetting something. "I'll give you until the end of today to deal with your PMS symptoms. You had better be at that B&B, bright and early tomorrow morning or else you will have *two* swollen ankles!"

Magnus rushed through the French doors, slamming them behind him. Erica returned her defiant gaze to the ocean. She was going to take those days off, even if she had to book a hotel room or hide in one of their guest cabins, which was called Lush Haven. Such a bastard Magnus was, Erica fumed. He was in for a rude awakening if he thought he would plan their future without her. He should have never revealed that much to her. She punched in the number to the B&B and listened as one of her employees repeated the company's greeting.

"Good morning, Mr. Justin Knox. How are you doing?"

"I'm well, Mrs. Winthrop. How are you?"

"Not so well; that's why I'm calling. I will be out for a few days."

"Oh wow...I'm so sorry to hear that. Is everything alright?"

It would appear to be a silly question considering she'd just told Justin that she wasn't feeling well, but Erica knew Justin well enough to know he truly cared about her and that he would do whatever he could to ensure that the B&B thrived on excellence. He was only twenty-five years old and had been in prison for a short stint, but she trusted him more than she trusted all of her employees combined.

"I just need to take a few days off to recalibrate," she told him. "I'm gonna need you to hold things down for me. Do you think you can do that?"

"Of course. You know I will, and you know I can."

"Obviously, Sandra and Ian will be there to help you, but I lean more on you, when it comes to keeping things in order."

"Mrs. Winthrop, no worries. Ian has been slacking off a bit, but I'm dealing with it."

Erica didn't bother to inquire any further about Ian's situation because she was confident Justin would keep a firm hand on the employees. "Thank you, Justin, I truly appreciate you and all of the sacrifices you have made for the bed and breakfast."

"Don't mention it. It's me who should be thanking you. If you hadn't taken a chance on me, I probably would have ended up right back in prison. My loyalty is the least I can offer."

Erica smiled at those words. "How sweet of you to say that, but you've developed a great reputation and I am truly proud of you."

"You're making me blush, Mrs. Winthrop," Justin joked. "Thank you...I will be sure to send the financial reports by the end of the evening, so you can inspect them."

"Don't go through the trouble. I will have a look at them upon my return."

"Okay, my good boss...I pray you feel better real soon. And don't worry; I'll make sure everything stays in order."

"I know you will, Mr. Justin Knox. I have faith in you...Take care."

Erica disconnected from the line. The next call would be to her lawyer, a call she should have made a long time ago. However, it was the conversation she'd had with Magnus that opened her eyes to the sad truth: he was planning to divorce her or maybe even end her life someday. Why else would he tell her, *'You won't have the upper hand over me forever'?* Magnus didn't say things simply because he could say them. He was giving her clues of what was to become of her future. It was truly a wakeup call and it was time that she put her fears aside once and for all and follow through with her escape plan. She dared not allow Magnus to swindle her out of her own inheritance.

But before she called her lawyer, she was going to show Magnus who was the real negotiator in business. Call it her first act of defiance; she was moving ahead with her plans – despite any consequences that might befall her. Those white businessmen who came from Florida were scheduled to leave the island in a few days, and she had yet to receive a favorable response regarding the business agreement between them and Dean. She pulled up her address book and located the phone number for one of the men who gave her his name as Gavin Osprey. When he answered, she wasted no time with small talk.

"Mr. Osprey? This is Erica Winthrop calling."

"Yes?"

"Whatever my husband has promised you," she said firmly, "I will double it. My only interest is that you follow through with your promise to Dean Ripley."

"Mrs. Winthrop, I don't know if it is wise for you to have called me," Gavin said. "Your husband made it quite clear that he doesn't want you to interfere."

Erica could detect nervousness in Gavin's voice, which she knew was the result of Magnus' threats. But she refused to allow Magnus to outwit her – not this time around.

"When it comes down to acquisitions, mergers, and establishments in virgin territories," she pointed out, "my husband cannot settle any business transactions without my signature. I'm sure he mentioned that to you. No?"

"Mrs. Winthrop, please don't drag me in the middle of your and your husband's personal affairs."

"I'm not dragging you into anything. I'm simply offering you the better deal. And if this is any consolation to you, this conversation between us will never go beyond this phone. All I ask is that you and your business partners honor your contract with Dean Ripley. I know you guys are impressed with his craftsmanship and what he produces is very marketable."

There was a marked pause in Gavin's voice before he continued. "I am afraid that this won't end well. If I'd known we would be faced with a bidding war over Mr. Ripley's work, we would have cut our losses from the start and selected differently. Our vision is simple: Provide international exposure and funding for promising entrepreneurs. We invest not in just the ideas of a person, but in the person themselves. We have little tolerance for undisciplined lifestyles, lack of focus or shadiness from our potential prospects."

"Point taken. But I guarantee you, you can search this entire island but you won't find such talent, along with excellent character like what we've found in Dean. He is ideal for the platform you're representing."

"Not according to your husband."

"My husband has a personal vendetta against Dean and I don't feel it is professional of you to allow that to be one of the determining factors of your decision."

Gavin gave a long drawn out sigh into the phone. "I don't know what we've gotten ourselves into. But you seemed pretty taken with Mr. Ripley and I do mean that in the purest form – so, based on that, I will reconsider. However, I won't make any promises."

"That is all I'm requiring of you," Erica said. "Will I hear from you before you return to the United States?"

"You certainly will."

# CHAPTER ELEVEN

## *Butterfield Offshore Bank*

Lily had about fifteen minutes left of a long nine-hour work day. She wanted to use it to do some private investigating of her own. So when her boss explained to her he had to leave early for his daughter's tennis match, she was overcome with relief. The bank she worked for upheld a strict, professional atmosphere, where casually searching the Internet was heavily looked down upon. She could have waited until she got home, but the thoughts suddenly came to her and being one who usually gave in to her impulses, she wanted to address her thoughts right there and then.

Her eyes roved her surroundings and once she deemed it was safe, she pulled up Internet Explorer and typed into the search bar: *Gucci tiger head bracelets*. A number of searches came up but very few produced an exact wording. The link three rows down caught her attention. When she clicked on it, a simply-designed website materialized in front of her. The name, *Elites*, suggested to Lily that it was geared toward the affluent. It shimmered in diamond-studded letters, boldly seducing its viewers into a world of luxury. She quickly navigated through the website, locating the section, 'Men's Fine Jewelry.' There were two sections, 'custom -made' and 'shop now.'

For some reason, she went straight to 'custom-made' and was immediately dazzled by a collage of photos, showing some of the most exquisite designs ever seen by her eyes. She nearly jumped out of her chair when she came across several photos showing crafted white gold bracelets with the distinctive tiger heads designs. They looked like the one Dean wore. In fact, two photos down, she saw an exact replica. The tiger's ruby red eyes and its white mane. Her eyes popped open widely when she saw the estimated price of having one made like it. Four thousand, eight hundred dollars. If indeed it was the bracelet that Dean wore, the buyer paid a hefty price.

Two questions slapped Lily at once: Who would purchase such an expensive, custom-made piece of jewelry for her man? And why didn't Dean want to reveal who the buyer was, who'd bought the piece when he was only sixteen years old? Such a heavy gift for a teenager. Its value exceeded more than her monthly salary, and she could see why Dean cherished it so much. It was not only costly, but it was gorgeous. She sat back and allowed her mind to take it all in. She hadn't intended to go behind Dean's back and play amateur sleuth but ever since she'd had that last conversation with her mother, she was feeling somewhat insecure.

Not that she didn't trust Dean, but her mother's words had a way of staying with her, taunting her and threatening to suffocate her happiness. Her mother had told her the reason men ran away from her was because she was too shrewd. And then she had the guts to say that even if Lily got a man, she wouldn't be able to keep him because she was too uptight. As much as Lily didn't want to believe that, she couldn't help but consider those statements. At fifteen she'd graduated from high school as class valedictorian and by the time she'd turned nineteen, she was finishing her MBA and had landed a top-level position with the offshore bank she currently worked for.

However, the one guy she'd dated in the past didn't seem intimidated by her brainpower. But rather more interested in playing the field. He was her high school sweetheart and for the first ten months of their relationship, he showered her sweet words, wined and dined her until she refused to give up her virginity. Soon after she discovered he had gotten two different girls pregnant, the babies being only one month apart in age. Maybe her mother's words held a bit of credence in that incident, but when it came to her relationship with Dean, they didn't apply. Because Dean was not intimidated by her, nor, to her knowledge had he been unfaithful to her. Yet, in spite of this reassurance, her mother's words prevailed:

*...you will never keep a man if you don't loosen up and act like the rest of us...*

But deep down, Lily knew she couldn't blame her mother for Dean's reticence when it came down to that bracelet. The mere fact that he refused to tell her who'd bought it suggested that talking about the bracelet was off limits to her. She'd seen how he would get tense each time she mentioned the bracelet. He wouldn't even look her in the eye as if his eyes would somehow reveal something he didn't want her to see. Now Lily didn't consider herself to be a troublemaker or one to put much confidence into misfortune, but she couldn't help but feel as if the bracelet was an ominous sign of bad things to come. How else could she explain this sickening feeling at the bottom of her gut?

She bit down on her bottom lip in sheer angst. *Why can't I get my mother's crazy voice out of my head? My relationship with Dean is going so well. There is no need for the paranoia...*

And in the same vein of thought, she prayed:

*Dear Lord, I don't know You all that well, but please help me not to make a mess of this relationship. I'm really in love with Dean, and I don't want us to break each other's heart.*

*6:24a.m.*

The B&B rarely had a lull at any point in the day but when it did, Justin and the other employees tried to take advantage of it. It was the end of the work day, for Justin anyway, and he was only lingering around for Ian and Sandra to settle in to their shifts. The three of them stood around the Cappuccino machine, each sipping on the flavor of their choice. Sandra, as usual was chatty, but Ian was unusually quiet, almost distracted, even though he laughed at Sandra's jokes. Justin couldn't help but take notice of the great change he was seeing in Ian.

"You think boss lady will give me the weekend off?" Sandra questioned with a smirk on her apple-shaped face. "I met this hot stud online and he asked me to take the ferry with him to Bimini Bay. Just for one night, though as he has to get back home before his wife comes back from her trip to Norway."

Both men gave Sandra the you-must-be-crazy look. "You expect me to believe that garbage?" Ian commented first. "You just trying to find an excuse to duck work."

Sandra gave a toothy grin. "You should be the last person to allow something like that to come out of your mouth. Because who ducks work more than you?"

The rebuke was sharp, and the only thing Justin could do at that point was try to soften the blow. After all, Ian wasn't a bad guy. It just seemed as if he'd gotten into something over his head that he refused to share with anyone else.

"First of all," Justin said. "No one should be trying to duck work. Erica has been very good to us, paying us all a decent salary and allowing us to build our leadership skills."

Sandra ran a hand over her low-cut hair, as words of disgust fell from her thick burgundy-painted lips. "Speak for yourself, Mr. I'm-In-Charge. Erica doesn't trust anyone else but you. I can't say that I'm happy with my salary. It's chicken feed compared to what I know I'm qualified for. And what hurts me the most is that this place makes a lot of money, and I couldn't get a twenty-dollar raise if I put a gun to Erica's head."

Justin didn't like Sandra's tone, especially when she mentioned the word 'gun' in the same sentence with Erica. "I don't hear you complaining about the bonus at the end of the year," Justin said, "which far exceeds what an additional twenty dollars can do to your salary."

"I even have a problem with my bonus," Sandra said. "It's all chicken feed, and I'm only basing this on two things: my qualifications and the arsenal of money this place generates."

"Really, Sandra?" Justin said in shock. "I can't believe you are saying these things right now. That's pure greed."

Sandra shrugged. "It is what it is."

Justin cast his gaze on Ian, who had his eyes glued to the floor. "I guess you agree with Sandra, because you're not saying anything."

Ian made brief eye-contact with Justin before looking toward Sandra. "She's right, in some ways. Erica digs you and you can do no wrong in her eyes. She treats you with distinction. I'm not really griping, but you have to see things from our point of view. Three hundred and twenty dollars a week could barely sustain anyone on an island like Barracuda Cove when the cost of living is so high. I, myself, have to look for other means to supplement my lifestyle."

Justin didn't know what to say because his salary was almost twice the amount of Ian's and Sandra's. And he'd always assumed it was that way because of the greater responsibility that Erica placed upon his shoulders. However, after listening to Sandra's and Ian's complaint, he could understand their position. He made a mental note to talk Erica about it. But what did Ian mean when he said he had to look for other means? Could it be related to the change he saw in Ian over the last six months? He was coming in late frequently and had even missed a couple of days in this month alone. Justin didn't buy the 'my-car-broke-down' excuse anymore. Ian was probably moonlighting undercover.

"I'm cool with working here," Ian was saying, "It's something to do and it help pays the bills. I just feel Sandra and I and the other employees are being taken for granted."

"I couldn't have said it better myself," Sandra said and then added quickly, "But we have no problem with you, Justin. You are just doing what your boss tells you to do."

Sandra walked off with Ian falling in behind her strides. That conversation didn't sit well with Justin at all. His shift was over, and he should have been heading home to catch up on some much-needed sleep, but he decided to stick around for a few more hours to monitor Sandra and Ian. Because clearly, they were embittered toward Erica. Not that he thought they would harm her or do anything stupid. He just wanted to observe their work habits and see if they were actually qualified to receive a raise in their salary.

# CHAPTER TWELVE

*Vancouver, Western Canada*

T avian Winthrop was a focused young man, intent on fulfilling his God-given assignment. When he told his mother that he'd abandoned marine engineering for theology, it wasn't to score points with her or to make him feel as if he was doing something charitable for the human race. He honestly believed God was positioning him to confront the religious spirit of his birthplace. Barracuda Cove was bound by wickedness from one end of the island to the next, so entrenched in the hearts and minds of the people that even his father, Apostle Magnus Winthrop had been unable to escape it.

It wasn't a shock to Tavian that the church his father founded was the only church on the island. From a spiritual perspective, it had been designed that way by those controlled by power, greed, and deception. That way the truth of God's word and the power it had to liberate would be suppressed. There were more Satanists and warlocks living in Barracuda Cove than there were genuine Christians. At least, in Tavian's mind. His father's church should not have been the only church on the island. Had there been more Christians not afraid to challenge the spirits assigned from hell, Barracuda Cove would have been a central hub for Jesus Christ.

Tavian pushed open the driver side of his white Toyota Rav4 and made his way through the single entrance of World Embassy International Church. It was a dazzling name for an organization with little less than three hundred people in membership, but it was big on following the Word of God as closely as possible. Evangelism and discipleship were enshrined in the mission plan. The mere fact that the church was not only excited about soul winning but was successfully practicing what they preached, scored huge points with Tavian.

He had searched for months for a church like this and when he found it, he made it his mission to learn all he could for however long God kept him in Canada. Once his training was completed, his next move was to return home and establish a church of his own. One that would mirror the church of the Bible and its holy order. No doubt it would ransack the status quo of the island and would catapult him squarely in the path of his father's wrath. But it was the least that Tavian was willing to suffer to ensure that the people's eyes were opened to the truth of God's Word, upon which true deliverance would be experienced.

He walked the short hall that led to the pastor's office and gave the door a few raps. He heard the welcoming baritone of a man who carried an ancient anointing that made Tavian feel as if the pastor was much older than his thirty-seven years.

"Good morning, Pastor Coleby," Tavian greeted. "I just stopped by to say hello before I went into the sanctuary."

Pastor Coleby gave Tavian an appraising look. He loved Tavian's amicable personality, but more so, his enthusiasm for the Lord. When Tavian expressed his desire to be mentored just a mere two weeks after attending the church, Pastor Coleby was visibly impressed. Especially when he learned that Tavian was only twenty-one years old. Not many young men of such a crucial age would pursue a path overshadowed by sacrifice, discipline and deep commitment.

"Come in and have a seat," he said, beckoning to Tavian.

Tavian quickly stepped into the office and closed the door behind him and took a seat as instructed.

"Ever since you started attending this church," the pastor continued, "you've been causing a stir."

The only reason Tavian didn't take the pastor's words as a rebuke was because of the smirk that twitched at one side of his mouth. He'd recently discovered that the pastor loved to tease him. But Tavian went along with it to see where the pastor was steering the conversation.

"Sir," Tavian said, "my only intention is to complete my assignment. I can't afford to be distracted with anything else. So whatever it is, please let me know so that I can promptly fix it."

The pastor's smirk didn't match the concern in his eyes. "Sister Rosita stopped me on the way to my office and told me that she saw you having a very intense exchange with one of the ladies from the youth prayer squad. According to Sister Rosita, it looked rather romantic."

It was Tavian time to smirk. "Sister Rosita is such an instigator," he said. "What else did she say? That I got down on one knee and proposed to the young lady?"

"I see that you find this funny."

"I'm sorry, sir. I don't mean to make light of the situation. But you know Sister Rosita's perception is a little shaky. The young lady and I were role-playing for the prayer summit that's coming up next month. I didn't want to do it, but she insisted –"

"I understand, Tavian, you don't have to explain. I only brought it to your attention because I have a strong feeling that Sister Rosita is smitten with you and is probably plotting to make a decisive move toward you. I have seen this played out before with her and another young man who used to attend here. It didn't end well."

"What happened?" Tavian asked.

"That's irrelevant. What's important is that you be wise. Don't confront her or ask her advice about anything. Watch your smiles and your friendly gestures because she is certain to misinterpret them as something else. And for heaven sake, don't be caught alone with her. It is what she wants and will do anything she can to make that happen. You are poised to become a great leader someday and it will serve you well to keep your integrity intact."

"Yes sir, it is my desire to remain above reproach."

"And with the help of the Lord you will. I have seen great men succumb to the temptation of assuming they are invincible, as if sin could never get a hold of them. And while it is good to have confidence, having too much of it in yourself and less of it in God is a recipe for disaster. Do you understand what I'm saying?"

Tavian knew exactly where Pastor Coleby was coming from. His father was that sort of leader but had been blindly given over to all kinds of sins. He couldn't see anything wrong with what he was doing. Tavian didn't need another deterrent to dissuade him from such an ungodly hypocritical lifestyle. But he did appreciate Pastor Coleby for being kind enough to share his concerns. It meant the pastor truly cared about his spiritual well-being.

"I do understand. I've told you that my father is an apostle, but I kept my views silent about his leadership up until this time."

Pastor Coleby held a hand up to stop Tavian. "I don't need you to divulge anything about your father. I trust what you learn here will aid in your assignment when you return home to Barracuda Cove. And speaking of Barracuda Cove, when do you plan to return? You've been here almost eight months." When the pastor noticed the wilt in Tavian's expression, he wanted to take his words back. "Not that I'm rushing you or that I'm not happy that you're here. To be honest, I could use you around here on a more permanent basis."

"I wish I didn't have to go back home," Tavian said. "Your leadership has empowered me in ways I never thought possible. I have always sensed that the Lord wanted me to stand up against the corruption prevailing in my country. But I struggled to know the platform or medium that the Lord was calling me to."

"You need not plant a church to be a voice crying in the wilderness," Pastor Coleby said.

"I know, but you must understand the spiritual climate of Barracuda Cove. My father's church is the only church on the island, but it is not effective. The people are worldly, self-absorbed and spiritually dead."

Pastor Coleby stared at Tavian with a newfound appreciation. While he could detect a sense of purpose in Tavian's words, he also saw great disappointment in his eyes over the way he felt about his father's leadership.

"So you're planning to start a revolution when you return?"

Pastor Coleby may have asked that question jokingly, but it wasn't a joke for Tavian.

"If that's what it will take to turn the island upside down," he answered gravely, "then I'm willing to put my life on the line. You have been most instrumental to me and someday, I will take what I've learned and enforce it with the help of the Lord."

Pastor Coleby sat back and steepled his fingers on his desk, his mischievous smirk returning. "So I guess a wife is nowhere in the picture for you?" he asked and then added quickly, "I mean, at least in the foreseeable future."

"I have not given it any serious thought," Tavian answered truthfully, "but I will leave that part of my life in the hands of the Lord. Right now, my focus is to fulfill my God-given assignment."

Little did Tavian know from the supernatural perspective, when he said those words, the forces of darkness hastily moved into position to thwart or to stop Tavian's assignment from ever coming to fruition.

# CHAPTER THIRTEEN

Dean didn't usually encourage Lily to spend late hours at his home because he'd been tempted more than a few times to take her to his bedroom and have his way with her. And he really didn't want to do that before they were married. Lily was a virgin and he wanted their honeymoon night to be special for her. However, there were times, like now, as Lily sat on one of his knees, going through their wedding guest list, he craved to satisfy his sexual appetite.

He was not a virgin and he'd told Lily as much. Yet, she insisted on teasing him with her soft, pale skin, rubbing against his face. Several times he had to recalibrate his thoughts to suppress his erection. He couldn't even focus on what Lily was saying to him because the only thing he was thinking about was how good she smelled and how her delicate weight pressed against his thigh. Lily hadn't any idea how serious of a temptation sex was for him.

"You okay, babe?" she asked him, her eyes still glued to the guest list.

"Yeah? Why'd you ask?"

"Because you keep shifting your legs. If I'm too heavy let me know, so I can adjust my weight."

"To be honest, it's your weight that's stirring fire between my legs."

Lily tossed her head back against Dean's chest and laughed.

"You're laughing, but I am so serious," Dean said. "Why are you staying over here so late anyway?"

Lily quieted her laughter, but there was still a smirk pulling her lips askew. "It's only nine-thirty," she said, giving Dean a side glance. "Why? You're trying to get rid of me?"

"No, I mean, yes..."

"Which is it?"

Dean gently pulled Lily up by an arm and sat her in the empty chair next to him. "I'm trying to stop us from getting pulled into the devil's playground. My mother could walk out here any minute."

"If you're so worried about our privacy, we should have gone to my apartment like I suggested. We've made a vow that we won't have sex until we're married, right?"

"And I do stand by that vow, but girl, you have a lot to learn about a dude who has already had sex and knows what it feels like. My groin is on fire right now."

Lily playfully rubbed Dean's thigh in a suggestive manner. "Is sex really all they say it is?"

Dean caught Lily's hand and held it. "Why do I get the distinct impression you're testing my limits tonight?"

Lily's gaze zeroed in on the bracelet that was on Dean's wrist, wilting her good mood. She'd spent a good amount of time searching the Internet for information on the expensive piece, only to come to the realization her man wouldn't part with it. Why would he? It was an original design, obviously, given to him by someone he considered special to him. She thought she could remain quiet about it and that her jealousy would have eventually assuaged. But the truth of the matter was, she'd stayed up late last night, tossing and turning over the stupid bracelet. She must get to the bottom of this mystery before it made her crazy. *Good going, mother. You are the blame for my paranoia...*

"Can I ask you something?" she said, dragging her gaze upwards to Dean's.

"You can ask me anything."

"You won't get upset, right?"

"This sounds important to you, so I will listen to what you have to say."

"Alright then." Lily reached over and gently tugged at the bracelet on Dean's wrist. "This is a very costly piece of jewelry. Ask me how I know."

Dean was wary of the confidence he saw in Lily's eyes, which meant she was on a mission to get him to reveal who'd bought him the bracelet. He suddenly wished he hadn't given her the green light to express her concerns.

Dean shrugged and said lightly, "Maybe because it'd been designed by Gucci? It's engraved right here on the band, which you could have easily seen with your two, bright beautiful eyes."

Lily gave Dean a playful spank. "I said to ask me how I know; not guess your answer."

Dean was not interested in knowing how Lily knew because he knew where the conversation was heading. So he tried one more attempt to get her off track.

"If the bracelet bothers you that much," he said, "I will take if off and sell it."

"You are a smart man," Lily said. "But not smarter than me."

Dean suppressed his grin. "Why do you say that?"

"Because you think you're gonna get away with not telling me who bought you that bracelet."

Dean couldn't hold in his grin any longer and ended up exploding in laughter. "It's just a bracelet; why does it matter to you so much?"

"It's not just the bracelet; it's your evasiveness that frightens me." Suddenly, all of Lily's smirks and her playfulness vanished away, being replaced with a perplexed expression. "I don't understand why you won't tell me who bought it? Does the person mean that much to you?"

The question and the concern in Lily's voice certainly threw water on Dean's flaming libido, but he was also forced to examine his intentions. What was the real reason he didn't want to tell Lily that it was Erica who'd bought the bracelet for him? It wasn't as if he and Erica had anything going on between them. Erica was like a mother to him, who'd supported his dreams with no strings attached. Well, that was what he and Erica choose to abide by because it was highly improbable that they would ever be an item. So he should be free to put Lily's mind at ease. But for some strange reason, he couldn't.

And it could be explained that he didn't want Lily's godly perception of Erica to be tarnished, or that he didn't want to risk putting Lily at odds with Erica. But deep down, Dean knew those reasons were a far cry from what was truly going on in his heart. He took Lily's hand in his and pressed his lips against it. The gesture seemed to soften the anxiety in Lily's expression.

"Put your mind at ease, babe," he told her. "I don't have any attachment to this bracelet. It was a gift given to me when I was sixteen years old and it never really crossed my mind to get rid of it until I discovered it makes you uncomfortable."

Lily's eyes dithered with regret. "I didn't mean to –"

"It's cool. I have no problem getting rid of it." Dean unlatched the bracelet and handed it to Lily. "You wanna hold on to it? Maybe you can sell it to get some extra cash. It can help with our wedding plans."

Lily stared at the bracelet. It was such a regal piece of jewelry, one of a kind that could certainly start a bidding war. The dazzling red eyes of the tiger seemed to pierce through her soul. She really felt horrible now, knowing that she was forcing Dean to part with it.

"You keep it," she said weakly.

"No..." Dean pressed the bracelet into her palm and closed her fingers over it. "I want you to be assured that no one in this world means more to me than you," he said. "I don't plan on living life without you by my side. In fact, I don't think that's an option for me. Do you believe what I'm saying to you?"

A smile sprang into Lily's eyes. She pulled Dean toward her and kissed him on the lips. "Of course, I believe you, silly willy. I just hate that I made such a big deal over it."

"Anything that concerns you, concerns me. I love you, Ms. Lily Rose Tremblay, soon-to-be Mrs. Lily Rose Ripley. There's nothing I will allow to stand between you and me."

Lily couldn't keep from smiling. But a part of her still felt as if Dean was keeping something from her the way he shrewdly sidestepped her question. However, not wishing to exacerbate the issue any further, she stood to her feet, grabbing her wedding paraphernalia from the table.

"It's late and I should be going," she said. "Besides, I really don't wanna deal with your momma's wrath if she happens to stumble out here. She's just too old school for me."

Dean laughed. He stood to greet her with a parting kiss. He walked her to the front door and they said their goodbyes. He returned to the dining room table and embraced the silence. His thoughts were spinning. He'd truly loved that bracelet and was now kicking himself mentally for giving it to Lily. But he would rather part with it than to deal with Lily's insecurities. He just prayed it was enough to keep her questions at bay.

Sighing, he pulled out his phone from his pants pocket and clicked into his email app. He noticed Erica had responded with a second message, twenty-four hours after she'd responded with the first one. It simply read,

*I don't think you should buy Lily the same bracelet. It was a gift given to you.*

He clicked out of the second message and then reread the first message:

*How sweet of you, wanting to surprise Lily with such a special gift, though it will cost you a small fortune. However, if you need my help, I'll be more than willing to assist. But knowing how independent you are of receiving 'donations,' as you would call them...lol...you'll probably sell your entire kiosk to secure what you desire for the love of your life (Smile). I ordered the bracelet from an online catalogue called, "The Elite." And you do realize that the bracelet was custom-made, right? Of course, you do. I told you that it was.*

Dean never intended to buy Lily the same bracelet. He just wanted to confirm that the anonymous letter he received a few days ago had actually come from Erica. It was just strange she didn't make mention of the proposal. The one offering him fifty thousand dollars in exchange for something she wanted. He decided to ask her about it outright. He pressed the reply button and typed:

*What do I have to do for fifty thousand dollars? Not that I will do it. I just wanna know.*

He closed his email app, his heart pounding with anticipation of Erica's answer. Because in his mind, he could only think of one thing she wanted. Sex.

"I foresee that you want to play hardball."

The words fell from the lips of the male accomplice as he read the intercepted email that had come from Dean. Magnus was sitting in front of his laptop, pretending to be busy writing out his Sunday sermonette, but he was secretly panting for an opportunity to seduce the young bloke. The only reason he didn't make a move was because he was always in fear that the female accomplice could show up any minute and vehemently disapprove of his actions. A terrible thing to happen when they were smack dab in the middle of destroying his wife. His randy hormones would just have to hold out until he could take a calculated risk.

"What is it?" Magnus called out to the accomplice.

"I got a direct response from Dean. He wants to know what he has to do for fifty thousand dollars."

"You mean, he's relaying that question to my wife," Magnus said.

"Obviously. I would like to hold on to the belief that Dean has no idea we are monitoring the emails between him and Mrs. Winthrop."

Magnus snapped, "Why do you insist on calling that whore by my family name, as if she holds some type of respect in your eyes?"

"What do you want me to call her?"

"Slut, heifer, whore...any one will do."

"I won't argue with you over what I should call your wife. The thing I need from you right now is this: What do you want me to do with Dean's response?"

"Don't add or take anything away from it," Magnus spat. "Send it just the way it is."

"You do realize at this point that your wife could figure out her emails are being intercepted? We could lose the leverage we have now."

Magnus stared at the young man, unfazed by his insinuations. "Send it and watch them find their way to each other like two dogs in heat. This is the stage of the game where we put our cameras in place, which we should have already done a month ago. Because I assure you, we will be handsomely blessed with scandalous footage that will rock Barracuda Cove to its core."

The man turned his gaze away from Magnus so that Magnus didn't see him cringing in disgust. If Magnus' offer hadn't been so sweet, the accomplice would have thought twice about ruining the life of such a lovely woman. But money talks.

# CHAPTER FOURTEEN

Erica pulled her overnight bag from the back seat of the Mercedes and walked up the three wooden steps to one of five cabins she and Magnus owned in an area known as Lush Haven. As the name suggested, it was a canopy of vibrant greenery that stretched for miles against the Caribbean Sea. It was a secluded spot reserved for hiking or camping groups looking for an adventurous experience. The cabins provided ample technology for the modern occupant, but at the same time catered to those who preferred to be one with nature without the technological distractions.

It was the best of both worlds that drew people from all over during the summer months because they knew they would not be able to find such a spot anywhere else on the island. Fortunately for Erica, the summer months had past, and the cabins were vacant, especially now that the autumn breeze was starting to attract cooler temperatures. However, it was the perfect getaway for deceiving Magnus into thinking that she was slaving away at the B&B. He had no reason to think of her staying here because he was too busy gambling and crooking people out of their hard-earned money.

Besides, she'd instructed Justin to cover for her for a few days. He knew how to handle Magnus if he called or came to the B&B

inquiring about her. There was no way she was going anywhere limping on one foot. She was going to put her feet up, drink some coffee and relax her mind. She hobbled to the kitchen to check the pantry. The shelves were empty, save for a jar of coffee, a few boxes of Kraft macaroni, crackers, cans of tuna, mosquito repellent and a half bag of pure cane sugar.

There was a convenience store not too far back from the main road, but Erica didn't feel compelled to go because it was not as if she was staying during the night. She'd told her lawyer to bring her some food on her way to the cabin as they discussed her escape plan and possibly, her new life, far away from Barracuda Cove. In the meanwhile, she would snack on some crackers while watching a Netflix movie to kill some time. But as she proceeded to get comfortable on the chaise, her attention was pulled by the sudden bell-like sound of her email notifications.

Irritated, she reached for her phone and attempted to put it on silent. But her gaze caught Dean's name in the cascading email address. Her irritation melted right away as she was quick to recall his unusual inquiries of the bracelet she'd bought him for his sixteenth birthday. She would like to think she'd responded appropriately and that her words hadn't been misinterpreted, but knowing how unpredictable Dean had been in the past, it was possible that he just may take the situation out of context. When she clicked into his response, she did a doubletake.

*What do I have to do for fifty thousand dollars? Not that I will do it. I just need to know why you would ask a question like that.*

The first reaction that hit Erica was confusion. Why would Dean ask her such a question? It didn't correspond with her last message to him. Furthermore, Dean was responding in a way as if she was the one who'd propositioned him. Where did he get such a ridiculous idea that she would give him fifty thousand dollars? In exchanged for what? She would never ask Dean for any favors that would exploit his good character, much less put herself in such a compromising position. Maybe this email was not meant for her. Dean had mistakenly sent it, which would explain the confusion.

She clicked the reply button to respond but was simultaneously jolted by a light bulb moment. About two years ago, she remembered downloading an electronic diary onto her cell phone. She didn't even know why she'd downloaded it because she was not one to express her personal thoughts on paper. But once she had recorded her first entry, she realized how therapeutic it was to release her deepest, darkest secrets without having to share them with anyone and chance them making a mockery of her sadness. Her diary was her friend, her version of a true confidant who would never betray her.

Up until about six or seven months ago, she'd 'intentionally' forgotten about the app. It was during this time she'd found out that Dean had gotten engaged to Lily and that night, she poured her heart out about how it made her feel. But ironically, the thing that had brought her the most comfort, soon became a snare to her soul. It was because the truth of her heart regarding her feelings for Dean had been revealed, which became too embarrassing for her to continue writing about them.

It was as if writing about them, as opposed to denying them, forced her to accept that she was jealous, or maybe even heartbroken over the fact that Dean had moved on with his life. How strange it was to be entangled in such an emotional battle because it was what she wanted for Dean – to find someone in his age bracket. Yet, she simply couldn't understand why it hurt so badly.

She minimized Dean's email for the moment and then opened the app titled, *Memoire*. It was the only app on her phone that had a password attached to it, which ironically, was Dean's first and last names. She hadn't any idea what she was thinking when she did that. She just remembered being in a place of feeling totally hopeless and abandoned, with a gloomy future ahead of her. Now her behavior seemed so juvenile and so ungodly. Scanning the entries in her electronic diary, her gaze settled on the last entry she'd typed:

*I am so unhappy in my marriage; I wish there was a way out of this misery without killing Magnus. He's driving me toward violence with the constant physical and verbal abuse. He is so controlling and so manipulative. I often think about Dean and the wonderful, loving man he's grown up to be. He reminds me so much of my son, Tavian. Both of them seem to have been cut from the same cloth.*

*I often joke with myself about the idea of infidelity because separation from or divorcing Magnus would be nearly impossible. At least if I cheated on Magnus, it would give me some sort of personal vindication. But how short-lived it would be if he found out. He would kill me for sure and then go after Dean. So it appears as if I'm stuck in this miserable life. How lucky Lily is to have a man like Dean. I imagine if I was an evil vixen, I would find a way to steal Dean from Lily.*

*I would have offered Dean fifty thousand dollars in exchange for anything he wants, so long as he gave me what I needed...one night in a hot, steamy shower...lol...oh Erica, such futile thinking that would only land you in big trouble. Lord, please don't take me seriously. I'm only venting because I am so sad...*

Erica paused, her heart feeling as if it would pound out of her chest. *Could it be possible,* she pondered, *that I mistakenly sent this to Dean?* How else would he have known about the fifty-thousand-dollar proposal? It was too much of a coincident for Erica to believe it was a lucky guess. Another option, which was probably the most farfetched of them all, was that someone may have hacked into her phone and manipulated her data by sending it to Dean. Her phone was always with her and no one had access to it, except maybe if she was asleep. And even then, no one would know how to figure out the password to her electronic diary. *Except Magnus...*

A chill ran from the nape of her neck to the center of her big toe as Erica thought of how wicked her husband truly was – if, in fact, he was the culprit. Who else possessed enough hatred to do such a thing and who would be happy to destroy her reputation? Magnus was a jealous, vicious man who'd expressed his aversion for Dean on many occasions. So it was only natural to assume that Magnus was the culprit of her suspicions. She rose to her feet and paced outside onto the porch. The blinding rays of the sun caused her to squint her eyes, but the rays weren't as blinding as the accusations from her husband that suddenly assaulted her thoughts:

*"Don't lie to me! I caught you drooling over him. How disgusting! He's just a boy – the same age as our son... You're nothing but a lying whore! One way or the other, I will beat this whoring behavior out of you if it's the last thing I do..."*

Erica felt her paranoia was justified and she realized she must act quickly before Magnus' wickedness caught up with her. A few minutes later, she limped back into the cabin and punched in Dean's number.

"Mrs. Winthrop?"

He'd answered on the first ring, as if he'd been expecting her call. Erica restrained herself from correcting him for being so formal when she'd repeatedly given him permission to address her by her first name. But she guessed it was the best way of keeping the respect between them.

"How are you, Dean?"

"I'm great. You?"

"I've seen better days..." There was a pronounced pause in Erica's voice before she switched to the issue at hand. "I need to ask you something about that last email you sent."

"Okay...I'm hoping you are going to clear that up."

"I'm confused. Because we were discussing that bracelet I bought for you and how I feel you should purchase something different for Lily...not that I think she doesn't deserve one like it, it's just that that email threw me for a loop." Erica sighed to relax herself. "What I'm trying to say is that I don't know why you asked me that question. Why would I offer you fifty thousand, supposedly in exchange for something I want? It doesn't make sense. I have been supporting you since you were twelve years old. You could get anything from me – with no strings attached."

"That is what I said when I read that note."

"What note?"

Erica genuinely sounded stumped, which put Dean at considerable ease.

"A boy delivered a note to me the other day, saying that it came from you."

"I did no such thing!" Erica was so indignant her ears turned flaming hot. "I'm actually appalled that someone would lie so boldly on my name."

"That's what I thought, but then I began to get these emails from you – to which you confirm the answer to something only you would know."

"I only responded because I thought I was communicating with you. Dean, come on, you know I don't operate like that. I would never trust anyone – much less a fifteen-year-old boy – with such a message to hand to anyone. Obviously, someone is trying to set us up."

"I can't believe people are evil like that."

"You are so gullible when it comes to the motives of the human heart."

"What I mean is we don't trouble anyone. Why would anyone go through such an elaborate scheme to cause us trouble?"

Erica wanted so badly to tell Dean that she suspected her husband, but she held it for the time being.

"People are evil," she said. "And you must not deceive yourself into thinking that you are exempt from trouble. In fact, you don't have to go looking for it; it comes looking for you."

"I have heard that before, but still..." Dean sighed. "I guess what matters now is what we are going do with this information?"

"Well, you can start off by describing that boy to me who gave you that note. I will beat the pants off of him."

"And then what?"

"Hopefully, he will lead us to the person who enlisted him into their service."

"Is that necessary? We already know it was a setup."

"We would be in a better position knowing who's behind this."

"Not really...it's obvious this person has too much time on their hands and we don't need to waste our time playing their games. You didn't send the note and I think we should leave it at that."

Erica couldn't believe how disinterested Dean appeared to be. Didn't he know how big of a scandal this could be if it got out? But then again, she shouldn't be surprised. It was Dean's modus operandi to brush off any threat of confrontation. Or was it that Dean had some hidden agenda at the back of his mind? She would like to know what he was truly thinking as opposed to giving her this laidback attitude of his. The moment she went to attack him with her inquires, the front door of the cabin came alive with several rapid knocks. Knowing who it was, Erica shouted for the person to enter.

Kim Brighton, Erica's lawyer pushed open the door with a start. She was a heavyset woman, dark complexioned like Erica and dark brown eyes. "Girl, this place is gorgeous," she said in a squeaky island accent. "No wonder you're cooped up in here all day."

Erica gave her a weary smile and said, "Come right on in. You have no idea how happy I am to see you right now...give me a sec, let me end this call..."

With a firm tone, she told Dean to stay close by the phone, as she would call him back to finish their conversation. Because something told her that Dean was secretly reveling in that anonymous note he'd received from that fifteen-year-old boy. But little did he know, Magnus was behind it and he was banking on it to expose the inordinate affection she supposedly had for Dean.

Erica turned to Kim and said dejectedly, "Please let's get on with this; I have a strong intuition my husband is setting me up for one of the biggest falls of my life."

# CHAPTER FIFTEEN

"I think my wife is planning to divorce me."

Magnus had two domino tiles left in his hand, he made a pretense of studying the board for what seemed like forever and then slammed one of the tiles on the table. There was a five and two at both ends, causing him to win the game by default. He eyed his playmates with a smug look on his face. They began to protest because it meant that they all had to give up five thousand dollars to Magnus.

"You intentionally blocked the game, didn't you?" one of them seethed.

"You old scallywag," another one vented. "How the hell did you win six games back to back?"

Magnus rubbed his head and gave a hearty laugh. "I told you: I am king of this game and you can't beat me. And it is not just the luck of the draw; it's God's anointing on me to win at everything I put forth my hands to do."

"Let me see that last tile in your hand," the third guy challenged. "Because I'm sure that I have the lowest count."

Magnus tossed the tile toward the guy and laughed. "Why can't you accept that I won?"

Indeed, Magnus had the lowered the number: a double one. Grudgingly, each man pushed their stack of fifty and one-hundred-dollar bills into the middle of the table. Magnus rubbed his hands together with pure satisfaction and then in one swoop, he raked the piles into a waiting leather bag.

"Thanks!" Magnus kissed the bag and then jammed it between his feet. "Now, let's reset the atmosphere with something more interesting. As I was saying, I think my wife is planning to divorce me."

All three of the men stared at Magnus in a way as if to say that they wouldn't blame his wife for wanting to leave. He deserved every bad thing coming to him. But of course, the men were diplomats and they would never say anything to jeopardize their money-making schemes, even if it meant having to tolerate an animal like Magnus. So they played along, just to see how much Magnus would reveal about his married life.

"You'd be a fool to let a woman like that walk out of your life," one of the men said.

Magnus laughed. "And you're a fool for believing that innocent mask my wife wears to deflect from her true personality. That heifer is as lethal as they come. You know, she keeps a diary on her phone, which pretty much reveals her lust for a boy half her age."

"I don't know if we should ask how you got a hold of that information."

"While she was asleep," Magnus gloated, "I swiped her phone and figured out the password to her diary."

"Come on, man. Where's the trust. That's evil."

Magnus grunted. "No, it's my wife who's evil. If I hadn't punched her in the head, she would have chewed my thigh to pieces with her teeth."

The expressions on the men's face suggested that they were not convinced.

"You don't believe me?" Magnus spat, as he unbuckled his pants, allowing them to drop to his ankles. On his right thigh, there was a reddish incision, which looked worse than it actually was because of Magnus' fair complexion. "What you are looking at, gentlemen, are the bite marks of my wife's incisors. She attacked me while I was driving us to church almost two Sundays ago."

"Come on, man, I don't believe your wife would attack you for no reason," the men said.

"Of course she would," Magnus retorted. "When I told that heifer I was not going to stand for her whorish ways, she punched me in the head and then sunk her teeth into my thigh. I had to defend myself by punching back, just so she would back the hell off."

The men still didn't seem convinced. Two of them were at the Winthrops home the other night when Magnus slapped his wife in front of them. That action alone told them what kind of man Magnus truly was. But they were not man enough to rebuke Magnus' lies.

"So, maybe a divorce might be the best option," one of the men said. "It seems as if you and your wife are beyond reconciliation. You can correct me if I'm wrong, but I'm only going by what I see."

"I don't care if she leaves," Magnus spat, as he grabbed his leather bag from between his feet. "But I will be damned if I let her walk away with anything. She will be like a bum on the street by the time I'm done with her."

One of the men shook his head in a deprecating way. "Erica is a good woman."

"And I am a good man," Magnus fired back. "Why the hell don't you marry her once she divorces me? Maybe then you'll see that heifer for who she really is."

The men hung their heads, knowing it was pointless to change Magnus' evil perception of his wife.

"Well, if there's nothing else to be said," Magnus simpered, cracking one of the malicious grins he wore whenever he'd win a large sum of money. "I will see you gentlemen tomorrow night after Bible Study. Same place; same time."

As soon as Magnus disappeared through the door, one of the men stood and went in search of the bathroom. He locked himself inside. He was one of the two white men who'd traveled from Orlando in hopes to seal a contract with Dean. Pulling his cell phone from his pants pocket, he called his partner, Gavin Osprey.

"You were right," he said to Gavin. "Mr. Winthrop is not someone we should invite into our circle. He is ruthless, untrustworthy and downright disrespectful to his wife."

"I've known that from day one," Gavin said. "I just needed to be certain that we were making the right decision in throwing our support behind the wife. She seems to be the one who is more genuine about Dean's character."

"I agree. The only challenge I foresee as we move ahead with our plans is letting Magnus know that we want no part of the empire he's supposedly built. I think we would be better off without a man like that."

"You know I have no problem doing the dirty work," Gavin said. "I will handle Mr. Winthrop. Continue to keep a low profile until we get back to Florida."

✳✳✳

Magnus refused to leave his gambling spot until he'd thoroughly counted his winnings for the night. So, there he sat behind the wheel of his Land Rover and meticulously verified every bill. His stack added up to nine thousand five hundred dollars. Not exactly ten thousand dollars, but he was okay with that. He just needed to make sure he accomplished his goal next time. If he started shortchanging himself now, it would take him a longer time to amass the amount of wealth needed to control all of Barracuda Cove and not just portions of it.

As he brought his hand up to crank the engine, his cell phone dropped onto the floor of the car. He reached for it and was a bit taken aback when he saw Tavian's face staring back at him. It was a photo of his high school graduation four years before. Tavian was not smiling in the photo, but that didn't minimize his good looks in the least. Tavian had his father's fair complexion, but his mother's attractive facial features. Staring at the photo soon began to stir a feeling of pride within Magnus. This was his son – his only seed – poised to walk into a great inheritance if he abided by Magnus' rules.

Magnus closed out the 'gallery' app, which his fingers must have accidentally pressed when he reached for his phone. How strange it was that Tavian's photo had been selected. Magnus took that as a sign he needed to call his son, but he didn't know how to get over the fact that he hadn't called his son in almost two years. Excommunicating Tavian was his punishment for defying Magnus on the doctrines of the church, and for pointing out Magnus' sins at every opportunity. But if Magnus was to be honest with himself, he would have to admit he missed having his son around.

About two miles into the commute, Magnus finally built up the courage to call Tavian. He listened as the phone rang through. When Magnus heard his son's cultured voice on the other end of the receiver, he felt a lump swelling in his throat. Magnus couldn't determine if it was because he was nervous or because he was reliving his anger for the reason he'd had to ship Tavian off to Canada.

"It's been a long time," Magnus said to Tavian's silence.

"It has..." Tavian cleared his throat. "What prompted you to call?"

"I don't know; I just thought I should."

Silence.

"How's school going?" Magnus asked for lack of a better way to continue the conversation.

"School? Fine, I guess."

"You sound unsure. You are still in school, right?"

"What if I'm not?"

Magnus held the phone away from his ear for a second. He couldn't believe Tavian had just countered with that stupid question.

"Don't play with me, son," Magnus warned. "I send a lot of money to you every month so you can attend one of the top colleges in the world. I have great plans for you when you return home to Barracuda Cove. You should have two years left of your B. A. in Marine Engineering, but that doesn't mean you can't go for your Masters..."

"Dad," Tavian interrupted with a quiet call. "Your money is not going to waste; I am putting it to good use."

"What do you mean by that? That could mean anything."

"Couldn't you just call to say "Hi, son, I love you," instead of browbeating me with your shortsighted views of my life?"

"You don't have enough sense to make decisions which are *best* for your life," Magnus countered. "If I allow you to run wild with your silly notions, you will be another Martin Luther King or another Malcolm X, trying to stir up some senseless disturbance."

"Those men changed the face of history," Tavian said. "You should not trivialize their platform and what they stood for –"

"You don't tell me how to –"

"What do you stand for, Dad; how will your legacy be remembered? Will I be able to say at the end of your life that I'm proud to follow in your footsteps?"

145

"I am not getting into semantics with you," Magnus spat. "This is the same problem that got your disrespectful behind shipped off to Canada. Nothing has changed with you!"

"And I could say the same about you, Dad."

Magnus disconnected from the line without saying goodbye. He was so enraged that he sped through the red light and would have totaled a white van had it not swerved out of the way. If Erica had been next to him, he would have body slammed her through the windshield. Because it was Erica's divisive rhetoric that had made Tavian into the man, or rather the rebel, he'd turned out to be. Well, Magnus thought to himself, Tavian could forget about receiving any more financial support from him. As of tonight, he was done with trying to steer that boy straight.

# CHAPTER SIXTEEN

## Vancouver, Western Canada – Ten Hours Later

It seemed no amount of warnings or prayers could keep Sister Rosita away from Tavian. Ever since he'd come to World Embassy Church, she'd been following his movements, trying to get him into a compromising position. His stance on holiness and his desire to socialize with only the intercessors of the church made her uncomfortable. She found it difficult to figure out his weakness. Out of all the young male ministers she'd managed to lure from the pulpit, Tavian appeared to be unfazed by her tactics. At first, she thought he was gay, the way he shunned the women, only to spend all of his time locked away with Pastor Coleby. But she had come to the conclusion that Tavian was simply a strange character who was obsessed with God.

Pastor Coleby had never taken to any young man the way he'd taken to Tavian. In Rosita's eyes, Pastor Coleby was showing favoritism with his members and she was not going to stand for it. The longer that young man stayed at World Embassy, the deeper his convictions would amalgamate with Pastor Coleby's. Their church already a strong proponent of righteous preaching, and having Tavian as the poster boy for saintliness, would stamp out the little influence she had with the weaker men. Especially the younger, more impressionable ones, which Rosita believed was part of Pastor Coleby's plan all along, to have them follow Tavian's example.

If she couldn't seduce Tavian into his own downfall, then it was time for him to leave their church. When Pastor Coleby told the congregation to stand for the benediction, Rosita sneaked out through one of the side entrances. She knew Tavian would head to Pastor's Coleby's office after the service. So she went there to wait for him in an attempt to catch him off guard. If she didn't act now, she was bound to miss a great opportunity to incite a disturbance. As she suspected, Tavian exited the church and made a beeline toward Pastor Coleby's office. When he spotted her, he paused in his strides and began to backpedal as if he'd seen a ghost.

Rosita hurled her steps after him, her strong Spanish accent proceeding ahead of her. "Don't run now, you little pervert! Last night I saw you coming out of a porno shop on Cartwright Street!"

Tavian looked over his shoulder, as if to confirm whether Rosita was truly directing her rantings at him. He knew it was impossible for her to refer to him in such a distasteful manner.

"I'm talking to you, Tavian Winthrop," Rosita said. "I saw you and don't you dare deny it! I knew you weren't who you said you were. Preaching one thing and living another."

Pastor Coleby had told Tavian to keep his distance from Rosita and avoid her at all cost, but he couldn't let her run on with such foolishness. His reputation was at stake. With a holy anger, he spun around to confront Rosita.

"I bind your lies, in the name of Jesus!" he spat at her. "Your foul mouth will go no further!"

"I bind you!" Rosita fired back. "You have no authority over me, you nasty little pervert!"

Tavian pointed two fingers in her direction and shook them with force. "You are of your father, the devil, who is the father of lies. I pray the fire of God will come upon you suddenly."

Those words turned Rosita's face beet red; she was shocked that Tavian had the balls to challenge her. A gush of heat came upon her, but she dismissed it as adrenaline running through her veins. She did not dare believe that Tavian's words were taking effect. When she spotted Pastor and First Lady Coleby, along with some of the parishioners rushing toward the commotion, she turned up the accusations against Tavian.

"You preach against holiness, but you're not living one ounce of it!" she ranted. "These young men who look up to you should be ashamed. You're no example for them. You came in our church to spread your deception –"

Pastor Coleby stepped in between the two parties. "I can hear this noise from the pulpit. What in the world is going on here?"

"You need to get this young man out of this church," Rosita said, giving Tavian the evil eye. "He's corrupt and he's gonna contaminate the whole lot of us."

"I have no idea what Sister Rosita is running on about," Tavian answered in his defense. "I was attacked the minute I came out of the sanctuary. There are witnesses who can vouch –"

"Don't you dare use that piousness of yours to score points with Pastor Coleby," Rosita spat. "You're nothing but a hypocrite!"

"Both of you, in my office right now!" Pastor Coleby ordered. "It's unnecessary for you to involve the entire congregation."

Rosita smirked, as she and Tavian fell in behind Pastor Coleby's strides. First Lady Coleby excused herself because she wished to have no part in the drama. She'd told her husband a long while ago that he was spending too much time with Tavian and people were going to start taking notice. Once the three were behind closed doors, Rosita erupted again into another tantrum of lies.

"I want him gone!" Rosita said to Pastor Coleby in her heavy Spanish accent. "He's a negative influence and will soon dismantle our church."

Tavian turned an angry eye on Rosita. "What have I ever done to you for you to hate me so much?"

"It's not what you're doing to me because I won't allow it," Rosita replied. "It's what you're doing in secret that concerns me."

"What do suppose that I'm doing?" Tavian rejoined.

"I can spell it out for you if you want." Rosita looked toward Pastor Coleby as if to obtain his approval. "But I respect the man of God too much to be so vulgar in his presence."

"Speak your mind, Sister Rosita," Pastor Coleby said. "I believe in hearing all sides of a story."

"Well if you insist, Pastor. I was just trying to be respectful. This young man is not who he says he is. I was driving past Cartwright Street to pick up my son from work, as he works the late shift at McDonald's. And I noticed a car like Tavian's coming out of the driveway of a porno shop. I got a good look at the driver and I'm 99.9 percent sure that it was Tavian. Can you imagine how hurt I was to see something like that? Thank God it was me who saw him because if it had been anyone else, the entire church would have known."

Pastor Coleby was taken aback by Rosita's words, considering the racket she'd stirred moments ago in the church's foyer. He looked at Tavian and asked, "What do you have to say about this claim?"

"It's all lies," Tavian said. "And it would have been her word against mine if it weren't for the fact that I was with you in all night prayer."

Confused, Rosita stared at Tavian and then at Pastor Coleby. "What is he talking about?"

"It is true, Sister Rosita," Pastor Coleby said. "Tavian, along with three other young men joined me for all night prayer last evening. We left the church around 4 a.m. this morning."

Rosita stepped back in disbelief. "I can't believe you're covering for Tavian. I know what I saw, and no one can tell me otherwise."

"You can call the other young men and verify what I've told you," Pastor Coleby said. "I have no reason to fabricate lies. In fact, the church's security cameras should be able to track when we entered and left the premises."

At that, Rosita's resolve began to melt. There was no way she could contend against technology. But that didn't mean she was giving in. She just had to find a more effective way to get rid of Tavian.

"Well, if the church's security system can verify your story," Rosita said grudgingly, "I guess I stand corrected. It's just that I won't tolerate a hypocrite, especially in a Holy Ghost filled church such as ours."

Pastor Coleby smiled patiently, but internally he was pleading with God to give him the wisdom to deal with this wicked woman. Her tithes and offerings were significant, helping to pay at least thirty percent of the church's expenses. So she felt as if she were in control. Pastor Coleby hated when people tried to make him feel as if he or the kingdom of God had to depend on their money to survive. All that was needed was one more major disturbance from her and he would tell Rosita to take her money and go to hell with it.

"I understand your concern, Sister Rosita," he told her. "But if God was like man, none of us would have been worthy to stand in His presence. I would advise the next time you encounter such a situation with any member of this church, don't go broadcasting it for everyone to hear. Rather, prayerfully take it to the Lord, or in strict confidence, bring it to my attention if you feel the person needs some spiritual guidance. Matthew 5:7 says, 'Blessed are the merciful, for they shall obtain mercy.'"

"What are you trying to tell me, Pastor?" Rosita asked.

"I'm sure you understand what I'm getting at, Sister Rosita. We all live in glass houses, so be careful how you throw your stones."

The axiom was enough to drive Rosita out of Pastor Coleby's office. Tavian collapsed in a chair opposite the pastor, breathing a sigh of relief.

"Thank you, sir," Tavian said. "I don't know how this situation would have gone if you hadn't been here to intervene."

Pastor Coleby's pensive gaze settled on Tavian. "Young man, the devil is after your assignment. Be on your alert even more so now because I sense Sister Rosita is not done with this situation. However, I will do my best thwart her plans."

About half an hour later when Tavian got home to his apartment, he dropped to the carpet of his living room. He'd questioned God all the way during his commute from church: Did God really call him to be a preacher? Did God really call him to start a revolution? His father certainly thought he was wayward and hadn't any sense to make the right decisions for his life. And to make matters worse, it seemed as if there weren't any other twenty-one year olds who Tavian could identify with, or who he could lean on for emotional support.

To Tavian, it felt as if the weight of his destiny was crushing his confidence. Especially after experiencing that episode with Sister Rosita today. It shook him up and made him realize that Sister Rosita's antagonism toward spiritual awakening was only a shadow of things to come once his feet touched back down on Barracuda Cove. He was not simply challenging a small group of teenagers to live holy, but he was about to address the ruling demonic prince of his birthplace. He was about to bring to light the sins of his father and show the island that God was displeased with their lip service and darkened hearts. God wanted the entire island to repent or He was going to destroy it – like He did Sodom and Gomorrah.

Tavian must have wept for over an hour. He sat up and leaned against the wall, draping his arms around his knees. It was in the quietude, Tavian began to feel a strong impression upon his heart to go to the book of Isaiah, the fifty-eighth chapter. He grabbed a Bible that was resting beneath the coffee table and followed his impression. Tavian knew from experience when the Holy Spirit was trying to get his attention. The very first verse in that chapter read:

*Cry aloud, spare not; Lift up your voice like a trumpet; Tell My people their transgression, and the house of Jacob their sins.*

Tavian needed not to read any further to know that God had answered his questions concerning his destiny, but he couldn't stop himself from reading. Because every verse appeared to be speaking to him or to the people of Barracuda Cove. He stopped at verse twelve to fully embrace all that verse was saying to him:

"Those from among you shall build the old waste places; you shall raise up the foundations of many generations; and you shall be called the Repairer of the Breach. The Restorer of the Streets to Dwell in."

Tavian had heard this verse preached by Pastor Coleby, but the revelation of it hadn't gripped him like it did now. Was God truly saying that he (Tavian) would be called the Repairer of the Breach? That he would be used as an instrument in the Hands of the Lord to convert many souls? That he would be used to restore the holy ordinances and admiration of God's Word in Barracuda Cove? It was an eye-opening verse that brought immediate comfort to Tavian's wounded spirit, but also a sense of humility. That God would use him to accomplish such a sacred task was enough to make Tavian weep for months.

However, the enormity of the assignment still left an unsettling feeling in the pit of his stomach. Tavian wondered how he was going to go about effecting such change, or how the Lord would use him to bring to past His word. Another impression began to resonate in his heart and soon, he found himself reading Isaiah Chapter forty-one. But it was verses ten and eleven that pretty much wiped away every remaining doubt Tavian was experiencing at that moment:

"Fear not, for I am with you; Be not dismayed, for I am your God. I will strengthen you; yes, I will help you, I will uphold you with My righteous right hand. Behold, all those who were incensed against you shall be ashamed and disgraced; they shall be as nothing, and those who strive with you shall perish."

Tavian lifted his hands in surrender and began to worship God.

# CHAPTER SEVENTEEN

After locking up the cabin and tossing her overnight bag into the truck, Erica swung the Mercedes into the main road. The conversation she'd had with her lawyer yesterday still left a distasteful feeling in her gut. Divorcing Magnus was not so clear cut, especially if Erica wanted to part from him still holding on to her family's inheritance. Their monies had been commingled, more than half of it being made in the marriage as business partners. Add twenty-two years of Magnus ripping people off and opening several private accounts overseas to transfer the excess profit accumulated from their various companies, and it created a quagmire of where all of their monies were truly located. Erica doubted that Magnus would ever confess to the totality of their wealth.

But she was the fool for marrying Magnus without allowing him to sign a prenup. Her fears of pushing the issue made her feel as if she would lose Magnus to other women. Back then, Magnus was considered a real catch. He may not have been the most handsome man on the planet, but he was a promising preacher, very charismatic and influential. He was the kind of man who could make things happen at the drop at a hat. Her family loved him for that and advised that she marry him, even though there was great risk in him not signing a prenup. They trusted he would treat Erica well and never imagined they would have to deal with the issue of divorce.

But look at her now. In a marriage that was a shell of what she dreamt it would be. Between her discussion with the lawyer and her recent conversations with Dean, Erica was more certain than she had ever been that Magnus was out to destroy her. He was only using her for his gain and she was sure when he'd gotten his fill of her, he would strike. But if she struck first, Magnus wouldn't know what hit him and she would be the one with the upper hand. As she limped toward her front door, her cell phone vibrated in her handbag. She fished for it and noticed that it was Tavian calling.

"Hi Mom," he greeted. "Can you talk now?"

Whenever Tavian asked that, Erica knew it was important. She brought her movements to a halt and then sat on one of the steps.

"Is everything okay?" she asked.

"I think it's time for me to come home," he said. "But I don't know how to. Dad is still unaware that I ditched engineering to become a preacher. He called me two nights ago."

Erica didn't know how to process that because Magnus hadn't called Tavian in nearly two years, when he'd promised he wouldn't until Tavian was done with college. In Erica's eyes, that meant Magnus had something up his sleeve.

"What did he say to you?" Erica asked.

"The same old, same old. Berating me and trying to control my life."

"You don't worry about your father," Erica said. "You just come on home and we will deal with the situation together. I told you a few weeks ago how badly I need you by my side. That still stands. Your father is doing some strange things and I don't know how much more of it I can take."

There was a pronounced pause in Tavian's voice, which suggested he'd swallowed the bile that had rushed to his throat. He hated the way his father treated his mother and the way his mother seemed to accept it.

"It seems as if strange things are happening all over," he said, "which is causing me to believe that it's time to come home."

"What do you mean?"

"Let's just say the devil is mad about my assignment and he will use anyone to stir up trouble. I'll tell you all about it soon enough. I'm simply alerting you of my decision, so you will have time to talk to Dad."

"How much time do I have?"

"I don't know, maybe by the end of the month. I have to tie up some loose ends over here in Canada."

"That's three weeks away," Erica confirmed. "That's more than enough time to talk to your father about your decision. Frankly, I'm glad you decided to follow your dream of being a preacher. Engineering was never your cup of tea. It was your father's, trying to live vicariously through you."

"Wow, Mom. Watch that big word," Tavian joked.

"Oh please, I taught *you* how to spell big words. You remember?"

"Of course, I do...you are the queen of big words..." There was another pause on Tavian's end before he continued in a guarded tone. "Does Dean still come around the house?"

Erica didn't hurry to answer the question because Tavian wouldn't just ask a question out of the blue like that. "Why'd you ask that?" she queried.

"I'm just asking. I haven't heard from him since we had that huge blow up between us."

"I assumed you two had resolved that issue before you left for college."

"I tried to, but he kept avoiding me. I even tried calling him a few times after I left for college, but he wouldn't answer his phone. After two years of trying to make peace, I don't see the point. It's obvious he's still holding a grudge."

Erica knew exactly the grudge her son was alluding to. Tavian felt that Dean was harboring romantic feelings for her and he and Dean got into a fight about it. Sad to say, it ruined their six-year friendship.

"Well, you know how Dean is. He would give you the shirt off his back, but he can be a little stubborn when it comes to apologizing, especially when he feels he's right."

"But according to him, he has no problem with forgiving people."

"He really does have a forgiving heart; I just think you two need to sit down and have a heart to heart conversation. Sometimes it's difficult to resolve issues over the phone or when separated by millions and millions of miles."

"And there you go defending him," Tavian said.

"I'm not defending him, I'm just stating a fact."

"Call it what you want, Mom. I will be at peace, knowing he doesn't communicate with you like he once did."

"Don't even go there with me," Erica spat. "You know my stance on the situation."

"Yeah, but does Dean know?"

"Of course, he does. He's engaged now – to a beautiful young lady."

"That doesn't mean anything. You just be careful."

"Don't I always, Mr. Grumpy Pants?"

Tavian laughed at that. "Seriously, Mom. I worry about you."

"Thank you, my sweet boy, but I will be okay, even more so when you return to Barracuda Cove."

"Well, let's see what the Lord does in the coming weeks. Until then, let's continue to pray for each other."

She disconnected from the line and eased to her feet. Had she looked up at the encasement window to her immediate left, she would have seen that it had been left open. She would have also seen her husband stealthily leaning against it, listening in on the entire exchange between her and their son. But before she could push the key into her front door, he'd vanished upstairs to their bedroom. Five minutes later when he heard Erica enter, he closed his eyes and pretended to be asleep. He could feel her leaning over him, inspecting him.

As badly as he wanted to spring up and grab Erica's neck for the treachery found in their son, Magnus held his composure. If he lost it again now, it could work against him. Erica was on a mission to divorce him and he would be a fool to give her any more leverage at this point. He would bet a million dollars that she had already met with a lawyer and may have installed her own hidden cameras to catch him in a compromising position. But little did she know, he was working swiftly behind the scenes too to expedite her demise. How unfortunate their twenty-year-old marriage had been reduced to a competition, the survival of the fittest.

About an hour later, assuming that Erica had fallen asleep, Magnus climbed out of bed. He jogged downstairs to one of the guestrooms, locking himself in it. He punched some numbers into his cell phone and then placed it against his ear. A female voice answered.

"It's time to up the stakes," he said to her. "Get Erica to sleep with Dean and get her to do it now. We're running out of time. I've already told that young man to install the cameras."

"I'm doing my best," the voice hissed. "But your wife is not as weak as I'd assumed, or it could be that her affections for Dean are really platonic, like she has been telling you all along. I can't get her to take the bait."

Magnus fired a string of invectives. "That heifer wants Dean more than she values her integrity. Just get her in the right place, at the right time and she will give in to her lust."

"You truly are the devil," the voice said.

"When I'm through with Erica, the devil won't have anything on me. She's even gotten our son on board with her wicked plans.

But I will see to it that none of it ever sees the light of day...such a disrespectful heifer...I don't know what possessed me to marry her."

Line disconnected, Magnus sat on the bed and took in the silence. It wasn't long before his thoughts strayed to the male accomplice and soon, he began to brood over what the young man was doing at this precise moment. Was he awake or asleep? Was he in the shower or was he having sex with someone? Magnus couldn't shake the young man from his rumination. Moments later, he clicked into his Facebook account and pulled up the object of his affection. A shirtless pic of the male accomplice came into view, which immediately awakened Magnus' lust to dangerous levels. For the next hour, he painstakingly flipped through every photo of the young man's rugged appearance.

Magnus then pulled up his WhatsApp and sent the young man a text:

*Let's go for drinks tomorrow; I have a proposition for you I'm sure you won't be able to resist.*

When Magnus finally left the guest room, the demonic presence that had hovered over him, disappeared through the floor. It would return, knowing Magnus had set up a shrine and was now directing his ungodly desires to it – the god of lust.

# CHAPTER EIGHTEEN

Netty sashayed into the B&B, expecting to see Erica behind the front desk. Instead she saw one of Erica's cherished employees, Justin Knox, a young man Netty had flirted with in the past. But she didn't get too far with him – for various reasons. Justin was a levelheaded young man, who was outrageously loyal to Erica. And even though Netty was not one to be discouraged easily, because her track record would show she'd conquered the willpower of every man she'd set her sights on; she was simply not interested in pursuing men who'd spent time in prison. If she wanted Justin for herself, she was confident she could win his affections.

However, she'd had a terrible experience with an ex-inmate, who nearly choked the life out of her during their very first disagreement. He had a scar that ran from his right ear to his mouth. Eyes that appeared to have seen the horrors of hell. Similar features, though not as threatening, spoiled Justin's handsome face. But it was more so the look of distrust in Justin's gaze that tripped Netty up every time. She couldn't figure him out and that was a red flag in her book. Taking a deep breath, she perked up her breast implants and then cat-walked in the direction of the front desk. Justin connected his gaze with hers as she approached.

"Ms. Edmonds," he greeted professionally. "What can I do for you?"

Netty cracked him a Botox smile, which amazingly looked real enough to make her appear normal. "Hey, sexy...I'm looking for your boss. She around?"

Justin returned a smile, but his tone was politely dismissive. "I can take a message for her and make sure she gets it."

"I didn't ask you to take a message," Netty snapped. "I asked you...anyway, forget it. I'll call her on her cell phone. I happen to be her best friend, you know."

"Yes, ma'am."

"Yes, ma'am?" Netty looked as if she was going to melt right there on the spot. "Look at this body. Look at this face. Perfection! Do I look like a ma'am to you? You young boys have no idea who you are messing with." She flipped her fingers at him. "Go back to whatever it was you were doing."

Justin smirked as he turned away to address a guest's concern. He was not going to give out any details about Erica, especially when she didn't tell him to. Besides, Netty was not a true friend to Erica, and Justin had discerned that from the first time he'd met her some two years ago. There was some underlying issue with Netty that Justin couldn't place and although he tried to warn Erica about her, Erica appeared nonchalant about his claims. She felt if as Netty was a harmless spinster who preyed on young boys. But Justin sensed Netty was much smarter than she was leading people to believe.

Once he was done with helping the guest, he grabbed a stack of empty boxes that he'd been meaning to throw away in the main garbage disposal. As he exited the glass doors, he felt his cell phone vibrating in his pocket. He sighed inwardly, indicative of his mounting frustration with the caller. He knew exactly who it was because the individual had been texting and calling him for months, almost every day. He tossed the boxes in a huge green barrel and decided to check the messages anyway. As soon as he'd read it, he deleted it. *You just won't stop, will you, Magnus?* Justin hissed under his breath. *I've had enough of your harassment and today it ends...*

Furtively, Justin trotted down a dirt path and then slipped through an opening in the lush landscape that edged the main road. There was a navy blue Land Rover parked across the street, waiting his arrival. Justin was about to make his way over to unleash his wrath but stopped in his tracks when he saw Ian jump out of the passenger side. The scene confused the hell out of Justin because if Magnus had just instructed him to meet him at this location, why was Ian exiting Magnus' SUV? Furthermore, what business did Ian have with Magnus? Ian, as far as Justin knew, was a straight shooter and had never gotten himself mixed up in any sort of dishonest gain. Then again, Ian had been acting a little strange lately.

This had to be Magnus' doing, because he'd been blowing up Justin's phones for months, trying to pull Justin back into his old life of crime. But Justin was working hard on getting his life together and he wanted no part in whatever Magnus was offering. Still, Magnus refused to leave him alone for the simple fact that Erica trusted Justin with her life. With a strong connection like that, Magnus could use Justin to tap into Erica's head like no one could. He was around her ten hours out of the day and could obtain minute-to-minute details of Erica's daily agenda.

When Justin's phone buzzed with another text, he flinched. It was from Magnus, and read,

*Where the hell are you? I'm here waiting on you in the hot sun.*

Justin texted: *As I've said to you a dozen times, I am not interested!*

*I got you out of prison; you owe me. Either you join my team, or I will make your life a living hell. That's not a threat; that's a promise.*

Justin texted back: *I don't wanna join your team. What part of that don't you understand?*

*You will wish you had,* Magnus texted back.

Justin fired off some choice words under his breath. He hated to be reminded of his past life; much less be threatened to relive it again for some bastard who refused to take no for an answer. How could he go against everything Erica had done for him? She didn't deserve to be betrayed like that. Before Ian spotted him, he slipped back through the opening and jogged back to the B&B. Now he had his answer as to what Ian was into. Magnus had made Ian an offer he simply couldn't resist.

∗∗∗

True to her melodramatic behavior, Netty flounced her way out of the B&B and onto the wraparound porch. She was too bothered to take in the serene beauty of the island or to inhale the crisp air that so many tourists seemed to be enjoying just feet away from her. She dug into her handbag and began to fish for her phone. Her gaze happened to flutter upwards, only to catch

Dean running shirtless in the sand. His skin gleamed in the sun like he'd spread baby oil all over him.

The tips of Netty's ears exploded with heat, a sure sign that her lust had been sent into overdrive. The boy was so fine that Netty knew she would not be able to control herself around him. Her penchant for young men, especially the sexy ones who were trying to make something of themselves, was the gamechanger for looking and feeling younger than her forty-one years. She was at a loss as to why Erica had not given in to her cravings for Dean. Because it was obvious Dean liked her a lot and it would not take much for Erica to seduce him.

Netty had to restrain herself from running behind Dean in the sand. She simply watched with rapt attention as he curbed his speed at his kiosk to service the waiting tourists. His smile was easy, and his disposition relaxed. From where Netty stood, she could see the tourists enjoying his welcoming personality and the expedience with which he presented them a full tour of his craftsmanship. He was a stud who just couldn't help being a stud. Netty reached for her phone a second time and pressed in Erica's number; she answered a few rings later.

"Girl, I'm drooling all over myself right now," she exclaimed into Erica's ear. "So much sexiness in one package."

"O Lord, why did I answer my phone?"

Netty detected the annoyance in Erica's voice, but it didn't matter to her one bit. As far as Netty was concerned, Erica had nothing to be annoyed about. She had everything a woman could ask for: a powerful husband, wealth, fame and influence. And that didn't include the young men who fell prey to Erica's motherly charms. Though Netty would prefer to think that Erica used her money as a door to these young men's heart. If it wasn't for Erica's money, Dean wouldn't have had that kiosk on the beach. And Justin wouldn't have been paid such a generous salary every week.

Netty exhaled into the phone. "Two words: Dean Ripley."

"Why do I need to be concern about him?"

"Because he's concerned about you."

"Seriously? Is that what you called me for?"

"Why are you intentionally playing stupid with me? You know full well you are strongly attracted to that boy."

"Netty, please. I'm not in the mood for your loose talk. I have a lot going on with my life right now."

"That's why you need to embrace my advice. You're getting older by the minute and young men like Dean aren't going to stick around. I'm giving you one last chance to make up your mind. After that, I'm going to go after him and I *will* turn him into a ravenous sex beast."

Erica let out a brusque sigh. "I'm hanging up because you're not making any sense."

"Don't you dare hang up on me. You need to face to the truth —"

"Bye, Netty."

"Erica..."

"And don't try to contact with again until you've learned that there are more important things to talk about than sex."

"Erica!"

Upon hearing the familiar *click* sound in her ear, Netty rolled her eyes. She despised Erica's holier-than-thou attitude, acting as if she'd never given in to her sexual desires before. Erica was a cougar, just like she was, and no one could convince Netty otherwise. It was just that Erica was subtler in her expressions. In fact, Netty could recall an incident during their final year of high school when Erica kissed a fourteen-year-old boy who was just in the ninth grade. She did it under the pretense that she was teaching the boy how to be a good kisser, preparing him for his first kiss with his future girlfriend.

But rumor had it that Erica and the boy did more than kissing. Though Netty never had any concrete evidence, she believed it. Especially the way that boy followed Erica around as if he couldn't get enough of whatever she was dishing out. He begged to spend time with her, foregoing his lunch to ensure that he had enough money to buy Erica her favorite snacks. Netty knew from experience that those were the signs of someone who'd been devirginized. In today's generation, they would say that the boy was whipped. Giddy from having experienced sex for the first time.

Granted, they were all under eighteen years old at the time and were still in the process of transitioning into adulthood, but that three-year difference between Erica and that boy gave Netty a clue into how Erica's mind truly worked. Armed with the knowledge of that memory, she hastened her steps through the sand and made a beeline to Dean's kiosk. His back was turned to her, as he was making a sales pitch to a new group of tourists who'd joined the earlier ones. It would be nearly fifteen minutes that Netty would have to wait before Dean was free. But she didn't mind because it gave her an opportunity to fantasize about his glistening, toned body.

"Hey, handsome."

Dean turned in the direction of the voice, and noticing that it was Netty, he took a step back. He knew all about her thirst for younger men and how she put hexes on them to keep them under her control. He wanted no part of that.

"Miss Edmonds," he greeted. "What drew you to my neck of the woods?"

Netty smirked. "I don't think I should answer that; however, I will tell you, I'm here on Erica's behalf."

Dean folded his arm over his chest, making his pecs bulge more than they were already bulging. Netty unconsciously licked her lips.

"First Lady Winthrop knows how to reach me," he said.

Netty batted her wrist at Dean and said coquettishly, "Oh, she won't tell you what I'm about to say. She's too *holy* for that."

"Then maybe we shouldn't be having this conversation."

"Geesh, Erica must have you niggers under a spell," Netty snapped. "First Justin and now you. You do know that she is attracted to you, right? That's the reason why she supports you so much. I'm sure you're not blind to that fact."

The words struck Dean in the gut, but he was reasonably good at keeping a straight-face. "What do you want, Ms. Edmonds? Because as you can see by the influx of tourists flocking my kiosk, I can't entertain you right now. I have to tend to them before I lose them."

"I'm done. I just wanted you to know that you could do much better than Lily. Or the least you could do is explore your options with Erica, or with yours truly before tying yourself down to that white girl. White girls can never please a black man the way a black woman can."

With that, Netty pirouetted in the sand and left Dean standing in shock. He merely noticed when Lily came up behind him and pressed her lips against the back of his neck.

"What was that all about?" she asked, gently turning his face toward hers.

Dean shrugged. "Beats me...the ramblings of a crazy woman, I guess."

"You are too handsome to be so evasive."

"I thought you loved your man with a little intrigue."

"Intrigue is sexy, but evasiveness is unsettling. A vast difference."

Dean laughed and then said to Lily, "It would be in our best interest to stay far away from Ms. Edmonds. She doesn't mean us any good. I'm sure you've heard by now that she is the queen of the cougars, who prey on men half their age."

"Thanks for telling me. That was much better. Do you see how easy it was to tell me what's going on with you?"

Dean held back his reply when he noticed that Lily was wearing his Gucci bracelet. When he looked up and their gazes connected, he could see a dozen questions dancing in her grey eyes. He also detected a measure of sadness that seemed to have been with her for the past several days and no matter how much he assured her of his love, the sadness remained. Maybe it was his fault because he refused to tell her who bought him the bracelet, and her wearing it was a way to compel him into a discussion about it. But Dean still held on to his belief that it was better that Lily didn't know. He pulled her into him and pressed his lips against hers.

"I love you. You do know that, right?"

"I know…" Lily pulled away.

"What is it?" Dean asked.

"My job is sending me back to Canada for three weeks." The sadness in her eyes quickly turned to full disappointment. "But I don't want to go, especially with our wedding coming up."

Justin took the news in stride. "When does your job want you to leave?"

"In a few days, but I don't want to go. Could you help me come up with an excuse to stay here on the island? Going back to Canada is not good for me right now. It brings back so many bad memories being that close to my parents again. They still have no idea that I'm engaged to you and up to this point, I don't care if they ever know."

Dean didn't know what to say because if he assisted her in her ruse, there was a possibility she could be found out and lose her job. If he encouraged her to go to Canada, she would want him to go along with her. Honestly, he wouldn't mind going as a pillar of support, but he couldn't leave now – not when the secrets between him and Erica were looming over them, threatening to be revealed by an unknown source. He could handle the scandal – if there was to be one—it was Erica whom he was concerned about. She would die if her reputation was ruined.

"I was thinking you should come with me," Lily said, seeming to read Dean's mind. "It's only for three weeks."

Dean smiled. "I just knew you were gonna suggest that, but I'm not sure that's a good idea."

"Why not?"

"For several reasons."

"Like?"

"Well, for starters, you almost ripped my clothes off the other night while my mother was just twenty feet away in her bedroom. I can't imagine being locked away with you, thousands of miles away with no accountability."

Lily playfully punched Dean on the arm. "You're making me sound like an out-of-control sex maniac."

"Please don't take me seriously; I was only kidding with you. But three weeks is a long time for me to be away from my business. Extra money is coming in, which we could use to plan this wedding the way we want."

"I have money too, you know. I could sustain you for those three weeks."

"I cannot allow you to do that. What kind of man do you think I am? A gigolo?"

That generated a smile from Lily, but that restless concern was still coursing through her expression. "What about my parents?" she asked. "This would be a good time for me to introduce you to them."

"You really believe that? You haven't even told them that we are engaged. And by the way you described your parents, they will not be so accepting. I told you to break the news of our dating months ago, but you kept dragging your feet."

"That's because you don't know how cruel and wicked and disgusting my parents are."

"Even so, they are your parents and they have a right to know."

"Then come with me. With you there by my side, it would be easier for me to tell them about us."

"Lily..."

"No more excuses, Dean," Lily spat and then looked at him with exasperation. "Are you sure your reasons for staying don't have anything to do with this bracelet?"

She raised it up so that Dean could see it, making it harder for him to shun talking about it.

"I thought we settled the issue," he said.

"We did...I'm just thinking that if I have to go Canada all by my lonesome, this bracelet is going to give me nightmares."

Dean gave Lily a puzzled look. "Then why are you wearing it?"

"Because I'm trying to face my fears."

"Fears of what?"

Lily cocked her head at Dean. "Just tell me: Was it a male or a female who bought this bracelet for you?"

"What does it matter?"

176

"You see? You're being evasive again."

Dean looked over toward his kiosk and noticed tourists were picking up his masterpieces and inspecting them. It was the perfect excuse to get away from Lily's pressuring tactics.

"I have to go and entertain my customers," he said. "Can we talk about this later?"

Lily refused to bargain with Dean. "Just tell me if it was a male or female and I'll leave the issue alone."

"Lily Rose..."

Lily smiled sheepishly. Whenever Dean called her by her full name, she knew she'd upset him, but she simply could not let Dean go on sidestepping her questions. It only added to the doubts her parents had interjected into her self-worth since she was a little girl.

"I'm sorry that I'm making a big deal about this," she told him, "but it's really bothering me, and I can't go to Canada in this mood. Especially when you've already decided you're not going with me."

Dean gave her a patient smile. He hated to put her through this agony, but he refused to tell her that it was Erica who'd bought him that bracelet. It would open up a brand-new can of worms.

"It was a female," he answered and then quickly added, "Now enough about this bracelet. You're gonna drive me crazy with it. Call me later?"

Dean planted a kiss on Lily's cheek and hastened away before she had time to come up with another way to detain him. He knew if she didn't have to go back to work, she would have waited on him until he was through with his customers. Once she was out of view, Dean subtly raised his gaze to the glass window of the B&B, expecting to catch Erica staring at him again, but to his disappointment, she was not there. He could have kicked himself for letting his emotions embarrass him like that. How could he do this to Lily? She didn't deserve this – this divided heart of his, which was making it increasingly more difficult to decide where to focus his affections.

How strange it was that Lily was staring up at the glass window too as she trekked slowly through the sand. Her mind was on Erica as well, though for a totally different reason than Dean's. If there was one person who knew Dean better than anyone, apart from his mother, it was First Lady Winthrop. Certainly, Lily surmised in her mind, Erica would be able to tell her something about Dean's past girlfriends. As she made the five-minute walk back to her job, she called Erica and booked an appointment to meet with her at her earliest convenience. Because there was no way she was going to Canada without the name of that female.

# CHAPTER NINETEEN

Freda normally didn't have dreams, but when she did, they were vivid and very detailed. For at least fifteen minutes she wrestled with sordid images involving her son and First Lady Winthrop. They were so real that Freda thought at one point the scenes had actually happened, leaving her muttering in shock. *It can't be true...not my son...how could he let this happen?* The last time she'd had such a detailed dream was months before her husband had been murdered. She'd warned John repeatedly of the events she saw in her dreams, but of course, her husband didn't take her seriously. Eventually, she began to slack off from covering her husband in prayer when the dream seemed to fade into her subconscious.

It was the biggest mistake she could have made. She would never forget that night when she received the heartbreaking news of husband's murder. The dream suddenly came alive and depressed her spirit for months. This time round, however, she wasn't going to allow the devil to win. She didn't need to ask the Lord what direction to take because there were alarm bells already ringing off in her spirit, especially being a woman of much discernment. Freda knew this was not the kind of dream to let stew. Those alarm bells meant that she had to directly engage the enemy on the spiritual battlefield.

Suddenly fortified with holy anger, she slipped out of the bed and began to pace around her bedroom, rebuking the plans of darkness. It didn't take long for the atmosphere to become heavy with demonic spirits trying to block her prayers. But the more resistance Freda felt, the harder she prayed!

*"Satan, I bind your agents in the name of Jesus! You will not destroy my son and bring him or the first lady to open shame...I plead the blood of Jesus, against you, Satan and your evil workers! I demolish your plans, I paralyze and frustrate your diabolic schemes! In Jesus name!*

Freda continued praying like this, even while she bathed and got dressed for work. By the time she'd walked to the church, she felt as if the heavens above her were open and that her prayers were finally having some real effect. That was when she saw Apostle Winthrop had pulled up into the church parking lot. He jumped out and merely acknowledge her as he rushed past her into the building. He was on his phone, having an intense conversation about some business deal. Freda waited a few seconds before she walked in behind him. He was about fifteen feet ahead, standing with his back to her. She would have gone on about her business had she not heard her son's name in the mix.

"...if you allow Dean to sign that contract," Magnus spat, "I will personally see to it that you lose every one of your business connections. Gavin Osprey will be history. In weeks your investments will dry up and neither you nor your partners will ever recoup from the loss. Trust me, you don't want to contend with me because I am a ruthless man when it comes to my territory. You should have not entertained a conversation with my wife, because I gave her clear instructions to keep her hands off of this deal..."

Freda dashed into the women's bathroom when it looked as if Magnus would catch her eavesdropping. All of a sudden, that dream she'd had of Dean and First Lady Winthrop began to make sense. This persistence of Erica's to ensure that Dean got that contract would be the magnetic force that would pull them together. Freda could only imagine how Dean would react to know that Erica had made his dream come true. He was quick to show gratitude, especially in ways that could make Erica feel as if he was coming on to her.

Freda could already see the steps of their sin playing out before her. Her son was a very good-looking man with a huge heart that women often fell prey to. Over the years, Erica had been very instrumental in helping her son, and there were times that Freda suspected that their relationship had crossed the boundary, but without proof, she chose not to make an issue of it. However, having such a dream caused her suspicion to resurface. God wouldn't show her anything for naught. There was much trouble on the horizon and she must warn her son.

### ✳✳✳

This defiance of his wife's had Magnus jaw-swollen mad. How dare she go against his commands, knowing the repercussions. She must not be afraid of him anymore and that thought made Magnus even angrier. He wouldn't be able to control her the way he had been doing through domestic abuse. Somehow, Erica found the courage to fight back. *All power to you, you black heifer,* Magnus thought, *there's no way in hell I will let you mess up the plans I've worked so hard to contrive. There are other ways to get you to do what I want – without me laying a finger on you.* Magnus grabbed his cell phone and called Gavin back.

"Give my wife what she wants," Magnus said.

"By that, you mean you're agreeing to let us ratify the contract between Dean Ripley and ourselves."

"Just do it before I change my mind," Magnus spat. "She shows more loyalty to that boy than she does to me. How can I contend with that?"

"Okay, it is settled then. I will call your wife with the good news."

Gavin couldn't hide the excitement in his voice and it peeved the hell out of Magnus. Dean appeared to have captured Gavin's heart almost as much as Erica's. But both Erica and Gavin were in for a rude awakening to believe that he would sanction Dean's contract without an ulterior motive. When Gavin disconnected from the line, Magnus clicked into his WhatsApp contacts, and pulled up the male accomplice's number. For a few seconds, Magnus stared at his photo, completely smitten by what he saw. The young bloke had updated an image of himself, more alluring than the previous one.

*Where are you?* he typed.

*Lush Haven*

*Are the cameras and audio feed installed and working as they should?*

A few seconds later the reply came: *Just about...I'm testing the last cabin as we speak. I had to wait until your wife left the premises. She's been coming here in the mornings and leaving in the evenings.*

Magnus hadn't any idea that Erica was doing that. She had completely gone against his commands, which was an obvious show of defiance. This also suggested to Magnus that Erica may have some inkling he was behind the anonymous note he'd given the fifteen-year-old boy to give to Dean. But knowing how terrified Erica was of confronting him, she was working undercover to undermine him. It didn't matter anyway because he would still outwit her. A blast of hot air flew out of his nostrils, indicative of how exasperated he was with his wife.

He texted: *That heifer will soon get what's coming to her. Are you sure no one saw you?*

*I'm sure...I was very careful.*

*You had better be. I'm paying you a fortune.*

*Thanks for the reminder.*

Once Magnus was finished with the conversation, he deleted it, sat back and laughed. Because he anticipated that the real action was about to begin.

# CHAPTER TWENTY

By the time Freda got home from work, she was overwhelmed with dread. She'd gotten off at three-thirty that afternoon, but Dean was still at the kiosk. If she went according to how she felt, she would have marched down there to the beach and emptied her fears on Dean. But she felt she needed to calm her spirit because she could do more than good. She was actually more shaken about what she'd heard Apostle Winthrop discussing on the phone than the dream itself. Because it meant that the events of the dream had already been set in motion.

Erica was not going to relent until she made sure Dean got that contract. It was the way she'd always operated when it came to Dean, ever since he was a twelve-year-old boy. Always giving Dean what he wanted. Back then, Freda never understood why Erica doted on her son like that, but she understood now that it was the plan of the enemy all along to bring disgrace not only to the Ripley name, but to the Winthrop legacy. The enemy was just waiting for the right time for all of the chips to fall into place.

But what a pity it was that the Winthrops were allowing themselves to be pawns in Satan's game. And what a greater pity it was for Dean to be willingly dragged into the middle of it. In Freda's eyes, Dean didn't need that contract – not if it was going to lead him into sin with the first lady. He was better off hustling his way with his fiancée by his side. Together they could make their own future and avoid Erica's generous handouts altogether.

But Freda kept thinking: What if she couldn't stop her dream from coming to pass, no matter how much she prayed? And if there was such a secret to be exposed, it would destroy the only church on the island, which was already suffering from doctrinal error, worldliness and spiritual decay. Undoubtedly, there would be a nasty divorce between Erica and Magnus and their businesses would take a huge hit. Then the economy on the island would dive soon after, along with her janitorial job. The Winthrops were too powerful for things to remain unshaken around them.

The magnitude of her thoughts forced Freda to sit on the edge of her bed, but seconds later, consternation made her jump to her feet. She couldn't sit still and do nothing. God was depending on her to be a righteous voice and to expose the kingdom of darkness. Ten minutes later, she was marching through the sand toward her son's kiosk.

Fridays and Saturdays were always an excessively blessed day for Dean as the cruise ships around the world had made Barracuda Cove one of their main tourists' stops. The vendors on the beach could expect a goodly number in the thousands, from those who were eager to spend their money on rare merchandise. For some reason, Dean's kiosk seemed to be located in the right spot, because his kiosk would be among the first that tourists flocked to. This was what Freda had to contend with when she curtailed her speed several feet behind the crowd.

She barely glimpsed Dean, as he was totally immersed in giving the tourists his attention. She watched as he laughed and threw sales pitches at some, while he bagged wooden sculptures being purchased by others. He made being ambidextrous look like a walk in the park. Freda couldn't help the smile that pulled at the sides of her lips. Her boy was a natural businessman who would do exceptionally well without Erica's constantly throwing her support at him.

As soon as some of the tourists began to clear away from the kiosk, Freda made an attempt to get her son's attention. She stood to his immediate left, wringing her hands in anticipation of the talk she needed to have with him. She knew it would be a difficult conversation because her son was so naïve when it came to the human heart, but she felt no way deterred in her mission. Dean must be warned about the impending doom. She smiled when their gazes suddenly connected.

"Mom." Dean grinned, wiping sweat from his thick brows. "What wind blew you this way?"

*The Holy Spirt,* Freda wanted to say, but instead she replied cautiously, "The concern of a mother who loves you very much."

Dean gave her a confused smile. "When are you not concerned about me?"

"True, I can't say when I'm not, but this one is rather different..." Freda stepped closer to her son so that the few tourists milling around them wouldn't hear her. "I had a dream and I believe the Lord is sending us a message."

The look on Dean's face suggested that his mother had had a little too much to drink. "Well, in that case," he joked, "I had better call it a day and shut down my kiosk because whenever the

Lord gives you these messages, they are long and full of depressing woes. Can't you wait until I get home? I'll be done by five o'clock."

"This is the weekend," Freda reminded him. "You know full well you're not coming home until seven o'clock this evening. But I'm sensing in my spirit I should talk to you now, rather than later."

"Mom, c'mon...I'm making money, which Lily and I need to pay off some bills before the wedding. Our cake alone is costing us two thousand dollars."

Freda held back her biting retort, only because she wanted to deliver this message that was burning to get out. She did not see the necessity in spending all that money for a cake and she had already told her son that much.

"Well," she said, "I'm not leaving. I must obey God."

Dean said in a resigned tone, "I must say, you really know how to pull my strings, especially when you throw God into the mix. Give me a few minutes and you're all mine."

Freda stepped back and allowed her son to wrap up his final sales. Not long after, her gaze moved upwards and to her befuddlement, she saw Erica and a white man briskly walking toward Dean's kiosk. Their expressions were animated and although Erica walked with a small limp, their gait was purposeful. Freda could only assume they were preparing to give Dean some sort of news. He spotted them before she could pull his attention back to her, which was fruitless now, considering how much Dean revered Erica.

"Wow, what is so special about today?" Dean questioned, as he greeted Erica and Gavin with a handshake. "I don't usually get such visits all at once from people I honor and respect..." he craned his neck toward Freda. "Mom, what are you hiding from me? Are you a part of this surprise?"

Freda shrugged, as her pensive gaze connected with Erica's. Something told her that her talk with her son was about to be short-circuited and there was nothing she could do to stop it.

"Your mother has nothing to do with our visit," Gavin said. "But we are glad that she is here...Mrs. Winthrop, do you want to tell Dean the news or should I?"

Erica stepped forward, ignoring the slight twinge of pain in her ankle. She was too excited to even care. She parked her eyes on Dean and was almost swallowed by that irresistible smirk that was plastered on his face. His mohawk haircut sealed the deal for her, as it added a sense of edginess to his already striking appearance. Dean hadn't any idea of how well-loved he truly was. That was why it gave Erica great pleasure to see that smirk explode into joyful laughter.

"I think you should hold your mother's hand," she told him. "Because I'm not sure you will be able to stand on your two feet when I'm done saying this."

"Just go on and spit it out already," Dean said. "You're killing me with the suspense."

"Well..." Erica paused for dramatic effect. "Mr. Osprey and his partners have agreed to offer you a contract to showcase your work around the world. Complete funding will be provided, along with your travel expenses, living arrangements, food, and any reimbursements deemed appropriate. It all will be covered in the clause. Your first tour will be held in Paris..."

Dean locked his fingers over the top off his head and dropped to his knees. Tears welled in his eyes as Erica went on and on about the money and the business side of what he was about to walk into. The only thing he could think about at that moment was how long and hard he'd worked, and the immeasurable hours of sacrifice he'd put in to stay a step ahead of the competition. It all had finally paid off.

"By the end of the first year," Erica continued. "You will be rewarded with an entrepreneurial check of half a million dollars.And depending on how well your work is received around the world, that will be increased to one million, which will be used as seed money to establish you as a household name."

Dean threw himself back into the sand and laughed. He couldn't stop from laughing, even though the tears were falling. He kept screaming out for Freda, but she was too stunned to move. The amount of money alone that Dean had been offered was staggering and Freda had to shake herself from beneath its grip. She had come to warn Dean about this contract but as she looked on at her son, rolling over in the sand, she thought about how cruel it would be to break his heart. Especially since he'd been waiting for a breakthrough like this since he was sixteen years old.

*God, Freda prayed silently. Tell me what to do concerning this situation! Is this Your voice speaking to me or is it just my imagination running away with me? One million dollars is a lot of money to ask Dean to turn down for just a dream. He will certainly think I've lost my mind...*

Gavin extended a hand to pull Dean up from the sand. "I know this is a lot to take in right now and I know you will need some time to talk things through with your support systems. Plus, you have a wedding coming up. You will be given time to organize before your first tour."

Dean was giddy with joy. "I don't need a lot of time," he said. "I'm certain Lily won't mind pushing up the wedding date when she hears about this."

Erica laughed, but there was a wilt of disappointment in her eyes. "No need to push up your wedding date," she told him. "The offer is pretty much written in stone; so you can take your time getting things sorted out here before you leave for Paris."

"Can I take Lily with me?"

"Of course, you can," Gavin said. "In fact, I would encourage that she goes along with you. Your honeymooning days would have just gotten started."

Gavin laughed at his own joke, but Erica didn't find any humor in it. She was not an advocate of mixing business with pleasure. But if Dean wanted Lily to accompany him, it was his choice.

"Before I fly back to Orlando," Gavin concluded, "I'm going to have you come to my hotel and sign an official document. Of course, we will go over any questions or concerns you may have during that time."

"Thank you...I don't even know what to say right now," Dean said, still holding on to Gavin's hand with a firm grip. "I'm beyond speechless that something like this could happen for me."

"Believe it, buddy," Gavin said. "Your work speaks for itself."

Dean walked toward Erica and greeted her, then allowed his palms to cup her elbows. He stared into her eyes and offered her his deepest gratitude. The exchange was far from romantic, but it didn't look that way to Freda. She shifted her weight from one foot to the next to stop herself from reacting in a foolish manner.

"I will call you later so we can officially celebrate your success," Erica said, as she and Gavin turned to leave. "Congratulations, Dean! You deserve it."

When Dean's gaze returned to Freda's, his smile dried up almost immediately. It was the unspoken rebuke in Freda's eyes that told Dean his mother was not happy about the news. A strange reaction, he thought, because if anyone who should have been happy for him, it should have been his mother. She knew the hell they lived through, suffering financially because of his father's gambling habits. Now they would have no need and he couldn't understand why that would depress her.

"Why the long face?" he asked her.

Freda didn't bat an eye when she replied, "Because the devil is out to get you. Tell Mr. Osprey you don't want the contract."

Dean did a double take to make certain those words had really come out of his mother's mouth. His lips parted and then closed. Too hurt to respond, he walked off and left Freda standing alone in the sand.

# CHAPTER TWENTY-ONE

*Thirty Minutes Later*

Although the B&B was only footsteps away from Dean's kiosk, Lily could only remember going there twice. Once when Dean introduced her to Erica and the other time being when Erica took her for a tour of the grounds. Working as much as she did, she really didn't have time to visit otherwise. Her lunch hour was used to spend time with Dean. That was why she'd requested that Erica set their appointment for late afternoon when she would get off from work.

Moving stealthily up the walkway toward the entrance, Lily tried to appear as inconspicuous as she possibly could so that she wouldn't chance running into Dean. Because she wouldn't be able to explain to him why she'd gone behind his back to get information about his past. She didn't like this idea of sneaking around at all, but she simply could not go to Canada for three whole weeks with her doubts spinning out of control like this. What a pity Dean didn't seem to understand this side of her. As soon as she stepped into the vestibule, she was relieved to see Erica waiting on her.

She extended her hand to Erica. "Thanks for meeting with me," she said. "I came straight here as soon as I got off from work."

"It's fine," Erica said. "Please, let's go to my office so we can have some privacy."

Lily kept her strides about three steps behind Erica, which gave her the opportunity to observe the way Erica's jeans gripped her coke-bottle figure. A perfect butt that could give a fit twenty-year-old woman serious competition. Her crochet-style braids were pulled back into one and dropped to about eighteen inches behind her off-the-shoulder blouse. A pair of brown leather, open-toe sandals completed the look.

To the casual observer it was average urban wear, but because everything about Erica exuded class, and a regal confidence that Lily could only hope someday to develop in her own character, anything Erica wore looked aristocratic. And she smelled good too, leaving a scent trail that reminded Lily of lavender and vanilla. If Lily didn't already know that Erica was a woman in her early forties, she could have easily mistaken her to be at least ten years younger.

"You can have a seat right here," Erica told her, as she moved two huge binders out of a swivel chair and placed them on her desk. "Forgive my untidiness; I haven't had time to clean up this space."

Lily waved Erica off. "Oh please, you should see my apartment, which really hasn't had a proper cleaning since I moved into it. Too busy."

"That seems to be the catchword these days. I'm surprised we still look as good as we do for as hard as we work."

"But you do look good for your age," Lily said. "What's your secret?"

Erica gave Lily a dubious stare. "You're serious?"

"Yes...please forgive me if I'm being too forward. I in no way came here to dwell on your appearance."

It was Erica's turn to wave Lily off. "I'll take it as both a compliment and an encouragement, because I haven't been feeling anything like myself these past several weeks. I've been under a lot of stress and I can feel my body deteriorating from the inside."

"I would have never known," Lily said.

"But let me not take credit. It's all God. Without Him I would have come to nothing by now."

"Amen...spoken like a true first lady. I hope to take a page from your book someday."

There was a transient pause, which was the perfect cue for Lily to poke into Erica's personal life, but she refrained herself from crossing that boundary. Instead, she took a deep breath and got on with what she had come to talk about.

"Again, I want to say thanks for meeting with me," she said, continuing only after Erica prompted her. "Here's the thing: My job is sending me to Canada for three weeks to oversee a project. I don't want to go, but I have to. The reason I don't want to go has to do with Dean. Well, just let me be brutally honest with you, I believe he's keeping something from me...I know it seems as if I'm rambling, but I'm really worried."

"Take your time...I'm listening," Erica prompted.

"Thank you. I must say that Dean is a wonderful man and I love him more than I've ever loved anyone in my life. And I can't wait to become his wife. But there's this side of Dean that really concerns me...I was hoping you could shed some light on his upbringing. I understand you came into his life when he was just twelve years old and helped to rear him into the man he is today. So if anyone truly knows him, apart from his mother, it is you."

Erica hoped Lily didn't see the wilt in her expression, which was a manifestation of the protective walls going up within her. She didn't want Lily to think she would spill her guts just because she was Dean's fiancée. Lily needed to relax and not bog Dean down with her insecurities, especially with the life Dean was about to walk into.

"So you want me to be a snitch?" Erica tossed at her.

Lily rested a hand across her breasts, as if the accusation had pierced a hole in her heart. "Oh Lord, no. I'm not asking you to delve into Dean's past. I simply want to know what he was like growing up and why you think this bracelet means so much to him?"

"What bracelet?"

Lily reached into her handbag and pulled it out to show Erica. The same one Erica had bought for Dean's sixteenth birthday. Erica did a doubletake. It took everything in her to conceal her confusion and her hurt because Dean had promised her he would never take it off. She took it from Lily and inspected it as if she were seeing it for the first time.

"It's a lovely piece of jewelry," she said. "I've seen Dean with it on."

"And he would have never taken if off," Lilly added, "if I hadn't bugged the hell out of him about it."

Erica felt a little better when she heard Lily say that because it meant Dean had only given Lily the bracelet to distract her from revealing the truth to her. For some reason he didn't want her to know. Likewise, she would follow Dean's example. She was not about to complicate this situation any further than it already was. Especially now that Erica had discerned Magnus was working hard to embroil her in a scandal.

"I don't see why you need to make an issue out of it," Erica said, handing the custom-made piece back to Lily. "It was a gift given to him when he was just sixteen years old – way before he met you."

"I agree with you; I should leave it alone and not stir up trouble. But I just can't get rid of this unsettling feeling at the pit of my stomach. I feel there's so much more Dean isn't telling me about this bracelet. I think he still has strong feelings for the person who bought it for him."

Erica leaned forward toward Lily. "Listen to me, my dear. Take it from someone who knows a little about being in a relationship that isn't all that I hoped it would be. You're not going to find anyone as kind and as loving and as patient as Dean. I can't tell you who bought that bracelet for him, but I know for a fact it meant the world to him. And if he gave it to you, it says that you mean more to him than anything, much more than a little old bracelet he's been unwilling to give up. I need you to think about that for a minute. Don't go creating problems that aren't there."

Lily could hear her mother's voice in her head at that point. *I told ya, you're too stupid to keep a man...no man will ever want you...you're too insecure, you're too emotionally-attached, you're too..."*

Erica tapped the desk a few times to bring Lily's attention back to her. "Lily? Did you hear what I said?"

"Yes..."

"Really? It seems as if your mind was somewhere else."

Lily jumped to her feet, tears threatening to burst out of her eyes. "I have to leave now...but thank you for your wonderful advice. I will do my best to apply it. Please, don't tell Dean that I came to see you about the bracelet."

"I have my faults, but being a troublemaker is not one of them."

"Thank you. You don't know how much that means to hear you say that."

"No problem." Erica stood to her feet. "Come, I'll walk you out.

✳✳✳

Netty jumped out of her car when she saw Erica escort Lily through the exit of the B&B. She'd been waiting around several days for Erica to show because no one would tell her where Erica had been hiding out. Now she dared anyone to lie to her and she wouldn't hesitate to read them their last rites because she'd seen Erica with her own eyes. That thought hadn't yet left her when she noticed Justin Knox coming toward her. A bag of trash was in each of his hands, indicative of his work shift nearing its end.

Netty held her head high, intending to walk right past him. But to her shock, he stepped in front of her, blocking her movement. His rough-looking exterior always put her off and reminded her of his stint in prison, but she was ready to go head-to-head with him if he so chose to go down that path with her.

"Mrs. Winthrop isn't here," he told her.

"Did she tell you to say that?" Netty retorted. "Because I just saw her walk back into the building with my own eyes."

"What can I say? Your eyes have deceived you."

"Boy, please! I could be your mother. Move the hell out of my way before you get run over."

Justin kept a cool demeanor, although he was burning on the inside with hatred for this woman who claimed to be Erica's friend. "You know I don't like you, right?"

"That makes two of us...now move! I've got business to tend to and you're interfering with that."

Netty bumped Justin aside and sashayed her voluptuous curves through the glass entrance. Justin swallowed his rage and continued on toward the garbage site. In his peripheral, someone had jogged past him. He focused his gaze on the person, only to discover it was Ian, trying to appear inconspicuous as he escaped to the main road. Unable to control his impulse, Justin took off behind Ian. He just knew Ian was up to no good, the way he'd been coming to work late, and disappearing certain times during the day without any legit explanation. Justin already sensed that Ian was on Magnus' payroll. Justin vowed that he would make Ian tell him, even if he had to beat it out of him.

He dropped back behind the hedges when he saw Magnus' navy blue Land Rover pull to the curb. Ian hurried to the passenger side, nervously looking around as he settled in. Five minutes later, Ian emerged with a guilt-ridden disposition. Magnus sped off, leaving Ian to wipe away his tears. Whatever it was, it was enough to throw Ian into a tailspin. Justin had to find out what was going on. He waited patiently as Ian made his way back across the street. As soon as Ian was within reach, Justin snatched him by his shirt collar and swung him up against a thick wall of bramble.

"I've been watching you for months and now I see where you've been running off to. What the hell is your business with Magnus Winthrop?"

Ian's eyes were popping out of his head because he'd truly been taken by surprise. It affected the flow of his speech. "I... I, don't know what you're talk... talkin' about."

Justin was so angry that the scar on his face seemed to take on a life of its own. Looking like a thin stream of water moving back and forth. "Don't lie to me! I saw you coming out of his SUV. I swear I will go to Erica right now and rat you out. But not before I knock all of your teeth down your throat."

Ian tried to fight his way out of Dean's grip, but it was a futile attempt. It only made Justin become more incensed. He jammed his forearm into Ian's throat, cutting of his oxygen.

Tears streamed down Ian's face. "I needed the money," he shrieked.

Justin loosened his grip. "What?"

"I said I needed the money, man...please don't tell Mrs. Winthrop."

"Why is Magnus giving you money? What does he want from you?"

"I can't say, man...I can't say...it's too embarrassing."

Justin tightened his grip again, but when he saw Ian's eyes roll to the back of his head, he let go of him altogether. Expended from the onslaught, Ian dropped to his knees on the ground. At that moment Justin saw a broken man who needed guidance, not to be judged or condemned. But Justin was too upset to give any friendly advice.

"If you want to continue working for Erica," he spat at Ian, "you had better cut your ties with that bastard! This is your only warning."

Justin spun on his heel and marched back to the B&B.

\*\*\*

Erica was at the front desk instructing one of her guests on how to locate the spa center. Netty's fiery gaze zeroed in on them, and in alignment with her brassy nature, she walked right in between them and interrupted their conversation.

"Why won't you answer my phone calls or tell me where you've been hiding?" she spat at Erica. "Instead, you have everyone lying about your whereabouts."

Erica gave Netty a patient smile, and then turned her attention back to her guest. She apologized to them and directed their steps through one of the side exits. There was not a hint of a smile on Erica's face when her gaze flew back to Netty.

"You know that was downright rude and very embarrassing," she scolded her. "Couldn't you have waited until I was done with my guest?"

"No, because you're always avoiding me. I had to strike while I had the chance."

Erica looked Netty up and down like she'd just been let out the Looney Bin. "It makes no sense contending with you because you don't understand what it means to be civilized. What do you want?"

"First of all, I need you to lose the attitude. I didn't do anything to you."

"Really? You're a bloody pest."

"And what are you? A selfish snob who thinks the world revolves around her."

"You know, Netty," Erica said irascibly, "I've had enough of your –"

Netty pushed two concert tickets in Erica's face, bringing an instant halt to her ranting. "If this don't get you out of your funk," she told Erica, "I don't know what will."

Three letters, printed in a red, bold design captured Erica's attention right away. 'Bez.' He was a Nigerian artist whose music was categorized as alternative soul. Actually, a hybrid of soul, rock, jazz and R&B. He was featured in Pulse Magazine as the first on the list of "Top 12 Musicians to Look Out for in 2014."

202

Erica was waiting in the line of a high-end retail store when she first heard a song sung by Bez.

The musical arrangement was the first thing that captured her attention, then the lyrics, which focused on the passionate love of a man for a woman. When she got to the counter to pay for her items, she asked the cashier if she knew the name of the artist. To her amazement, Bez was one of the cashier's favorite artists, the cashier herself being of Nigerian descent. The name of the song was titled, "There's A Fire." Erica went home that evening, pulled it up on YouTube and listened to that song at least a dozen times that evening.

"I knew this would get your attention," Netty said, pulling Erica back from her walk down memory lane. "For some reason you love this Nigerian dude and when I read that he was coming to Barracuda Cove this weekend to do a concert, I thought of you."

Seeing those tickets may have taken the wind out Erica's sails, but that didn't mean she was back on friendly terms with Netty.

"You must have lost your mind purchasing those tickets," Erica snapped. "I am the first lady of First Family Worship Center and I won't attend something so inappropriate."

Netty let out a dramatic sigh. "Oh gawd, you're such a fake! There is nothing inappropriate about this concert. It's being hosted by the Red Cross and all proceeds will go toward the Kids Cancer Foundation. I hope you didn't make me buy these tickets in vain because they are not cheap."

"How much did you actually pay for them?"

"Enough."

"How much?"

"Why do you need to know?"

"So I can reimburse you," Erica said. "If I can't attend, I know someone who will."

"Sorry, but these tickets are not for resale," Netty said. "If you won't go with me, then I'll go alone."

"That doesn't make any sense."

"And it doesn't make sense that you're being so mean and disgruntled when all I'm asking is that you indulge me for three hours. I will have you back home before anyone sees you from the church. Chances are, we may see half of the congregation right there, swooning to Mr. Bez's velvety voice."

Netty cracked a huge grin, but Erica didn't find humor in that at all.

"You're doing a good job convincing me that this is not a good idea," Erica said. "Why in the world would I be happy about my members seeing me in a place like that?"

"Girl, relax your tired bones. It's just a concert. When will you get another chance like this to see one of your favorite artists live on stage? I will even help you get his autograph."

When Netty said that, it looked as if Erica's resolve was starting to crumble. She loved Bez's music and she didn't need Netty to convince her any further that it would be a real treat to meet him in person. It was just her reputation that she was worried about.

"By that sly smirk on your face," Netty said, "I can tell you wanna go."

"I don't know –"

"Come on, Erica, live a little and stop being such a wuss."

Erica gave Netty a warning with her eyes. "I hope I don't regret this…"

That was all Netty needed to hear. She lunged forward and pulled Erica into a bear hug. She was screaming so loudly that it got the attention of passing patrons.

"I promise you won't regret this…It will be like old times, hanging out before you met Jesus. You have no idea how happy you've made me…" Netty pushed both tickets into Erica's hand. "I think you should keep them because you know I have a habit of forgetting where I put things."

"At least we can agree on that." Erica began to goad Netty toward the exit. "Now please, leave my establishment before you frighten all of my guests away. I don't know why you have to scream so loudly."

"Because I never imagined you would agree to go. You are so uptight and moody and –"

"Go," Erica instructed, "before I change my mind."

"Okay, okay, I'm leaving. I'll call you, so look out for my number because you're famous for avoiding my calls."

Erica shook her head and laughed as a giggling Netty cat-walked through the exit. And talk about phone numbers, Erica planned to pay a visit to her telephone company today to acquire a second cell phone number. She would keep the old number because so many people were connected to it, but she didn't trust communicating with Dean on it. Hence, the reason for the second number.

She couldn't think of any way to ascertain how Magnus had infiltrated her privacy, except that she asked him about it outright. However, she wasn't about to walk into the lion's den just like that. That didn't mean she couldn't work around the situation. In fact, it would be stupid of her to act as if her husband would ever be that loving, affectionate man she'd married so many years ago. He rarely looked at her without disdain in his eyes. His life's mission was to degrade her and keep her under his feet.

So it would be in her best interest to stay a few steps ahead of him to protect herself and Dean from being exploited by Magnus' venom. And one way of doing that was to keep her daily movements as untraceable as she possibly could.

# CHAPTER TWENTY-TWO

L ater that evening, Dean went to Lily's apartment. He knew he shouldn't be there because of the temptation of giving in to premarital sex, but he was too upset to go home. His mother hadn't any idea how much she'd hurt him when she told him to reject Mr. Osprey's offer. How could she find it in her heart to say that to him? This wasn't some fly-by-night deal. This was the big break both of them had been waiting for. What changed or who had fed his mother envy food? Because Dean refused to believe that his mother came up with this nonsense on her own.

"I know you don't drink champagne," Lily said, as she leaned over him and placed two wine glasses on the table. "But this calls for a celebration. You see? I told you that Mrs. Winthrop was going to come through for you. She has more influence than her husband, if you ask me. My baby is about to be a millionaire!"

Even though Lily was genuinely happy for Dean, she wondered why Erica didn't say anything to her about Dean landing the biggest contract of his life. It hadn't even been three hours since her meeting with Erica. The least she could have done was lifted her spirits. Why keep such information from her? But not wanting to darken her heart with cynicism, Lily kept her mood light. Because maybe Erica wanted to leave it as a surprise.

"Mrs. Winthrop is the best, isn't she?" Lily went on. "Someday, I hope to wield as much power as she does."

Dean cringed at the way Lily continued to toot Erica's horn. He was certainly indebted to Erica for the role she played in making this deal happen, but he wanted Lily not to get too caught up in becoming bosom buddies with Erica. The further Lily stayed away from her, the better it was for them both. He could not imagine the depth of betrayal Lily would feel if she discovered the bracelet was more than a gift to a sixteen year old. It was Erica's declaration of her love for him.

He could sense the jealousy in Erica's email tone when he told her he wanted to buy Lily a bracelet just like the one she'd bought for him. Why would Erica be jealous if she didn't have any romantic feelings for him? And talking about emails, Dean wondered if Erica had taken his advice not to pursue the culprit behind that anonymous note. Secretly Dean would prefer it that way because they could pretend they didn't know they were being set up and carry on with the ruse.

It was not like they were going to cross the line or do something crazy to jeopardize their relationship. Dean simply wanted more opportunities to communicate with Erica, so he could provoke her to admit she was in love with him. Because depending on Erica's answer, Dean didn't think it would be fair to marry Lily when he could have a chance to be with Erica. But of course, if she continued to deny her feelings, he would move on with his life.

"Baby..." Lily squeezed Dean's shoulders to get his attention. "You're not drinking your champagne."

"Thanks," Dean said, giving Lily an apologetic smile. "But I really don't feel like having any champagne tonight. My mother threw a monkey wrench in my good mood."

"Cheer up, my handsome beau," Lily cooed, planting a quick kiss on Dean's lips. "Your mother will come around. She's simply too stunned believe that you can – and you will – become a millionaire overnight."

"I don't think that's the issue. My mother is one of my biggest supporters. I feel someone has been filling her head with craziness..."

Dean paused, looking like he'd just received a divine revelation.

"What is it?" Lily asked.

"Well, she did mention she had a dream and she believed the Lord was sending a message. Maybe that's why she's been carrying on with this strange behavior."

"A dream about the contract?" Lily wanted to know.

"I don't know. She never got the chance to tell me. Mr. Osprey and Erica, I mean Mrs. Winthrop showed up to tell me the good news." Dean pulled Lily toward him and sat her on one of his thighs, hoping she hadn't picked up on his intimate tone by calling Erica by her first name. These last few days he'd been feeling very close to Erica, but he tried to keep up his formal pretense to avoid being bombarded with questions by Lily. "My mother is a strange woman," he went on, "but when she has these dreams, they fulfill exactly the way she sees them."

"Wow...then maybe you should have stayed and found out what the dream was about."

"I agree. But when my mother told me to reject the contract, my mind went blank. I was too hurt to say anything else to her in that moment."

"You can still ask her when you go home tonight," Lily suggested, but her eyes told Dean a different story. She didn't want him to leave. "Or, you can ask her about it in the morning."

"Now that I think about it, I don't know if I wanna know what the dream was about. It could be something I don't wanna hear. Why else would my mother tell me to reject the contract? I would rather not know."

Lily stared into her fiancé's eyes, loving how his long lashes curled slightly at the tips and how his mohawk gave him such a sexy appeal. "You really mean that? I mean, I won't want to know either because you've been waiting for a deal like this to come along for a long time. This could be our big break. I won't need to work anymore." Lily paused to address the lingering reservations in her spirit. "But suppose there's something sinister wrapped up in it – like a life or death situation? It would be like being warned ahead of time."

When Lily noticed the vacillating wilt in Dean's expression, she quickly added, "I'm not telling you what to do, baby, but if you respect your mother's dreams so much, you should at least listen to what she has to say."

It was Dean's turn to peck Lily on the lips. "That's why I love you so much. You not only know what to say, but your heart is so good toward my mother."

210

Lily blushed at the compliment. "I want you to know that I'm not with you because of the wealth that I have long suspected is coming into your path. I'm totally smitten by who you are at the core. A caring, loving and nurturing individual who inspires me every day. My knight in shining armor who has rescued me from my own selfishness."

Dean's eyes turned glassy with tears. "Now you gon' make me cry with that sentimental female stuff."

"I mean every word...I just wish you could come along with me to Canada, so I won't have to leave your side for so long."

*And there it is, Dean thought. A hint that Lily is still wary of being apart. It must be that bracelet that has her on edge. What else could it be?*

"But I know you can't go," she said, interrupting Dean's thoughts, but also saving him from an uncomfortable reply. "Especially now with you having to allocate your time between this new deal and making time to indulge your mother's dreams."

"I really wish I could go along with you," Dean said sincerely.

"I believe you, but your hands are full, and I wouldn't want to add to your frustration."

"You're not adding to my frustration...you're the best thing that ever happened to me and I'm more than willing to throw my weight behind this relationship."

That put a twinkle in Lily's eyes, but there was something else in her eyes that Dean noticed. Fear. But fear of what? Dean, however, needed not to ponder too long because Lily made her fears known in her next statement.

"I must be honest with you," she said, "I am still restless about this bracelet."

"Lily..."

"I know you're going to tell me I'm making a big issue out of it, but I want you to put yourself in my shoes for a minute. You've worn this bracelet since you were sixteen years old, without taking it off even once. This suggests you love it and it holds great sentimental value for you. I'm surprised you took it off and gave it to me, considering how costly it is. In fact, I was half expecting you to ask me to return it."

"It isn't that big of a deal, Lily."

"I think it is and you are too ashamed to say." Lily gazed into Dean's eyes as she gently locked her arms around his neck. "It's okay to tell me you were deeply in love with someone else before you met me. I know she must have been in love with you too, the way she invested so much time, money and effort into that gift. I've resigned myself to accepting that you won't tell me her name, but I would be at peace if you could assure me I won't be competing for first place in your heart."

With Lily sitting on his lap, smelling so sweet and gazing into his eyes, it sent a warm sensation to his groin. For a white girl, she had a pair of kissable lips that would rival Angelina Jolie's. Dean was drawn to them like a magnet, pulling him slowly to make contact. They'd kissed many times before, but this time the atmosphere was charged with an irrepressible lust. Dean carefully raised Lily out of his lap and then jumped to his feet. His pants in front of him looking like a tent.

"I'm sorry," he apologized, "I wasn't expecting that to happen."

212

Lily smiled mischievously and said, "I will take that as a sign then, that there is no one else in your heart except me."

Dean returned the smile, but added in a serious tone, "There isn't anyone else, Lily. I want you to believe that. It's just that I feel there are certain things that need to be left unsaid. It has no bearing on our relationship."

"I understand; you're trying to protect my feelings. But I will have you know, mister, I am not as delicate as you think." She drew close to Dean once more. "So that means you want your bracelet back?"

He did, but Dean was no fool. The Bible said that the ways of a woman were far past finding out, and Lily was no exception to the rule. She could be testing him, for all he knew.

"Nawh, you can keep it," he told her.

Lily grinned. "Well, if you insist. I will be wearing it when I leave for Canada tomorrow afternoon."

*Enough about this crazy bracelet, already...* "What time do you have to be at the airport, because I want to see you off?"

"About 10 a.m."

"I'd better go then," Dean said, "so you can pack your suitcase and then get some rest."

"I don't want you to go," Lily singsonged. "Can you stay just fifteen more minutes?"

Dean felt that warmth stirring between his legs again. "Please, don't take this the wrong way, but it's best that I go. I will see you in the morning, hopefully with my sexual urges under control."

Lily laughed. "I'm sorry that I'm making this so hard for you..." she dropped her gaze to his groin. "No pun intended, but I would be lying if I told you I'm not enjoying making you sweat."

"You, naughty little girl," Dean quipped. "Three more months to go and you're all mine. I hope you will be able to handle me then."

Lily blushed. Dean pecked her on the cheek and made a quick exit. He walked a little ways toward the road, pausing to answer his cell phone that had started to vibrate in his pants pocket. Retrieving it, he studied his WhatsApp notification. He noticed Erica had a new telephone number and that she had sent him a text from it:

*Hey Dean, this is Erica. I don't trust using those email addresses or my old number. So I went out today and got a new number. I suggest you do the same...just to be on the safe side. Anyway...call me as soon as you can. I need to talk to you.*

Dean's libido suddenly sprang into overdrive and he had no explanation for it other than the fact that he knew Erica was thinking about the contrived proposal as much as he was. A setup, undoubtedly, but deep-down if Dean were to be truthful, he didn't need an email to coerce him into Erica's bed. He would have gone on his own accord had it not been for these silly boundaries that Erica had established between them. Therein laid the secret of his heart, which was about to explode in his face big time. He speed-dialed Erica, placing the receiver to his ear in quiet anticipation.

"Hello, Dean," Erica answered in that calming voice of hers. "How are you?"

"I'm good. You?"

"I'm doing exceptionally well, and you should be too, considering you've just landed the biggest deal of your life."

"I couldn't have done it without you," he said and then added in a husky tone, "You are the kindest and dearest person to me. I love you."

Erica wasn't expecting that. She cleared her throat. "You shouldn't talk like that; people could be listening to our conversation."

"You had your number changed."

"But still..."

"It doesn't matter anymore. Someone knows about my feelings for you and they are hoping that we get together."

"Well, that's not going to happen, if only for that reason alone."

"Did you hear what I said? I love you and I don't wanna hide it anymore."

"Listen to me, Dean. You've got your whole life ahead of you. A beautiful girl who loves the dirt you walk on, a praying mother, and a blossoming career that is about to take off...this phase that you're going through will pass –"

"You've been telling me that since I was fourteen and nothing has changed in regard to my feelings for you. Now that I am a man, I want to explore them, but you won't let me."

"Because those feelings are not ordained of God," Erica hissed. "I am twenty years your senior. I am married and currently serving as the first lady of FFWC, alongside your apostle."

"Sounds as if you're trying to convince yourself that you don't feel the same way about me. You may be married, but I know for a fact that you're not happy. I noticed you were limping today when you and Mr. Osprey showed up at my kiosk. No one can convince me that Apostle didn't have something to do with your injury. I know more about your abuse than I've let on. You don't deserve to be mistreated like that."

Erica grew quiet on the other end, which suggested to Dean that he'd accurately hit the nail on the head.

"Why don't you leave him?" Dean prompted. "He shouldn't hurt a beautiful sweet soul like you. My respect for him has greatly diminished. Leave him and I'll leave Lily for you, as much as she means to me. In the long run, it wouldn't be fair to her anyway to build our marriage on a divided heart."

"I truly thought you were over this obsession of yours," Erica said icily. "I shouldn't have called."

"But you did, which shows you care about me more than you're willing to admit. I can't help what I feel for you. I've tried to rid myself of it over the years, but it's impossible."

"You were right when you said this is not fair to Lily."

"Since when do you care about Lily?"

"I do care about her; she's a nice girl with a good spirit."

"You're saying that, but I think you are jealous of her."

"I beg your pardon?"

"I know you are," Dean affirmed. "But you don't need to be because you have the key to my heart."

Erica sighed into the phone. There was no getting through to this young boy. "Dean, we must be extra careful about how we move, especially now that we are being targeted."

"I have a feeling Apostle is behind it and I know you think it's him too. That's why I told you not to pursue it. Confronting him is not the wisest thing to do because you know exactly what Apostle is capable of."

Erica wondered when Dean had the opportunity to observe so much about her marriage. She thought she'd been careful not to show any evidence of abuse when Dean came to visit her home. It made her heart melt the way Dean was so intimate with details of her life and yet, was being so mature about it. But Erica continued to hold strong to her views of this situation: She and Dean could never be together.

"All the more reason for you to forget this obsession of yours," she said.

"Stop calling it an obsession as if I'm sick in the mind," Dean spat. "You know that I'm in love with you. Trying to convince me otherwise won't work. I will fulfill my part of the bargain as long as you promise me you will find a way to get out of that unhappy marriage. Otherwise, you will lose me."

"What is that supposed to mean?"

"You know exactly what that means."

Erica said abruptly, "If you want to kill yourself over something like this, this time I won't stop you...I have to go."

"Of course, you always do when I force you to face the truth."

Erica disconnected without a reply. Dean calmly placed his phone back into his pocket and resumed his walk. Had he looked behind him right then, he would have caught Lily observing him through her front room window.

# CHAPTER TWENTY-THREE

## *Vancouver, Western Canada*

Sister Rosita was as calculating as she was evil. She knew she would not get any dirt to stick on Tavian except she did something more dramatic than the lie she'd told of him sneaking away from a porn store. Pastor Coleby admired Tavian, which was a roadblock in and of itself. It seemed as if Tavian could do no wrong with Pastor Coleby defending him at the drop of a hat. And what peeved Rosita more than anything was that Tavian was now being consistently used to teach Wednesday night Bible Study, as if there weren't anyone else qualified.

She sat in the first pew boiling with anger, not caring how her expression was interpreted by Pastor Coleby. In fact, she wanted him to see how angry she was and that she was not pleased with how Tavian was being shown such blatant favoritism. She almost jumped out of her Latin skin when the congregation suddenly exploded into a sonorous shout, only to discover the racket had resulted from the pomposity of Tavian's admonitions. Even Pastor Coleby was on his feet, waving his hands wildly in the air.

Rosita didn't get it. What was it about Tavian that people loved? Because his words were downright rude and accusatory.

"There is a heart cry for holiness!" Rosita heard Tavian exclaim. "Not everyone is messing around in sin. There is a remnant who dares to go against the status quo, who will stand boldly on the authority of Jesus Christ. But I say to the church at large – the ecclesia in this modern generation, we must get back to right standing with God, if we are to see the blind eyes opened, the deaf ears unstopped, and the sick, healed. It will take true repentance from the heart. Let us now lay aside every weight and the sin which so easily besets us, and let us run with patience the race that is set before us..."

Some in the congregation dropped to their knees in tears at Tavian's words. His voice was filled with conviction and power. Never had they seen a young man so in tune with the Holy Spirit. He was on fire and as he continued to project his voice in the atmosphere, more and more people began to genuflect before the presence of God. Pastor Coleby was undone. The only thing he could do was lay prostrate as waves and waves of the Spirit swept over him. His wife, unable to deny the power of God any longer, began to sob and to repent of her pre-conceived notions of Tavian. He was truly anointed by God and there was nothing anyone could do about it.

Young men, ranging from ages thirteen to twenty-five began to flock to the altar. With their hands raised, their faces softened by contrition. They cried out from the depths of their souls, *"Lord, wash us! Cleanse us! Sanctify us! We want more and more of You! Fill us with Your power! Fill us with Your love!"* A great mourning swept from the back to the front and soon a great move of the Spirit, unlike anything World Embassy International had ever seen.

220

When Rosita saw the results of what was happening, she sprang to her feet and marched out of the sanctuary in a huff. *What nonsense!* she spat beneath her breath. Everyone was getting carried away with that blasphemous imposter. He was controlling the church with his well-rehearsed words and crazy antics. What a crying shame that Pastor Coleby had allowed such a travesty to seep in, rolling over on the floor like he'd lost his mind. Well, she wouldn't stand for it. Something must be done to stop Tavian Winthrop – once and for all.

She retrieved her cell phone and logged into an alias Facebook account she'd set up a few days ago. This was the age of technology where a rumor could get around the world in minutes. If nothing else worked to shake the people's confidence in Tavian, Rosita was certain that this would.

✳✳✳

At the same time, at First Family Worship Center in Barracuda Cove, Wednesday night Bible Study was also underway. However, the atmosphere was like night and day compared to what was going on in Vancouver, Canada. Apostle Winthrop was pacing back and forth in front of the altar, rallying the congregation into a frenzy to sow a seed of two thousand dollars. Sometimes he stumbled forward, looking as if he was catching his fall. Then he would laugh hysterically and tell the congregation to laugh along with him. He was half-drunk with whiskey, but everyone assumed he was under the power of the Holy Spirit, except for Freda Ripley.

She sat in her seat, distraught over the circus show transpiring in front of her. She didn't know how much more of this she could take. There had to be a remnant in Barracuda Cove who were not deceived by this religious demon posing as a true son of God. Every service made her sick to her stomach and she kept promising not to return, but the Winthrops had blessed her with a comfortable-paying job and she didn't want to seem ungrateful.

But if the truth be known, it was only because of Erica that Freda still tolerated this demon-induced atmosphere. That and the hope that God would raise someone up with a true heart for souls and call Magnus out on his sins. But Erica was not so much a partner in this deception but rather a victim of Magnus' wrath. Freda felt sorry for her and many times she wanted to reach out to Erica and let her know that there was someone she could talk to. However, ever since Freda had that dream about Erica and Dean, Freda wasn't feeling so friendly toward the elect lady of the house.

Everything was being carefully planned by the devil for Erica and Dean to fall prey to an illicit affair. And if they didn't open their eyes to see the truth – no matter what anyone told them – they would be ensnared in their sins, which would end horribly for them. The mere fact that her son kept avoiding her confirmed to Freda that the devil had already gotten a hold of Dean's mind. It had been two full days since she'd seen or heard from her son. But Freda refused to rest on her laurels and let the enemy win this fight.

For every deceptive statement Magnus spat forth into the atmosphere, Freda reversed it with a rebuke or with a divine decree. She pled the blood of Jesus beneath her breath and began to war forcibly in the realm of the spirit with Ephesians 6:12 as her weapon of choice.

*"For we wrestle not against flesh and blood, but against principalities, against powers, against the rulers of the*

222

*darkness of this world, against spiritual wickedness in high places..."*

By the time Freda got through praying, the adjutant had to lead Magnus out of the sanctuary. He'd suddenly looked dehydrated and was unfit to continue. The praise and worship team stumbled into position, leaving the congregants confused.

# CHAPTER TWENTY-FOUR

W hile Magnus was at Bible Study, Erica took a chance on meeting with her lawyer at the cabin in Lush Haven. She wanted the meeting to be away from her house, just in case Magnus showed up unannounced. Her lawyer suggested that it was wise for Magnus to be left in the dark until they'd built a strong case against him. They sat on the porch in wicker chairs, enjoying the cool breeze blowing from the ocean.

In the back of Erica's mind, she thought that by having the conversation on the outside that her words were safe. But little did she know, there was a tiny red light flashing beneath the wooden porch. A high-tech listening device had been installed by the male accomplice to record the slightest of sounds.

"The best recommendation I can offer you," Kim said to Erica, "is that you split everything between you and your husband right down the middle. Especially if you don't want to be embroiled in a nasty divorce. You two are very powerful on this island."

"Magnus is not a reasonable man," Erica said. "He would want everything, even though it's my inheritance that gave us a head start and my hard work that sustains the life we currently enjoy."

"All the more reason for you to consider my suggestion. At least you may settle with half in as little as six months, as opposed to years. I've seen these things drag out in court because one party refuses to submit to a compromise. Furthermore, you did not sign a prenup with your husband, which automatically removes your ability to protect certain assets. This includes family heirlooms and businesses predicated upon what had occurred during the marriage."

Erica stared at Kim grimly. She shouldn't have listened to her family when they told her to marry Magnus on good faith. "So you're telling me without a prenup," she questioned, "I don't have any control over how our assets are divided?"

"Pretty much. You ratified that deal the minute you entered marriage without proper legal protection. It says your husband can legally lay claim to your inheritance. The courts will see it no differently. Look at it from this perspective: If you don't get a divorce, a prenup doesn't exactly matter, does it?"

"I am getting a divorce. No doubt about that. I just hate the fact that Magnus gets to walk away with half of something he didn't work for. All he did was use my money to gamble and to con people out of their possessions. He can have the church; I met him with it and I have no problem leaving him with it. What if I can prove that I'm being physically and emotionally abused? Will that have any effect on me maintaining the majority share of our assets?"

Kim looked thoughtfully at Erica. "Well, you may have something there to work with. I've worked a few cases where I had the victims prepare a complete domestic violence complaint, inclusive of reputable witnesses, medical reports, photographs, and other physical evidence that was used to support the victims' testimonies. The judge in all cases awarded the women more than half of the marital possessions. They were even allowed to keep the homes and the cars."

Erica loved the idea being presented to her and it showed in her eyes. "That sounds like a route I would want to consider."

"Well," Kim said in her buoyant tone, "we must be thoroughly prepared for this to work because I've seen where this technique backfired."

"What do you mean?"

"If your husband can discredit your character in any significant way or present the court with plausible evidence that the abuse was mutual, convincing a judge to totally side with you will be difficult." Kim looked away briefly before turning her attention back to Erica. "I had one client who presented herself as the victim in a very abusive relationship. She had ample evidence and her witnesses lined up to support her testimony.

"Two days before the divorce court proceedings began, the husband's lawyer walked into my office and dropped a manila envelope on my desk. He told me to look at the contents and then call him back when I was ready to strike a deal. The first thing I saw when I opened the envelope was a collage of photos showing the wife having sex with the husband's brother. And to make matter's worse, the brother recorded the wife petitioning him to kill her husband."

Erica looked harried all of sudden. It all made sense now as she thought about how Magnus had constantly accused her of carrying on an inappropriate relationship with Dean. Next, emails started coming from Dean, and she would have thought nothing of it had he not asked her about a proposal she supposedly sent him. Why would she offer Dean fifty thousand dollars in exchange for sex? The proposal may not have been so forthcoming, but it was certainly implied, along with the sense that she was using her money and her influence to pull Dean away from Lily.

This entire affair was an eye-opener. It was as if the Lord had given her a sign by allowing her to deduce that Magnus was behind the mix up and that he was trying to force her into a compromising position with Dean. An evil agenda designed to ruin her very existence. The fear alone of such thoughts made Erica even more determined to keep her distance from Dean.

"What happened to the wife in that incident?" she asked weakly.

"She got nothing. She was arrested and sentenced seven years for contrivance to commit murder. It was the best I could have done. She would have been given the maximum penalty of twenty years. Are you sure you don't have any skeletons in your closet?"

Erica slowly nodded her head at the question, knowing that she harbored secret feelings for Dean. If she remained married to Magnus, she would chance her reputation being destroyed by an evil plan Magnus had concocted. If she pursued a divorce, it could mean signing her death certificate. What was there to stop her husband from killing her before the divorce proceedings even began? She realized she was no match for the malicious intent of her husband's mind. Either way she was screwed.

"What are you thinking?" Kim asked.

"I don't know," Erica said. "I need a few days to think about my decision."

"Well," Kim said, lifting her leather bag from the floor. "I would tell you to take all the time you need, but you are embroiled in a very abusive relationship and the longer you wait to make a move, the greater the chance your life will be in peril. But I will throw this advice in for free. As soon as you go home tonight, I would encourage you to look for some inconspicuous spots to hide a few cameras. Provoke him, if you must, so that we can begin getting some footage of our own."

"That's if I make it out alive," Erica said. "Magnus shows no mercy when he gets into beast mode."

Kim's eyes wilted with regret. "I admit it's not great advice, but I promise you if it works, we will hit this bastard where it hurts the most."

Erica watched as Kim descended the steps and then climbed into her white Subaru. She sat with her feet curled beneath her and her arms folded tight over her breasts to generate some warmth. The winds had picked up a knot, but Erica refused to go inside. It seemed to help clear her head because she couldn't pray, and she couldn't think. All she could do in that moment was allow the tears to roll unhindered.

It seemed as if she would be stuck in this hell of a marriage for the rest of her life. She hadn't many options. Magnus would not stop until he utterly destroyed her, either by death or by stripping her of everything she'd worked hard to accomplish. Who could she turn to for help? It seemed as if God had checked out on her.

Her phone soon vibrated in her lap. When she noticed that it was Dean's number, she didn't hesitate to press the 'IGNORE' button. A minute later, her WhatsApp sounded off with a message. She eventually read it out of sheer curiosity:

229

*Don't avoid me; not when I need you more than ever right now. Call me, if you care anything about me.*

Erica's blood pressure went up a notch. For one, she wasn't certain if it was truly Dean who had sent her the WhatsApp message, even though she'd just seen him calling her new phone number a few minutes ago. No one else would have her new number, unless Magnus had found a way to hack into it. Was that even possible? Erica couldn't be sure. Her paranoia was one of the reasons why she'd had the meeting with her lawyer on the outside – to reduce the risk of their conversation being recorded if the cabins had indeed been wired. She didn't come across any in her search, but that didn't mean the bugs weren't there.

But what if the text did actually come from Dean? It could mean that he was in a very precarious state of mind at the moment. The last time Dean had sent her an email like that, he had cut his wrists and had to be rushed to the hospital. She regretted now telling him that she would not stop him if he tried to kill himself this time around. What if he had actually gone through with it? His blood would be on her hands and she would never ever be able to live with that on her conscience, knowing she could have stopped him. She replied to Dean's text in a very matter-of-fact way, regardless of the risk involved:

*I do care...and you know it. Where are you?*

An hour passed, and Dean still hadn't answered back.

"It's a good thing I bugged both the inside and outside of the compound. If I hadn't, we would have missed everything." The young male accomplice who was working along with Magnus sat next to him with a small listening device wedged between two fingers. "It seems as if your wife has significantly reduced communicating with her cell phone. I hardly get any WhatsApp messages between her and Dean."

Magnus stared at the young man, whom he had develop a strong attraction for over the course of a few weeks. From day one, he was convinced that he'd chosen the right man to be his mole on the inside of the B&B. The others were backups just in case he needed another pair of hands. In any event, it was mind blowing to have a team of young, handsome men, ready to obey his every whim. All he had to do was wave a few crisp hundred-dollar bills in their faces and they were his. Even now he fought to keep his inordinate affections to himself. But with every second that ticked by, Magnus was losing his restraint, especially when the young male did things that appealed to Magnus' flesh.

He spoke up when he was able to clear the husk from his voice, "I don't understand where you're coming from."

"Well, it's like I've said. I haven't seen any WhatsApp messages to Dean or to anyone for that matter within the last thirty-six hours. I told you she must have caught on to our game. I wouldn't be surprised if she's changed her phone number."

"She didn't," Magnus said confidently. "I called her on it today."

The young man shrugged. "I'm just saying that we won't need to depend on that as the only means to track your wife. I have planted the bugs in all the right places."

"That's what I'm paying you for," Magnus said. "And I have said to you repeatedly that I don't care if my wife suspects. She's not woman enough to confront me to confirm her suspicions."

"You have a strange way of doing things because if your wife suspects she is being set up, she will be more careful with her behavior."

"Not when it comes to Dean."

The accomplice didn't bother to comment on that. It was clear Magnus would believe whatever he chose to believe. "Well, at least you were right about your wife in one regard," he said. "She is planning to divorce you in grand style. It's all here when you're ready to listen to it."

"I'm always right," Magnus fired back. "That heifer despises me almost as much as I despise her. The minute she allowed her lust for Dean to mess with our money, I knew my marriage was over. She would spend thousands of dollars on him and think nothing about it. And when I asked her about it, she would lie to me and say she'd used the money to pay bills or to do some shopping."

The young male shook out a cigarette from a Morley brand, jammed it between his lips and then lit it. "And what about your son?" he asked.

"What about him?"

"How does your wife treat him?"

"Oh, she lavishes him with gifts too, but she only does that to win his affection. As she has with Dean."

"You don't talk much about your son, do you? It's always about Dean."

Magnus' stare became almost transfixed when the young man removed the cigarette from his lips and blew the smoke into

Magnus's face. "That's because my wife has brainwashed him to side with her," he finally answered. "I can't talk to him without him pointing out my mistakes or badmouthing my church."

"Your church?" the young man laughed. "I see that you're very possessive."

"I'm not possessive; I am just a stickler for being a good steward over those things I've worked hard to achieve. There will be hell to pay if anyone dares to put a finger on it."

The young man gave Magnus a knowing look. He'd seen the way Magnus had been ogling him and he was waiting for the right time to use it against him. Why settle for a measly ten thousand dollars when he could get five times more just by playing his cards right? Magnus was that type of pervert who would splurge on anything that brought him pleasure.

He said provocatively to the balding apostle, "I've been noticing the way you look at me. What do you want?"

"Excuse me?"

"Do I need to repeat myself because I'm sure you get where I'm going?"

Magnus' throat was suddenly parched, causing him to swallow several times because he was certain he'd detected sexual innuendoes in the young lad's tone. Even so, Magnus proceeded with caution. "I don't appreciate parables. So speak plainly."

"I don't have to. I know what you want, and you know what I want."

Magnus raised a brow as if to say he didn't appreciate the boy taking control of the situation, but Magnus was too far gone to turn back. "I'll pay whatever you ask," he said, but added quickly, "providing it is within my power."

"Oh I'm certain it is within your power. Let's not waste each other's time."

The smirk on the young man's face caused Magnus' lust to flare in his eyes. It emboldened him to reach over and put his hand on the young man's thigh. In what seemed to be the most inopportune time, the door to the hotel room pushed open and in waltzed the other accomplice. She slammed the door, and as she sashayed over to the men, Magnus yanked his hand from the young man's thigh, jumping to his feet.

She kicked off her heels and then began to unbutton her blouse. "I've had a long day and my body craves satisfaction. Who's first or shall we make this the usual threesome?"

The men shared a glance, which suggested nothing would be 'usual' after tonight. The demonized atmosphere of perversion cloaked Magnus like a glove, pulling him deeper into its death grip. His thirst for debauchery would only increase. But he dared not act upon his lust for the lad in front of the female.

"Turn on the listening device," Magnus demanded of the young man. The audio feed crackled to life but still wasn't loud enough for Magnus' ears. "Is that the highest it can go? I wanna make sure I don't miss one word coming out of that heifer's mouth."

The conversation that had occurred between Erica and her lawyer a few hours ago pervaded the room. A clear and crisp recording of the highest quality. On cue, Magnus pulled the woman into him, both of them landing on the floor next to the listening device. Ripping and scratching at each other in a heat of blind passion.

Knowing his presence wouldn't be missed for at least ten minutes, the young man slipped out of the room unnoticed. He hastened down the carpeted hall toward a garbage can where he hunched over into it and vomited the pizza he'd eaten thirty minutes before. He was disgusted by Magnus and his penchant for sex with men. Only one thing he wanted from Magnus and that was his money. But he would do anything to get it, even if it meant he had to tolerate the filth of a revolting man like Magnus.

*"For the love of money is the root of all evil; which while some coveted after, they have erred from the faith, and pierced themselves through with many sorrows."*

– Timothy 6:10

# CHAPTER TWENTY-FIVE

A meeting with the B&B staff was long overdue. But because everyone's shift either overlapped or all seven employees were never at work at the same time, Justin found it a challenge to get everyone to commit to a specific time. The excuses were outrageous, and Justin had had enough of it. When he sent an email threatening suspension for those not showing up to the meeting, he received a favorable response right away. They all convened in the conference room and sat around an oval table.

Justin sat in the head chair. To his immediate right was Ian and to his immediate left were Sandra and Derek. Tibo, Brenda and Rochelle filled the remaining seats respectively. The atmosphere was stiff and not a sound could be heard save for the Lasko fans blowing in the background. Justin took in a deep breath. He could already foresee that this meeting was not going to end well, but he had to do it. Erica was depending on him to keep things in order.

"First let me start this meeting off by thanking all of you for showing up," Justin started.

Sandra coughed into her hand and said sarcastically beneath her breath, "As if we had a choice. We were practically manhandled and forced to the gallows."

Everyone who heard it, laughed.

Justin ignored the comment and continued evenly, "There are a number of things we need to discuss among ourselves and better we do it now before it gets back to Mrs. Winthrop. I encourage you to voice your opinions. I am willing to listen and make suggestions that can benefit both you and the B&B."

"Awesome!" Rochelle exclaimed. Although she was stout with stubby limbs and made a snorting sound when she laughed, she was generally well-liked. "Can I get some help in the kitchen? The amount of cooking I do in a day is just too much for one person. How long do we have to complain that we need more workers?"

"I agree we need more workers," Brenda chimed in, her red and orange hair looking like her head had caught fire. "I have to clean 12 rooms a day by myself, each with two king-sized beds and a huge bathroom. Plus, I have to wash loads and loads of laundry. What do I look like? A bloody ox?"

Sandra smirked mischievously. "You actually do...that's probably why you get treated that way."

The entire table rippled with laughter, even Justin's mouth twitched, though he did his best to hide it. Brenda looked as if she wanted to cry. She vowed right then that she would keep her mouth shut for the rest of the meeting because it was clear everyone thought she was stupid.

Justin tried to quiet the table. "Let's stay on track and keep moving forward. And please, let's respect each other's opinions." His gaze settled on Tibo, who stared back at Justin with an indomitable look in his eyes. "What is *your* complaint, Tibo? You hardly say anything."

Tibo shrugged. The V-neck T-shirt he was wearing revealed the head of an angry boa constrictor. A tattoo that seemed to mirror Tibo's disposition.

"I've got nothin' to say," he rumbled in a deep voice. "I'm cool."

"Are you sure?" Justin prompted. "This is your opportunity to speak up."

Tibo stared at Justin a good while before he answered, "A job is better than no job. Let's leave it at that."

Justin had seen Tibo's type in prison, and he knew how far to go with such people. They were silent killers. They attacked swiftly and unexpectedly. Derek spoke up next, shaking his feet incessantly to control his nervousness. He was paranoid that Justin could detect that he and Tibo were on Magnus' payroll, making more money in a week than their monthly B&B salary combined. If he kept quiet about his complaints, Justin would become suspicious for sure.

"Well, I've got something to say," he said. "I don't think Mrs. Winthrop truly values all the hard work we do around here. I think I speak for everyone here, maybe with Tibo being the exception. But too many disgruntled employees are not good for any business. Sooner or later, we will begin working off the job one by one. I mean, would you blame us if we decide to look for another job to supplement our salary?"

"What is your suggestion, other than a salary raise?" Justin asked Derek. "Please think outside the box."

"There is no need to think outside the box, Justin," Sandra said. "There are only two things we're asking for: more money and more workers."

"You can't have both," Justin said. "That would increase the overhead expense of the B&B considerably. If, and that's a big *if*, Mrs. Winthrop agrees with what you want, how long do you think it will be before she realizes it was a very bad decision?"

"She will never know until she tries," Derek said.

"You guys have a very poor perspective of Mrs. Winthrop," Justin said. "She and her husband both own the B&B and from what I understand, it is her husband who makes the decisions concerning what is to be paid to the staff."

"But you're sitting comfortably, bruh," Ian spat. "Making way more money than us and doing everything Erica tells you to do. I doubt Mr. Winthrop knows that you're being paid more than us –"

Justin held up his hand to stop Ian. "Listen, we are not in this meeting to discuss my salary. It's off limits. It is mostly speculation and hearsay anyway. Though I can say we all are being paid way above the minimum wage."

Ian fired back, "Stop acting as if the Winthrops can't afford to give us a raise! They own half of Barracuda Cove. If you want to do something about our complaints, you can. You just choose not to so as not to ruffle the boss' feathers."

Justin furrowed his brows at Ian. The vehemence in his tone was shocking. Ian must have forgotten who he was talking to and that Justin knew about his secret meetings with Magnus.

"Ian, where did you get this sudden blast of defiance all of a sudden?" Justin asked. "You should be the last person to say something like that because you're hanging on to your job by a very thin thread. Missing days and days of work and coming in late several times a week –"

Ian jumped up. "Fire me, boss man and let me go on my merry way. I don't care what you people do anymore!"

Ian's anger drove him from the table and through the door, slamming it on his way out. The silence that fell afterwards was deafening.

Sandra stood up. "I'll go talk to him," she said to Justin. "Continue on until I return."

"I have a better solution," Justin said. "This meeting is suspended until otherwise announced. If we can't resolve our issues among ourselves, I will have to let Mrs. Winthrop handle things from here."

Everyone filed out, leaving Justin alone. He grabbed his cell phone from the table and clicked on Magnus' name in the WhatsApp message box.

*Stop messing with Ian's head, he typed, or I'm going to tell your wife.*

It was less than fifteen seconds when Magnus' response returned. *And you would have just bought your ticket back to prison. Have you considered being a part of my team?*

*Never! You may have gotten me out of prison, but it was Erica who took a chance on me and helped me to make something of myself.*

Magnus put several red angry emoji faces next his reply: *That all can change in the blink of an eye. You have one last chance to consider your rebellious ways.*

Justin cursed profusely under his breath as he exited the conference room.

# CHAPTER TWENTY- SIX

arly the following morning, Netty awoke with a terrible bout of dry coughs. It was the day of the Red Cross event or what Netty had termed, the 'Bez' concert. She was determined to attend, if only to lure Erica away from her prissiness and show her that everyone had some sort of darkness hidden in them. Erica's sanctimonious act could only last for so long. If she could get her in the right place, at the right time and with the right person, there would be nothing to stop her from giving in to her impulses. In fact, she would see to it that Erica did just that, hoping she would fall flat on her face, so Netty could laugh at her calamity.

But Netty wasn't prepared for what happened next. Without warning, her stomach heaved, and heat trickled from the top of her head to the tips of her toes. Soon chills spread throughout her body, causing her to tremble like the temperature had suddenly dropped to thirty degrees Fahrenheit. She crawled out of bed and managed to retrieve her cell phone from the tallboy. She called Erica, which was hard for her to do, considering how much she envied her, but Erica was the only person Netty would trust with her life.

She spat into the Erica's ear, "I need you! How soon can you get here?"

In less than twenty minutes, Netty's distress call brought Erica stumbling to Netty's apartment. When she saw Netty hunched over on the floor in pain, she started firing a barrage of questions at her.

"What did you eat? What have you been doing? Where have you been? How many times do I have to tell you to take better care of yourself?"

Netty was too nauseated to form a complete sentence. She groaned, "Help me...feel like I'm gonna die..."

"Stop saying that and tell me what happened."

"I don't know...so much pain...help me, Erica, help me!"

Netty's groans sent Erica scurrying through Netty's closet. She pulled the first dress she saw hanging in front of her. "Let me help you put this on," she spat. "I'm taking you to the hospital."

Netty protested. "I'll be fine; I just need some hot tea."

"Are you crazy? I'm not having anyone die on my watch. You're going to the hospital whether you want to or not!"

Erica worked Netty's arms through the sleeves of the dress and then pulled it over her head. She propped Netty up to her feet and steadied her by putting one of Netty's arms around her shoulders. By the time they got to the hospital, Netty was incapacitated. The paramedics extracted her from Erica's car and lifted her onto a gurney. They rolled her into the Emergency Room, with Erica following close behind.

Eventually, Erica floated to the waiting area. It was the first time she'd ever seen Netty in such a vulnerable state, which forced Erica to rethink how she really felt about Netty. Sure, she was obnoxious, ostentatious and had a strong fondness for younger men, but Erica had known Netty since they were in high school and to her, Netty had always had such a bombastic personality and appeared too independent for human support. And there were times she could become extremely brazen with her inordinate affections, but that was Netty.

So when people warned Erica of Netty's true intention toward her, she always brushed it off because Netty could have destroyed her years ago with secrets she'd shared with her and even now, with the craziness going on in her marriage, Netty had not exploited her, even though she could. Why would Netty call her in her time of need, Erica pondered, if she didn't value their friendship? It would be ludicrous of Netty to treat her as an enemy when it appeared that she didn't have any other person she could turn to for comfort.

Erica found a chair at the far end of the waiting room. She sat in it to prevent her incessant pacing back and forth. Something else was bothering her, though, and as much as she tried to keep her focus on Netty, her thoughts kept straying. After five minutes of vacillating, she could no longer stand it. She pulled her phone from her handbag and clicked in her WhatsApp messages. She read the last text Dean had sent to her eighteen hours before:

*Don't avoid me, not when I need you more than ever right now. Call me if you care anything about me.* She hadn't heard from him since and that was not like Dean. A feeling of déjà vu came over her as she recalled the incident that occurred a few weeks before Dean's eighteenth birthday.

She had just arrived at Tavian's high school graduation when she received a text from Dean, asking urgently that she call him. She had intended to do so, but she soon lost track of the time, trying to find a parking spot. She was already late, and she was trying to call Magnus to confirm if he'd saved a seat for her. By the time she remembered Dean's text, Tavian was walking across the stage to receive his diploma.

Half an hour later, she received a frantic call from Freda saying Dean had been rushed to the hospital after an attempted suicide. Without going into too much detail, she told her husband and her son to go ahead of her to Tavian's graduation party, saying she would join them later. Erica remembered that day as if it were yesterday, as she screeched out of the parking lot. Her conscience was heavy upon her because it had only been a few hours since Dean had confessed his love to her. They were in her office at the B&B:

*"So, do you like the idea?" He'd asked her, beaming with excitement. "I think I could make a lot of money selling carved wood."*

*"You should not call them carved wood," Erica told him. "They are masterpieces, deserving to be put into showcases around the world."*

*Dean grinned. "You really think so? I could never imagine myself on an international platform like that."*

*"You should...you have a brilliant mind and a brilliant gift. Someday, people will pay top dollar for your work."*

*"That's a nice dream, but I don't even have any money to get this business idea off the ground. Of course, I could work from home to cut expenses, but I still need money to buy material.*

Ever since my father was murdered, my mother and I have been struggling to make ends meet..." He paused, suddenly looking apologetic. "Don't get me wrong; I am grateful for the job you gave my mother and for all the times you've supported me. It helps a whole lot, but I can't depend on you or my mother to fund my dreams. I need to make my own way."

After a brief pensive gaze, Erica got up from her swivel chair and edged her butt on the desk, right in front of Dean. At the time, she didn't think anything of it or how that move would have affected Dean's psyche. She noticed he'd appeared nervous, but she assumed it was because he felt embarrassed having to talk about his impoverished background.

"Listen to me," she said, taking his hands into hers. "There is nothing wrong with asking for help. In fact, I don't mind at all giving you what you need to get started."

"I can't ask you to do that, especially in light of everything you have already done for me."

"You're not asking; I'm saying to you that I will be your financier. When you begin to make your own money – and you will – you can pay me back a percentage. All I'm asking of you is to work hard and stay focused. There's a strong entrepreneurial spirit inside of you that is going to bring you great success. Mark my words."

In one quick move, Dean pulled her off the desk and into his lap. Before Erica knew what was happening, he had pushed his tongue between her lips. The kiss quickly deepened, but Erica caught her senses halfway into it. Embarrassed, she stumbled to her feet.

"Why did you do that?" she tossed at him.

*Dean dropped his head toward his knees. "Sorry. I didn't intend to make you uncomfortable. But I couldn't control myself." He raised his head slightly but refused to look into Erica's eyes. "I've been thinking about that kiss since I was fourteen years old."*

*Dean's admission stumped Erica. She didn't even know what to say to that. For a boy that age to harbor such thoughts was eye opening, which revealed that sex seemed to be one of the prevailing interests of Dean's generation and boundaries did not matter.*

*"I don't understand if you truly realize what you've done,"* she told him. *"That kiss shouldn't have happened."*

*"Why?"*

*"Because it was inappropriate on so many levels. I, for one, can't believe that I allowed it to happen."*

*"You didn't allow it to happen; I took it. So, don't go blaming yourself."*

*There was a stiff silence between them as the reality of the moment began to sink in. Gone was the platonic structure that had kept the temptations at bay. In its place was an undefined space that threatened to turn their world upside down.*

*"I can understand why you're upset,"* Dean spoke up. *"I'm underage and getting involved with me could pose a legal problem for you."*

*"It's more than just your age, Dean. I am a married woman with the responsibility of the church as the first lady. I can't even imagine what this would do to you. You're seventeen years*

old with a full life ahead of you. This is not what you want. Trust what I'm saying to you; you will regret it."

Dean stared at Erica as if her words didn't penetrate his interior. "So, in essence, you're saying if these obstacles weren't in our way, you would have explored your feelings for me?"

"Speaking hypothetically is not the solution because it only produces false hope."

"Then what is the solution, because by now I thought you would have understood my feelings for you. Do you think I kept coming over to your house to play video games with Tavian for nothing? I wanted to be in your presence. I wanted to see you because I missed you like crazy when I had to leave. I can't just turn my feelings off for you. They've had three years to develop and they ain't going anywhere."

Erica's heart broke into pieces as she listened to this handsome boy pour his heart out to her. If only Magnus would have shown her just a smidgen of Dean's affection, she wouldn't have been feeling so vulnerable right now. And had Dean been just a few years older, she would have probably lost the battle against her resolve a long time ago. Dean was a hunk at fourteen as much as he was at seventeen.

"You're not thinking clearly," she told him.

"I am thinking more clearly than I ever have in my life. I'm well aware of your age and of your position on this island. I have no intention of making things difficult for you."

"Then why expose your feelings?"

"Because it's torment not knowing what the other person truly feels. And it would put my mind at ease to know I'm not delusional and I haven't lost touch with reality. Ever since you came into my world, I started to hope again. I started to believe in myself and dared to dream that I could be somebody in this life. What's wrong with wanting to spend the rest of my life with someone like that?"

Inside, Erica was crying, but she kept a firm exterior in hopes of discouraging Dean's silly notion of them being together. "You will find someone who –"

"I don't want anyone else; I want you."

"You're saying that because of how you feel right now. But there's a girl out there, tailor-made just for you who will bring a lot of joy to your world. You are an incredible, gifted young man and I am so proud of you and what you have become. But you must not construe my kindness as something else..."

Dean stood to his feet. "I have to go."

"Where are you going?"

Dean shot Erica a bothered look. "Make up your mind whether you want me or not. Because I can't promise you I'll be around for long."

Those words should have prompted Erica that Dean was not in the best of spirits and that not answering his text right away only made matters worse. When she arrived at the hospital and saw the bandages around Dean's wrists, she realized his feelings for her were more than a silly teenage crush. Possibly unhealed wounds he may have incurred during his formative years. Whatever the reason, she had to find a way to get through to him before he truly took his life.

"Excuse me..."

250

A man hurriedly brushed past Erica and brought her mind fumbling back to reality. Worry was etched in her expression as Dean was not responding to her calls nor her texts. Before she could stop herself, she dialed Freda's phone number.

"Hello?" came the reverential voice on the other end.

"Mrs. Ripley? I hope I didn't disturb you, but I need to know if you've heard from Dean lately."

There was a pronounced sigh from Freda before she answered. "I haven't seen my son for three days. But he did send me a text telling me not to worry about him. What have you done to him now?"

The question hit Erica so hard that she struggled to come up with an answer. Freda may not have said much about Erica's connection to Dean, but Erica knew Freda was a woman of discernment.

"I, er...I'm calling out of concern –"

"I know why you're calling," Freda cut in sharply. "And I don't care if I lose my job after this. But I'm not gonna stand by and let the devil steal my son from under my nose."

"Mrs. Ripley..."

"I need you to listen to me and listen good," Freda said. "You go back and tell Mr. Gavin Osprin, Osprah, whatever his name is, that my son don't need that contract. It is the plan of the devil to use it as a means to destroy his life."

"I will do no such thing," Erica huffed. "Your son has worked hard and put in tons of sacrifices for this opportunity. What in the world has brought this on? I thought you would have been excited for your son, knowing after all the hell you two have gone through."

"I don't care how much hell I've gone through. Your offer for a better life is rife with sin and if you don't be careful, you will be the cause of both your and my son's demise."

"Mrs. Ripley, you are very valuable to me, but I am losing patience with you. This is not you talking, which is the only reason I'm not hastening to fire you on the spot."

"My God shall supply all my needs if I do lose my job. I took the risk to obey His voice."

Erica couldn't argue with that. "I hope you know this is your son's future we're talking about and if you do anything to ruin it, Dean will never forgive you."

"Don't act as if you know my son better than I do," Freda said. "The devil is on your track and by your very words, you're not prepared to handle the storm when it shows up on your doorstep."

Erica heard that familiar *click* in her ear, meaning that Freda had disconnected from the line. Even if Erica wanted to be angry with Freda, she couldn't. Freda's words had rocked her to the core because Freda was one of those praying women who Erica feared. Their words held weight and rarely fell to the ground. However, that didn't lessen her anxiety for Dean's whereabouts. As far as she was concerned, he could be in a ditch somewhere, bleeding to death from self-inflicted wounds.

Erica swiped at the film of tears on her eyelids. The only thing that boy ever did was love her. And what did she do in return? Broke his heart – more than once.

# CHAPTER TWENTY-SEVEN

"Mrs. Erica Winthrop?"

Erica spun around to address the voice. It was a female nurse, who wore a grumpy-looking expression.

"The doctor will see you now," she said. "Follow me."

Erica fell in behind the nurse's brisk strides, which led them down a short hall, and through a pair of wooden doors that swung open automatically as they approached. Ahead, Erica could see Netty lying on a bed, much calmer than she'd been two hours before. But Erica assumed the prognosis must not be good by the way Netty's tears effortlessly flowed down her well-polished cheeks. The nurse said that the doctor would join them shortly before marching away in her white orthopedic shoes.

"You're crying," Erica said, drawing nearer to Netty's side. "Is everything okay? Are you still in pain?"

"I'm good for now. They put something in my drips to numb the pain caused by something totally unexpected." Netty cracked a half smile. "I've got some good and bad news."

Erica reached out and gripped Netty's hand. "You don't have to say anything if you don't want. I will respect your privacy."

"Away with that nonsense. You're the only friend I've got. Besides, I want you to know." Netty gave a light sigh. "I'm pregnant...with twins. That's the bad news. The good news is I'm not too far along to have an abortion."

Erica looked at Netty as if she had two heads. "You said so much in those few sentences, I don't even know how to process it. First of all, I can't get over the fact that you're pregnant...not that I'm not happy for you −"

"I don't want you to be happy for me. I want you to feel disgusted and tell me about my whorish ways. Tell me that I deserve it because I'm always running after younger men."

"Well, I could, but I won't. You don't need that right now."

"How do you know what I need? You don't even like me like that."

"That's not true and you know it."

"I don't know anything right now except that my life is a mess. I'm forty-two. What am I gonna do with two babies at this time in my life?"

"Being pregnant is not the end of the world. Of course you have options, but having an abortion shouldn't be one of them."

"If this is your way of encouraging me, it isn't working. I'm getting an abortion and that's that!" Netty's voice dithered into a high soprano, tears rolling down her face. "I feel so overwhelmed right now. I must have slept with more than seven men within the last two months. So it will be impossible to know who the father is."

"All of this doesn't matter right now," Erica tried. "There is a set of new lives growing inside of you and you must give priority to them."

"Even if the doctor told me that the pregnancy is considered high risk and that I would have to be on bed rest for at least six months? I can't submit to that...I just can't...my life is ruined! How could I have been so careless?"

Erica was at a loss for words. In all the years she'd known Netty, she'd never seen her look so helpless. Netty was always the one to look adversity in the face without a hint of intimidation. But it seemed as if the mere thought of being pregnant had turned her world upside down.

"I've ruined everything," Netty continued to bemoan. "I can't even go to that concert with you tonight."

"It's impossible for you to go; don't even think of it. In fact, *I* won't go; I'm going stay here with you."

"No...what sense does that make? Find someone else to take with you. I paid a lot of money for those tickets, you know. Don't make me regret it. Go and have a good time."

"I have no problem giving you the money back; your health is what concerns me right now."

"Listen to me, Erica, I will be fine. Go and enjoy yourself. And if I was you; I would ask Dean to come along. He would be excellent company."

Erica gave Netty a side glance. She wondered why Netty was so hell bent on her attending this concert. And to even suggest Dean as the one to take her place was equally weird. But then again, it was exactly the way Netty's mind operated. Always thinking about ways to ensnare the younger males. Even if she wanted to invite Dean to accompany her to the concert – which she really didn't want to do anyway – she couldn't. She hadn't any idea where he was.

"You have a very strange way of dealing with your depression," Erica said. "I hope you're not trying to get rid of me so that you can go and have an abortion behind my back."

Netty rolled her eyes. "Girl please, if that was the case, you wouldn't know when I got the procedure done. But obviously, it won't be today. Promise me that you will go to that concert and ask Dean to go with you. He loves you and he will not turn you down."

Netty was right about Dean's love for her, but Erica would never give Netty the satisfaction of admitting to that fact.

"I'll go..." Erica paused, her spirit heavy with indecisiveness. "And I'll ask Dean, but you have to make me a promise too."

"Oh Lord...what now?"

"I want you to carry these babies to term."

"Are you serious? All I'm requiring of you is a few hours of clean fun and you're demanding nine months of hell on earth. I won't put my body through that. My mind can't even accept it."

Erica folded her arms defiantly. "Well, I'm not going to the concert."

"Geesh! I can't believe you're forcing me to do this."

"I'll take that as a yes. I'll stay around a little longer to see what else the doctor has to say about your pregnancy."

Netty pressed the sides of her head in frustration. "Erica, I'm almost sorry that I called you. Get out of here; you have a concert to prepare for!"

"Alright," Erica chuckled. "But I'll be checking in on you first thing in the morning."

Netty pointed to the door. "Go, for heaven's sake!"

"I'm going already! You just don't go having no abortion while I'm gone."

Netty looked for something to toss at Erica, which made Erica picked up her steps and disappeared through the door.

# CHAPTER TWENTY-EIGHT

*Vancouver International Airport – 12:12 p.m.*

*"Final boarding call for flight 225 to Miami, Florida."*

Dean grabbed his carryon bag and made a mad dash toward the departure gate. He'd been so immersed in reading Erica's texts that he didn't hear the first boarding call. It was interesting to see what a few days of avoidance could do to a person. If Dean didn't know how Erica's mind worked, he would have viewed her texts as someone completely unhinged from reality, but he knew better. Erica was still in denial over the fact that she was head over heels in love with him. He would not show any signs of weakness by responding. Gone were the days when he ran behind her for her affections as he'd done when he was seventeen years old. She would have to face the music for herself and come to the realization that he was the only man who could make her happy.

The only reason he'd put Erica on the spot the other night, pretending as if he were suicidal, was because he wanted to test Erica's heart to see if she was ready to let go of her restraints. She texted him back a brief message, saying that she did care about him. But Dean knew she only did that to pacify her guilty conscience. She still thought of him as a little boy who needed to be delivered from his ungodly obsession. But he would show her that he was no longer a little boy, but a man who didn't have time to play games with his heart.

It was one of the main reasons why he decided to go to Canada with Lily and stay with her for a few days. A spur-of-the-moment decision that Dean hoped would work in his favor. He purposely didn't tell anyone (particularly Erica) where he'd gone, so as to create the illusion that something bad had happened to him. Hence the other reason why he was not responding to Erica's texts. He wanted her to fret herself into a frenzy. He did, however, sent a text to his mother telling her not to worry about him, but that was simply to buy him time and to keep his mother in check until he returned to Barracuda Cove. He needed to figure out his next move, which would be his decision on the contract offered by Mr. Osprey.

Should he accept it or reject it, as his mother had so adamantly told him to do? If he did accept it, he would be walking into the trap of the enemy, according to his mother's ominous warning. If he didn't accept it, he could kiss his dreams goodbye. He had yet to hear what his mother had dreamt that was so horrible. The thought alone kept his mind in limbo and he assumed by now after spending a few days with Lily, he would have had a clear path. But he was more frightened and more confused than he'd ever been.

And to make matters worse, Lily wanted him to stay in Canada with her for the entire three weeks of her job assignment. She didn't understand that he had a life to go back to and that her constant whining about the bracelet was getting on his last nerve. Every day that he was with her she pestered him to reveal the name of the person when she'd promised that she wouldn't pressure him to do it. To get Lily off his back, he lied, supplying her with a fictious name. He had to, if he wanted to keep himself from exploding in anger. And even though he could see in Lily's eyes that she still didn't believe him, she finally shut up about the stupid bracelet.

Once he cleared the gate and found his seat on the plane, he pulled out his phone and resumed his studious examination of Erica's texts. One thing that stood out to him about the last texts she'd sent two hours ago was that she was definitely worried about something:

*Your mother told me you contacted her; so I know that you're fine. Your not responding back to me, means you probably don't want anything to do with me. I understand...and it's probably for our own good. However, I need you to speak with your mother urgently...she is insisting that I cancel your contract with Mr. Osprey. Is that what you really want? You know your mother can be very scary when she gets these crazy notions into her head. I got the idea she thinks I will ruin your future. You don't have to say anything to me for the rest of your life, if that's the path you want to take. But please talk to your mother. I'm worried it will be she who will ruin your future and not me.*

Dean thumbed down to Erica's most recent text, which was sent half an hour ago.

*I don't mean to keep on bothering you, but I made Netty a promise. She purchased two concert tickets hosted by the Red Cross organization. One of the artists coming in is from Africa. It's the same guy you asked me about when you heard his song playing in my car. Netty was scheduled to go with me, but she had to be rushed to the hospital this morning and will be unable*

261

*to attend. For whatever reason, she insists that I take you along. You are not under any obligation to accept. I'm just asking because I promised Netty I would. In fact, I can give you both tickets and you can take Lily instead...but...if you decide to come, I will be sitting in the VIP section.*

"Good afternoon, ladies and gentlemen. Welcome aboard Air Canada, Flight 321 to Miami, Florida. My name is Susan Graham and I'm your In-flight Service Director. For your safety, all passengers are kindly requested to refrain from using portable telephones, televisions, CD players or FM radios in the cabin..."

Dean moved his gaze from the screen to the strikingly handsome woman, immaculately attired in her Air Canada uniform. She seemed to be smiling at him when she spoke, but Dean knew it was a part of her professional presentation. He wanted finish reading Erica's texts while she continued to speak; however, he suppressed the urge and shut his phone down. It helped him, too, from responding to Erica. He was trying to hold out as long as he could. Erica hadn't any idea what state of mind he was in and he wanted it to stay like that.

He leaned his head back against the headrest and closed his eyes for a few minutes. Gradually, his thoughts drifted away to the time when Erica picked him up from home in one of her luxury cars. It was January and the temperatures were mercilessly chilling to the bone. But that didn't faze eighteen-year-old Dean one bit as the anticipation of spending time with a much older woman warmed him from the inside out.

However, he was careful about how he should express his feelings this time around because a year before, he had been rushed to the hospital for attempted suicide after Erica had rejected his love. And ever since that time she had been trying to appease her conscience by lavishly spending her money on him. She didn't understand, though, that he didn't care for her money as much as he wanted her heart.

*Erica pushed open the passenger door and said, "I thought I should surprise you and take you for a drive."*

*Dean bent down until his gaze leveled with hers. "I'm heading to the bowling alley with some of my friends."*

*"Get in; I want you to see something," she told him, completely ignoring what Dean had said. "Plus, I got a gift for you."*

*Dean listlessly ran his thumb around the bracelet on his wrist Erica had bought him almost two years to the date of his sixteenth birthday. He knew whenever Erica said that she bought him a 'gift,' it would be a very costly investment. Now, if she'd simply said she had a surprise for him, then he could expect to be taken to lunch, or to a social event of some sort. This time, however, she wanted him to see something, which only could mean that this was her biggest investment yet. He hedged getting into the vehicle because he didn't want to send Erica the wrong message. He was not into her because of her affluent background or what he could amass from it. He simply wanted to spend time with her.*

*"Get in," Erica prompted. "You're going to be excited to see what I've bought you."*

*"Why are you always helping me and buying me stuff?" he asked.*

*"You don't want me to?"*

*"You didn't answer the question."*

*Erica smiled, which seemed to suggest that she didn't intend to. A brief silence ensued, highlighting a sultry R&B compilation that was playing in the background. The lyrics talked about a fire raging in a man that could never be extinguished by water. That fire, Dean perceived, as he homed in on the words, could be equated with the love he had for Erica. It was such a moving song that it began to mess with his emotions.*

*He turned to Erica and asked, "Who's singing this song?"*

*"I knew you would like it," she said. "I liked it too when I heard it for the first time standing in line at a grocery store. It's a new release by an African artist simply known as Bez. So I went out yesterday and bought it."*

*"It has a lot of soul."*

*"Yes, it does," Erica agreed.*

*Dean grinned. "I didn't know first ladies listened to this type of music."*

*"You would be surprised to know what we listen to," Erica joked and then added, "Truthfully, I bought the CD because –"*

*"You knew I would like it," Dean finished for her.*

*Erica blushed. "I wasn't going to say that. I was going to say that I loved the music arrangement and how it puts me in a place of reflection. I think about my marriage; my life, my future...and then there's you. There's a fire burning in all of us, but I don't know what to do with mine..."*

*Dean was about to comment, but Erica cut right back in with a switch of excitement in her voice.*

*"Look to your left!" she instructed him. "Tell me what you see."*

*Dean noticed that they were pulling toward the beach and as far as he could see were the colors, blue, green and aquamarine. Seconds later, Erica brought the car to a stop, which overlooked the Winthrop's B&B. Beyond that, Dean didn't take notice of the spot Erica was trying to get him to see.*

*"What am I supposed to be looking at? he asked. "Because the only thing I see is the ocean."*

*"You men never see anything," Erica said, shaking her head in a mocking manner. "You are looking at a prime piece of property where you will be able to sell your masterpieces, literally just steps away from my bed and breakfast..."*

"Excuse me, sir, the plane is getting ready to land in a few minutes. Please return your tray to its locked position."

Dean's eyes slowly blinked open and instinctively glanced at his wristwatch. It was twenty minutes to seven in the evening. He couldn't believe he'd dozed off for over two hours, thinking about Erica. He looked out the window, noticing the night lights of Miami were slowly coming into view. His connecting flight to Barracuda Cove would land him there in forty-five minutes or less. More than enough time for him to make it to the Bez concert tonight. But Dean wasn't certain he would attend. He never admitted to Erica that he loved Bez more than she did and he didn't want to chance getting caught up in his emotions, sitting next to her in such a romantic atmosphere. He knew his best bet was to avoid Erica and this concert at all costs because she would only continue to break his heart.

# CHAPTER TWENTY-NINE

*Same Hour*

W hen Erica walked through the front door of her palatial home, the air was piping with roasted garlic and cinnamon spices. Frank Sinatra was playing from the speaker above in the ceiling and Erica could hear the faint sounds of someone moving around in the kitchen. The feeling was so bizarre that Erica almost thought she'd walked into the wrong house. There was no way she would ever believe that Magnus was the one behind such an unusual gesture. The man had never cooked a full meal a day in his life. What would cause him to start now? There must be someone else – or rather some woman Magnus had brought in her house to disrespect her.

She moved ahead about fifteen feet and ran into a string of blood-red, rose petals. With her curiosity now in full swing, she decidedly followed the trail, which had started midway from the foyer, ending in her grand dining room. The kitchen was at the opposite side of the house, so she would be unable to see Magnus, if indeed he was in the kitchen preparing food. The dining table, however, was adorned with boutiques of the same blood-red colored roses from one end to the next. Wine glasses, along with a bottle of champagne on ice was set in the center of it all.

Now Erica was thoroughly convinced that she had unquestionably walked into the wrong house. Either that, or Magnus had set up one of his gambling revelries without telling her about it. But Erica thought to herself, *Why would my husband need roses for a gambling party? It doesn't make sense.*

"How was your day, beautiful?"

*Beautiful? This could not be the same man who calls me black and ugly and aloof...*Erica almost snapped her neck as she spun in the direction of her husband's voice. There he stood in front her neatly attired in a black tux, freshly shaved and smiling at her. The feeling of nostalgia washed over her as she remembered Magnus looking similarly on their wedding day, minus his balding head. His powerful personality shone through those beady eyes and gave him confidence to compete with any man on any level.

Magnus' voice rumbled into a quiet laugh. "You look stumped," he said to her.

"That's because I am," Erica shot at him. "What's all this about?"

"Let's just say that this is my way of apologizing for all of the nasty things I've ever said or done to you. I want us to turn over a new leaf and reconnect in the way we used to before all the drama got started. You must realize I am still very much in love with you."

Magnus closed in the distance between him and Erica, attempting to take her by her hands, but she flinched and pulled away. An automatic reaction it was, but true to his unsympathetic nature, he grabbed her hands anyway, locking them into his in the way he'd done when they said their wedding vows.

"Let's stop the fighting and start over," he said. "I hate to see the way our marriage is deteriorating."

"You said that the last time and the time before that," Erica said. "What makes you think it's going to be different this time around?"

"I can't say it will be different, but I'm praying that it will. Don't you want our marriage to work?"

"I don't know, Magnus. You can't come at me out of the blue acting all nice and stuff and expect for me to forget all the hurtful things you've said and done to me."

"I don't expect you to forgive me just like that; but I am asking you to give our marriage a chance. Have dinner with me. I've cooked you a very tasty meal."

*A very tasty meal...*Those words lingered in Erica's mind. The only thing she could think about why Magnus was being so nice all of a sudden was because he'd wanted to poison her, hoping she would die in her sleep. Magnus did not cook, which was the first red flag.

"I'm not hungry," she spat. "And furthermore, I have plans already set for tonight, for which I'll be late if I don't leave in thirty minutes. So please excuse me; I need to take a shower."

Erica was half expecting Magnus to draw back and slap the taste out of her mouth, but to her astonishment, he simply smiled, leaned over and kissed her on the cheek.

"At least I tried," he told her. "I won't detain you any longer. But know that I won't stop trying until you begin to trust me again. I will put the food in the fridge in case you want to eat later."

Erica didn't know what to say. The man standing before her was not the same man who had pushed her head in a toilet filled with urine a few weeks ago. He had to be an imposter, pretending to be her husband because Magnus would have never allowed her to talk to him the way she did. But she was counting on his negative reaction so that she could have some footage to give to her lawyer. She'd planted a few small cameras around the house the night before while Magnus was out with his gambling buddies. However, it looked as if Magnus was already onto her ruse because he was acting too nice.

"You're not upset?" Erica couldn't help but ask the question. She was just too suspicious of Magnus' calm behavior.

"Should I be upset?" he rejoined.

"I don't know...I've gotten so used to you knocking me about at what you perceive as the slightest disrespect, but all of a sudden, you're unbothered. Honestly, I find that very unsettling."

"I love you more than you know – both you and our son. I would do anything for you two, which includes taking a thorough introspection of my life. I've discovered that I haven't always been a good husband or father. But as of tonight, things will change. And to show you how serious I am, I want you to call Tavian and tell him that he can come home. I don't have a problem with him wanting to pursue his spiritual calling. Who am I to say that God hasn't anointed him to preach?"

The hairs stood up on the back of Erica's neck. "How did you know that? Did Tavian call you?"

"No..."

"Well, he told me you called him."

Magnus stumbled for the right words. "I may have called him, or he may have called me...I don't remember. But we did not get into any detailed discussion about his future. I just know my son. I've always known that he wanted to be a preacher like his daddy. I'm saying he can. Tell him I won't be upset if he decides to come home."

*If you knew our son wanted to be a preacher, why the hell did you ship him off to Canada and force him to study engineering?* Erica wanted to ask, but instead, she searched Magnus' eyes for his usual hints of deception, but she couldn't detect anything except for that unnerving smile. That smile, though, was all she needed to know that the real Magnus hadn't gone anywhere. Sooner or later, something would make him flip and he would return to beast mode.

"Well, I can't talk about any of this right now," Erica said. "I have to prepare for my event tonight." She walked off, but paused right after as if forgetting something. "And just in case some silly rumor gets back to you, I want you to know that Dean might accompany me tonight. We are going to celebrate his success."

"Oh?"

Erica rolled her eyes. "I'm sure you are aware that Mr. Osprey offered him the contract."

Of course, Magnus knew. He was the one who'd instructed Gavin to do it. He simply shrugged his shoulders as if it wasn't a big deal. "It's fine with me. That boy loves you like a son."

"That's really okay with you?" Erica asked. "Because for years you've been accusing me of having romantic feelings for Dean. And I've never known you to change your feelings about any matter overnight. Especially where it concerns Dean."

Magnus kept that crazy smile going. "I realize my jealous streak was only putting a wedge between you and me. You are a faithful wife. Call me blind, stupid, whatever you want, I just want you to know that I believe you would never cheat on me. I am trying to change for the better, so we can save our marriage."

*You must think I'm an idiot to believe that mess,* Erica said to herself. The fact that Magnus had alluded to her faithfulness in their marriage suggested to Erica that Magnus was up to something and that she should continually be on guard.

"I don't understand why you would even bring that up," she snapped. "You know I have been faithful to you from the day we got married. So let's not go there. It's your behavior that's questionable, coming home all hours of the night, drunk as a skunk. Belligerent and completely out of control. How can I be sure that you're not only gambling my money away but also using that as an excuse to sleep around? In fact, I'm inclined to believe that you are having an extramarital affair, though I can't prove it – yet."

Magnus chuckled. He sensed Erica was intentionally trying to bait him into a rage. Not happening, even though the tips of his ears were already burning with anger.

"It seems as if you're trying to get me to fight with you," he said measurably. "Go to your event, if you must, but I will not let you spoil a good evening with your unforgiving heart."

Magnus spun on his heel and walked out of the dining room.

Erica ran behind him and yelled, "I have every right to be unforgiving. You hurt me; practically destroyed my self-esteem and you expect me to forget what you've done? I can see through this phony display of a truce. You don't mean it...you must think I'm stupid if you believe I would ever trust you again!"

Magnus sped up his strides and disappeared through the French doors of his office. Had he turned to address his wife's impertinence, he would have shattered her nose into pieces. But he was not going to give Erica what she wanted, which was to trap him in an indisputable show of domestic violence. He was too smart and too close to embroiling Erica in her own lust for Dean to make such a dumb mistake.

Curbing her steps at the French doors, Erica squeezed her fists and screamed, frustrated that she'd allowed Magnus to get beneath her skin before she could get to him. The audacity of that man to point out her unforgiving heart when he had the heart of a beast! She could see that he was upset, but somehow he was able to display great control over his emotions. Such control could only last so long, Erica thought, as she marched up the stairs to her bedroom. She would not stop provoking him until he snapped like the weak twig he was.

✳✳✳

Thirty minutes later, Magnus was relieved when he heard the front door slam. He ran toward the eastern window of their living room and stealthy moved the blinds to one side. Erica had just climbed into the Mercedes and was reversing into the street. He waited a few more seconds before going back to the dining room. With the bottle of champagne and a tray of food, he walked out the kitchen exit toward the shed.

"The heifer is gone!" he announced loudly. "You can come out!"

The male and female accomplices stepped into view, both looking as if they were about to die from dehydration. They'd been hiding in the cramped shed, knowing it was the safest hiding spot. Minutes before Erica had arrived home, they had used a scanning device to locate audio or visual bugs in the house. They soon discovered that Erica had hidden cameras in several rooms. The device worked so well from distances that they needed not to go into the house, which worked perfectly for them. It meant their presence could never be detected.

Magnus popped open the bottle of champagne. "I think this moment calls for a celebration."

"I'm down with that!" the female cackled. "I thought that witch would never leave. I was sweating like a pig in that shed."

"I don't know if we should celebrate just yet," the young man interjected.

Magnus peered down at him. "Why not? My wife going to that concert tonight has practically signed her divorce papers. There is no way those two will be able survive that romantic atmosphere unscathed. They will give in."

The young man pointed at the female. "I guess she didn't inform you that Dean hasn't been seen for days. In fact, his kiosk has been shut down since Tuesday and he hasn't been seen around by friends and family. So, we are of the assumption that he is not on the island."

"Either that or he's lying dead in the pit somewhere," the female joked, squeezing Magnus' arm. "Lily must have found out about his obsession for your wife."

The female squelched her laughter when she saw the seriousness in Magnus' eyes.

"Don't be stupid," he lashed out at her. "Without Dean, the plan won't work. Why am I just finding this out?"

"Keep your pajamies on," she told Magnus. "I did my research and discovered that Dean has gone to Canada with Lily. Apparently, Lily's job sent her over there for a few weeks and I assume Dean wanted to accompany her to settle her in. But he will be here; in fact, his flight should be landing as we speak."

"How can you be so sure?" Magnus questioned.

Netty batted her eyes in a seductive manner. "Don't question my tactics. I have my ways. Those boys at the ticket counter will give you the information you want if you play your cards right."

Magnus didn't bother to question any further because he understood that they all did things they needed to for the good of the team.

"I'm not certain that Dean will be attending that concert," the young man chimed back in. "If his plane is just landing now, he's already half an hour late."

"You're missing the bigger picture," the female said. "Does it really matter if Dean makes it to the concert? Lily will be off the island for at least three weeks, which means we have a lot of time to work on our plan."

"I don't want to wait an additional three weeks for something to happen," Magnus spat. "We've waited long enough. I want to see results tonight and you two had better see to it that it does. I'm not paying you all of this money to procrastinate and have this plan blow up in my face. That heifer is determined to destroy me, and I'll be damned if I allow her to get the upper hand."

The young man told Magnus, "I will ensure you get the footage you want. So I'll go to the concert and keep tabs on your wife."

"No, send her," Magnus said. "I want you to stay with me."

The female glanced back and forth between the men in a suspicious manner. She got the distinct feeling that Magnus didn't want her around and she was quick to assume his reasons had much to do with his bloody lust for this pompous young bloke standing in front of her.

"And what good would that do?" she fired. "If Erica sees me at that concert, I am screwed."

"She has a point," the young man said. "It is better that I go. I will do my best to make sure she doesn't recognize me. I will have an alibi if I happen to run into Erica by accident."

Magnus grated his teeth in frustration. It seemed as if every opportunity he had alone with the male accomplice, was rudely infringed upon by this obnoxious chick. He was growing increasingly impatient with her. With a quick flick of his wrist, he agreed to the plan.

"Let's meet up tomorrow at our place of business," he said to them. "I need to be alone for tonight."

The female smirked and then walked off without another word. She knew Magnus would strangle her with his bare hands, if he could. But she couldn't care less about how he felt about her. She was not about to allow Magnus' sick obsession for this young boy rob her of her part of the deal. In fact, she had devised a plan of her own, which she was about to execute in short order.

# CHAPTER THIRTY

*Vancouver, Canada – Same Time*

The coffee and donut shop on 2902 Main Street was a cozy hangout spot for the local residents. It served some of the tastiest combinations, like Venezuelan Coffee and Pumpkin Cheesecake Donut, which were two of Lily's favorites. Before she'd migrated to Barracuda Cove, it was always what she ordered when she came to this spot. It was her comfort food, obviously not exactly the healthiest choice but she needed an outlet when dealing with parents like her own. She would sit here for hours, munching on her donut and drumming up ways to escape her miserable upbringing. It was only when she landed a 50-hour-a-week job at the bank that she was able to put some distance between her and her parents. So, this place was not unfamiliar to her.

The time on her wristwatch showed 8:11p.m. She'd not too long gotten off from work and she would have sat on the outside away from the bustling crowd, but the November chilly temperatures discouraged her. She found a recently-vacant table roughly ten feet from the cashier. Not the best view, but she was still able to observe her surroundings. It seemed as if everyone was involved in animated conversation with open laptops in front of them. Mind you, she had one in front of her too, but she hadn't any choice. Her presentation for a manager's briefing was due at eight o'clock tomorrow morning and she hadn't even gotten through half of it.

She was beginning to loath her job as an International Project Management Consultant. It took too much of her personal time. She hadn't a problem with it before meeting Dean and moving to Barracuda Cove because it was one way to avoid her parents. Now that her priorities had changed, her ideals were changing. She was not as career-driven as she'd been eighteen months before. In fact, when she'd opted to migrate to Barracuda Cove, part of the deal was that her traveling from one city to another would be scratched from her job description. But she'd been accosted by upper management to fulfil the assignment for one final time before tying the knot with Dean.

Even so, three weeks away from Dean was not what she needed right now, especially when she was still feeling suspicious about some areas of Dean's past. He'd blatantly lied to her and was beginning to treat her like she was a mosquito on his neck. When he offered to accompany her to Canada and spend a few days with her, she assumed that he wanted to smooth things over with her. But Dean remained evasive, short-answering her questions, even about the planning of their wedding. She soon discovered that he didn't really tag along with her to Canada because he really wanted to; he was using that as an excuse to avoid facing his mother. By the time he was ready to go back to Barracuda Cove, Lily was petrified over her future with Dean.

Right now as she sat sipping on her Venezuelan Coffee, her heart was heavy from the last conversation she'd had with Dean at the airport where she'd dropped him off several hours ago during her lunchbreak. His lies about the bracelet were not as hurtful as the way he seemed anxious to get away from her. She was seriously considering at this point if it was wise to even tell her parents she was getting married because there may not be a wedding anyway.

"I can't believe you're still not being upfront with me," she had said to Dean after a few minutes of stiff silence.

Hot air flew out of Dean's nostrils. "Lily Rose, I never knew how determined you were until I gave you that bracelet."

"I've told you, this isn't so much about the bracelet as it is about your attitude. You are being so overprotective of someone you consider to be in your past. What is it about this girl that is so special. Are you still in love with her? Let me know now so that I can make a decision on whether to go ahead with this marriage."

"What is that supposed to mean?"

"I want you to tell me the truth! Do I have your heart or not?"

"What else do you want me to say?"

"Start by giving me a name and convince me that I won't have to compete with this girl for your heart."

Dean's jaw tightened. "Wendy...her name is Wendy Fields. She was one of my high school crushes. The bracelet was a gift."

"Did you love her?"

"No."

"Then why did you accept the gift?"

*"I don't know...her father was rich, and she had no qualms spending the money. I was sixteen and I didn't think it meant anything."*

*Lily dabbed at her tear-filled eyes. She was crying because she knew Dean was lying to her and she couldn't understand why. Shortly after, she swung the rental car into the departure lane, parking in the offloading zone.*

*"Can't you stay a few more days,"* she asked in a saddened tone.

*"As much as I want to, Lily, I have to get back to the island. I have a huge decision hanging over my head and I'm not going to get anything done staying here. Please understand that. Wasn't four days enough? I can't stay, okay?"*

"Excuse me. I couldn't help but notice the bracelet you're wearing. My friend has one just like it."

Lily snapped out of her depressed thoughts and stared up at the young man's baffled expression. "I'm sorry, do I know you?"

The young man extended his hand for a handshake. "Pardon me, my name is Tavian Winthrop. I don't mean to intrude, but I couldn't help but notice that bracelet –"

Lily interrupted him, "I'm still stuck on your name," she said, pinning him with a studious look. "Tavian Winthrop?"

"Yes."

"As in the son of Apostle Magnus Winthrop and Lady Erica Winthrop?"

"Yes."

"And you're going to school here in Canada, right?"

Tavian managed a little chuckle and then jokingly said, "Do I need to call my lawyer? I feel as if am being accused of murder."

Lily laughed, despite her shock. She'd heard Dean mentioned Tavian a few times in their conversation, but she never got a chance to see a picture of him. The man standing in front of her could pass for Dean's brother. The only difference was that Tavian's complexion was two shades lighter and he donned a low crew cut as opposed to the mohawk that Dean wore.

"I'm sorry...my rudeness is so evident," Lily fumbled. "Do you want to sit? I am just blown away that I ran into you like this."

"Technically, I ran into you," Tavian quipped as he took a seat in the chair opposite Lily. "I feel rather uncomfortable that you know so much about me and I don't have a clue to who I have the pleasure of meeting. Could you please be so kind and put me out my misery?"

Lily couldn't stop the sides of her mouth from twitching. "You are so polite...I would have never known you were related to the Winthrops...I mean I can see your mother's eyes and your father's complexion, but your disposition is so different from theirs."

"I would like to comment on that, but please tell me who you are. The suspense is killing me."

"Oh...I'm running my mouth...I'm so sorry...such terrible habits. My name is Lily Rose Tremblay and I was born and raised right here in Vancouver. But I migrated to Barracuda Cove almost two years ago now, where I've met the man of my dreams. We're getting married in a few months."

Tavian smiled patiently at Lily as she rambled on again. She was easy to relate to and had the most beautiful grey eyes he'd ever seen on a white girl, which lit up when she talked about the man of her dreams.

"I'm still trying to figure out how you met my parents," Tavian said once Lily gave him an opportunity to speak.

"Didn't I tell you? I met them through my fiancé, Dean Ripley."

Tavian sat up straight. "Hold up...you're engaged to Dean?"

"Yes...he mentioned to me that you two were very good friends."

"I would like to think that we still are," Tavian said. "Dean is like a brother to me; he partially grew up in my house...this is a small world."

"Dean didn't tell you about me?"

Tavian didn't know how to answer that question. Right before his father had shipped him off to Canada, he and Dean had the biggest fight and ever since then Dean hadn't spoken to him. But what more could Tavian do if Dean refused to accept the olive branch? Obviously, Dean wouldn't have said anything about Lily because that would mean Dean would have to admit to Tavian that he was no longer obsessed with Tavian's mother. Tavian knew better. Dean avoided him because he knew Tavian would continue to press the truth out of him.

"Dean and I grew apart as we got older," Tavian said. "So I don't hold it against him why he didn't mention he was getting married."

"I understand..." Lily was too giddy with meeting another Winthrop for her to read anything deeper into Tavian's words. "So," she said in an inquisitive tone. "It makes sense that you would be familiar with this bracelet. Dean gave it to me – well, after I nagged him to death about who'd bought it for him. But he is being so tightlipped about it and I'm afraid I've aggravated him to no end. It's a very costly piece of jewelry to give a sixteen-year-old, and I know my perception is probably twisted because of the way I grew up, but I'm simply baffled by that."

Tavian said, without much thought about the repercussions of his response, "When it comes to Dean or myself, my mother doesn't care about how expensive something is. If she wants us to have it; she will make sure we do."

Lily felt as if the insides of her stomach had dropped to the floor. Had Tavian just implied that his mother had bought Dean that bracelet? If that was the case, it certainly explained the reason behind Dean's evasiveness. Why did he even bother to tell her that some Wendy chick had bought it for him when he could have simply told her the truth? She would have been okay with that, but Dean's action raised a lot of suspicion in her mind.

In fact, she'd even shown Erica the bracelet and Erica acted as if she'd never seen it before. That was downright evil and calculating in Lily's eyes. There was no way she could look at Erica the same way ever again. Something was going on between those two and they didn't want her to know.

"You look as if you've seen a ghost all of a sudden," Tavian said, his caring gaze piercing her. "Did I say something I shouldn't have said?"

Lily couldn't bring herself to speak for several seconds and when she did, she was choked with tears. "Both your mother and

Dean have played me for a fool...how gullible I have been to not see their lies for what they were." She stood up abruptly, knocking the remnants of her coffee to the floor. "I'm sorry, but I have to leave..."

Realizing the damage he'd done, Tavian sprang to his feet too. "I didn't mean to upset you. Please let me apologize and make it up to you."

"You've done enough," Lily said.

Tavian insisted, "I'm sorry...let me help...please..."

Lily glared at Tavian. She couldn't blame him for what he'd revealed, especially when she was the one who'd pushed him to reveal such information. Furthermore, she couldn't resist his handsome features, which were mixed with a distinguished air. She could tell that his apology was sincere and that he truly wanted to make things right.

"Give me your phone number," she said. "I will call you later. But I really need some time alone right now."

"I understand...I will pray for your strength."

"Thank you."

Lily grabbed her laptop and her handbag. She vanished through the exit before Tavian could say another word to her. When she made it to her rental car, she released a torrent of heart-wrenching tears. How could she have not seen this one coming?

# CHAPTER THIRTY-ONE

E rica was about ten minutes away from the Bez concert. She should be excited about meeting one of her favorite artists in person, but her thoughts were a cluster of confusion. The fact that she was still fuming over the argument she'd had with Magnus left her trying to figure out what was truly going on with him. He did not give in to her provocation, no matter how hard she tried to push him over the cliff. It was not like her husband at all to hold back his wrath and the only thing she could gather from that was Magnus was covering his bases.

Erica had to ask herself for the tenth time if Magnus had somehow found out about the cameras she'd hidden throughout the home. It was the only explanation she could think of that would prevent Magnus from acting out. And this angered her, because she knew if she didn't get any footage of her husband's abuse, she and her lawyer had no case against him. And God forbid if Magnus' plan to expose her secrets to the world ever came to light. The judge would toss her out of the court himself without giving her much of anything.

As grim as the picture appeared in Erica's mind, she refused to allow herself to slip into a defeated mindset. There had to be other ways to trap her husband in his own folly. Right now she needed to put these thoughts aside and focus on enjoying the concert. But it wasn't as easy to rally her emotions, especially when there were so many other things making her depressed. She looked down at the two concert tickets that were on the passenger seat. Letting out a deep sigh, she reached for them. It appeared as if she would be going to the concert alone. Netty was probably still in the hospital recovering from the shock of being pregnant and Dean had yet to respond to her texts.

It pained her to know that one of the tickets would not be honored because she knew Netty had paid a lot of money to get them. Maybe if she could sell one of the tickets to someone or get someone else to tag along with her, she wouldn't feel so bad. Her mind went to Justin Knox, who undoubtedly would enjoy an event like this, seeing that he didn't get to go out much. But Erica felt it was too late in the game to consider such an option. However, when she pulled toward the gates of the Red Cross compound and saw that there was a long line of vehicles ahead of her, Erica felt her hope returning. It looked as if it would be another fifteen minutes before she would be able to get in, which was enough time for Justin to make the commute from the bed and breakfast to where she was. She grabbed her cell phone and called her company's phone number.

"A pleasant good evening. Welcome to Winthrop's Bed and Breakfast; this is Justin Knox speaking. How may I serve you?"

Erica smiled each time she heard Justin repeat the company's greeting. It had taken him a whole day to perfect it. "Hey, Justin. How do you feel about accompanying me to a concert tonight?"

There was a slight pause on Justin's end. "Um, yeah...sure..."

"You don't sound too excited."

"I am. It's just that I'm the only one here, holding it down for now."

Erica's brows knitted with confusion. "What happened to Ian and Sandra? Ian's shift should have started an hour ago."

"Both of them called in. Ian said he would be late because he got a flat tire. Sandra said that her daughter suddenly came down with a high fever and she won't be coming in."

"This is crazy. Those two seem to be missing a lot these days. I will have to deal with that when I return on Monday."

"It's okay...I'm holding it down."

"But you've been at that place since ten o'clock this morning," Erica said. "I don't expect you to pull anyone else's weight."

"I know, but you know I have no problem watching over your place. You're the closest thing I will ever have to family."

"Justin, you don't have to feel obligated or keep on thanking me for giving you a job. You have already proven your loyalty in so many ways. I was hoping you would be able to accompany me to this concert tonight. But it looks as if that won't be happening."

"I am so sorry, Mrs. Winthrop. As soon as Ian shows, I will come."

"Whatever time that turns out to be," Erica said. "Don't worry about it."

"I want to come. Just tell me where to meet you."

Erica let out a sigh. "I will leave a ticket for you at the gate in my name."

Erica disconnected from the line with her frustration mounting. Nothing appeared to be working in her favor tonight. She couldn't help but think that this was a sign that something ominous was on the horizon and that there would be nothing she could do to stop it. She pulled up Dean's WhatsApp and sent him a text:

*Please stop ignoring me; you've made your point. I need you.*

### ✳✳✳

Dean felt his phone vibrating in the palm of his hand but made no haste to address it. His troubled mind, heavy with the woes of his future was beginning to tell on him, there was a sense of him wanting to be left alone. He did not wish to talk to anyone – Lily, his mother, Erica – none of them. Because of them he was currently undergoing one of greatest distresses he'd ever experienced in his twenty-two-year existence. It seemed as if none of them truly understood him or what he truly wanted out of this life. Couldn't they see that they were making things more complicated than they needed to be? He was a simple guy and he didn't ask for much.

His phone vibrated again, actually several times back to back, which eventually lured him away from the headrest of a taxi he'd gotten into after his flight had touched down at the airport in Barracuda Cove. He scanned the WhatsApp notifications. Despite himself, his heart leaped with excitement when he saw Erica's words loading in, even though they were nothing to get excited about. She was irate, and Dean could tell that she was at her wits' end:

*You're not the only one suffering, she texted. I sacrificed my feelings just so that you could be happy. But it is not enough for you, isn't it? You think by not responding to me it is going to change the situation? I will survive, as a matter of fact, I have survived. Even after you marry Lily, I will survive. So go on and throw your tantrums and see how far that gets you.*

Dean smiled. This was the moment he'd been waiting for. Erica was ready to embrace her feelings for him. Each of her words was laced with deep desire, blatantly exposing her vulnerabilities. She no longer cared to be discrete about how she truly felt about him. Feeling as if his heart would pump out of his chest, Dean leaned forward toward the taxi driver.

"How quickly can you get me to the Red Cross compound on Jobson Blvd.?"

The taxi driver looked at the clock on his dashboard. "In twenty minutes. Is that okay?"

"I will pay you double if you get me there in half the time."

The taxi driver swung to the left and made a hard U-turn. Dean flew back into the seat when the taxi driver stomped his foot on the accelerator. It was amazing, Dean thought to himself, what the love of money could do. The anticipation of seeing Erica was more than he could stand. He would give anything to hold her in his arms right now and for as long as the Lord would give him breath. He loved every single cell that had created the stunning Erica Winthrop and there was no way his love for her would ever be abated. Not now; not ever.

# CHAPTER THIRTY-
# TWO

It was almost nine o'clock in the evening when the male accomplice showed up to the Red Cross compound. The atmosphere was lit with excitement. People covered the grounds like ants and at that point the accomplice realized that it would be a challenge locating Erica. And it would be even more of challenge catching her in a compromising position with Dean if the young man did not show up to the concert. And even though the female accomplice had sent a WhatsApp update and told him that Dean's flight from Vancouver came in two hours ago, which should have settled his nerves, the young man knew Dean had a habit of being capricious. So he could not be dependent on chance, but could only hope the events of tonight worked out in his favor.

He jammed his ticket stub into his pocket and began his arduous trek toward the stage. The lady at the booth told him to hold on to it as there would be a grand raffle at the end of the evening. The accomplice paid it little mind because his mission was not to play games but to bring down a powerhouse, who undoubtedly was smarter than Magnus gave her credit for. No one could convince the male accomplice that Erica hadn't changed her phone number and had probably convinced Dean to do the same. This revealed that she was cognizant of Magnus' plan to destroy her. That was why he continued to warn Magnus to refrain from underestimating his wife. But Magnus was too pompous to take wise counsel.

The concert hosts announced that the main act was scheduled to appear on stage in twenty minutes. The crowd went ballistic and began to chant, "Bez, Bez, Bez, Bez!" Their hands striking the air in unison. The accomplice was temporarily paralyzed by the wave of excitement but soon felt someone jerking his arm behind him. He looked around and was stunned to see the female accomplice, giving him the biggest grin ever. She took hold of his arm and dragged him aside, as if that would minimize the noise of the crowd.

"What the hell are you doing here?" he yelled at her.

"I thought you would be happy to see me," she yelled back.

"But didn't you say it was risky showing up here? What if Erica sees you? It's bad enough that I'm here."

"She won't see me. The ground is too thick with people. Besides, I won't be staying long…"

The crowd simmered down as the final local act mounted the stage. Once they were through, the host announced that Bez would take over the remaining hours and mesmerize the crowd with his soulful ballets. The female accomplice was happy she didn't have to yell at this point because she'd come to this concert for one purpose – to strike a deal with her male counterpart.

"So," she questioned, her eyes infused with mischief, "how much is Magnus paying you to sleep with him?"

The young man slapped a hand over the female's mouth. "What the hell? You crazy? Coming up in here with that nonsense."

She swiped the young man's hand away from her mouth. "I am not stupid. I know you wouldn't do it unless Magnus made you an irresistible offer."

"I don't know what you're talking about."

"Boy, please! Don't lie to me. I see the way that pervert looks at you and the way he touches you when –"

The accomplice goaded the female away from listening ears. "What the hell do you want?" he hissed at her.

"I want half of whatever he's giving you."

"You must be stone crazy. Why can't you be satisfied with what he's giving you?"

"The same reason why you're not. Obviously, you have something Magnus wants that I can't give. And that's a problem. Either you consider my proposal or there will be hell to pay. I ain't loyal to no one when it comes to what I want."

The young man was not one who gave in easily to threats. He narrowed his murderous gaze at the female and spat, "Get lost! Because you have already crossed the boundary of my patience."

The female backed away, that mischievous smirk never leaving her eyes. The young man took a minute to recalibrate his thoughts. It was just like that ungrateful chick to distract him from the assignment at hand. She had no business inquiring into his private affairs and for that reason alone, he would ask

Magnus to pay her out and let her not be a part of the plan. She was too sneaky to be trusted. He sent a quick text to Magnus:

*Be on the lookout; we have been double crossed by our own.*

As the accomplice shifted his attention back to the concert, he was again distracted, but this time by the familiar gait of a young man. Walking with purpose and with an air of confidence that suggested to the accomplice that the man was indeed the infamous Mr. Dean Ripley. And if the young man's gait wasn't enough, the mohawk certainly sealed the deal. The accomplice fell in behind the strides of the young man, weaving in and out of the lively crowd.

Like a bee drawn to honey, Dean seemed to possess an uncanny ability to locate Erica wherever she was. Because it was not until the accomplice saw Dean moving to the very front of the stage that he spotted Erica, sitting in one of the VIP seats.

**✳✳✳**

Magnus couldn't sit down. He paced the floor of his living room back and forth, waiting for the news that his wife had taken the bait. He was already imagining how his life would be once that heifer was out of it for good. He'd even thought about taking a three-month hiatus from church leadership to enjoy an extended vacation on the other side of the world. Those bunch of scallywags wouldn't miss him anyway. He would then convince the male accomplice to tag along and they both could bask in their hedonistic desires for each other without having to hide it from anyone. Certainly, Magnus had his plan all figured out and he couldn't think of a single thing that could go wrong.

That was until he checked his WhatsApp message, which could have been the twentieth time in ten minutes. Finally, a text from the male accomplice, which simply read:

*Be on the lookout; we have been compromised by our own.*

Magnus' brows furrowed as he texted in response:

*What has that heifer done now?*

Several minutes later, the male accomplice responded:

*We can't trust her; she was here at the concert, threatening to expose us if we don't give her what she wants.*

*What does she want?*

*More money.*

Magnus let loose a string of invectives before he typed: *That ungrateful sea witch! We are too close for her to mess up all my hard work. Where the hell is she?*

*I don't know; she left almost thirty minutes ago.*

*Forget her! Focus on my wife.*

*I am...I'm sitting about thirty feet from her.*

*Is Dean there with her?*

*Yes.*

Magnus could have jumped up and clapped his feet at that point.

*What are they doing now?* he typed.

*Well, they are sitting next to each other; not really talking to each other. I guess the music is too loud. Wait...Dean just reached over and grabbed your wife's hand...and she did not reject him...*

Magnus' fingers shook with excitement, making it hard for him to type his response. He wouldn't get the chance anyway because when he heard his front door slam, fear caused him to drop his phone to the floor.

"Who the hell is that?" he yelled.

Magnus heard heels, tapping with a slow pace against his porcelain tiles. His first reaction was to run and hide, but the man in him wanted to prove that he wasn't a coward. He stepped toward the entrance of his living room and paused when Netty appeared in his view.

"I'm sure your boy toy informed you by now of my humble request," she said. "So I won't make this long. Whatever you offered him, I want you to match it. In fact, I will make you a better offer. Half a mil, and you will never have to worry about me exposing this wicked plan against your wife. Just in case you have forgotten; she is my best friend."

Magnus stared at Netty in shock before he suddenly exploded in laughter.

"This is not a laughing matter," Netty said.

"I have to laugh, because either you're plain stupid or stone drunk to walk up in here and put demands on me. Who the hell you think you are? You ungrateful, two-faced whore!"

Netty smirked. "Your wife may be afraid of you, but you don't intimidate me, Magnus. The mere fact that you're yearning to have sex with men – or maybe you already are doing it –the way you've been touching that young boy every chance we get together, not only shows how much of a pervert you are, but your penchant for filth. I could destroy you, just like that."

Magnus was smirking too, but inside of him every blood vessel was about to burst with rage. He may have his weaknesses, as Netty so wickedly pointed out, but there was another side to him that Netty had yet to experience. The devil himself.

Magnus said in an unhurried tone, "I am not giving you a dime more than what was agreed upon in your initial contract. Now get out of my presence while you have a chance to leave here alive."

Netty grinned. "Will you kill the mother of your unborn child? Actually, we will be the proud parents of two bouncing little angels. How can you deny me and our babies what rightly belongs to us?"

Magnus's fair complexion seemed to turn blue when he heard the shocking announcement. "You are a slut by nature," he growled in a seething tone. "Those illegitimate bastards could not and will never be mine. So to answer your question: a resounding yes, I will kill you and those undeveloped monsters without a second thought."

"You really must think I'm joking with you. Your threats don't mean a bloody thing to me! I have the power to bring you down and you dare stand there and defy me? I thought your lust would have been your biggest demon, but it seems as if your arrogance –"

Netty didn't get the opportunity to finish her rant. Magnus sprang forward punched her squarely in the mouth. She flew off her feet and landed on her back. Magnus straddled her and continued to rain down right and left hooks to Netty's face. They were coming so fast and so hard that she felt as if Magnus was going to punch her eyes out of her head. Her handbag hung loosely on her left wrist. She managed to single-handedly pull it toward her and fished into it for her handgun.

When Magnus caught wind of the weapon, it was inches from his face. Feverishly, Netty worked to pull the lever but Magnus was too quick. He grabbed her hand and tried to wrestle the gun away from her. Like two well-trained warriors they contended. Netty desperately wanted to live and Magnus desperately wanted her to die. Adrenaline pumped into every second, transforming the atmosphere into an animalistic showdown of unshakeable grit. The survival of the fittest would emerge with their life intact.

Suddenly, two shots rang out and then a third. Both bodies stilled on top of each other as blood quickly spread beneath them onto the floor. Three shots that would change the course of this night forever.

# EPILOGUE

Faint sounds from the 'Bez' concert could be heard all the way into the neighborhood where Dean lived, but the loud, prevailing prayers of Freda Ripley were able to drown them out. She'd been shaken awake by another one of those frightening dreams. It was not just her son's destiny that was in peril. This time, however, the images showed the entire island of Barracuda Cove trapped in a conundrum of sins, on the brink of total moral collapse. The affluent and poor alike would not be able to escape the encumbering forces behind gambling, sexual sins and religious desecration unless someone was willing to stand in the gap and intercede for the island.

The burden had rested upon Freda and at one point it became so heavy that she moved from her kneeling position and laid prostrate on the cold floor. Moaning like a woman with labor pains.

*Lord, she wailed, remember my island in the midst of Your wrath. I plead for Your mercies to prevail. We need You to intervene before we destroy ourselves. The devil is masquerading in the church as an angel of light, but there is gross darkness among the people. They are blind, wretched and deceived. Raise up true servants of Yours who will show the people their sins! You still expect us to live holy for You are holy.*

301

*This island needs to repent before You and ask for forgiveness. Help us, Lord! Help my son. Help the first lady. The devil is working overtime to deceive them. Don't allow them to be swept away by the corruptness that is on this island...Oh, Jesus, we need You! Oh, Jesus, we need You! If You don't show up, this island will surely perish in her sins!*

### ✳✳✳

In Vancouver, Canada the spirit of God had rested heavily upon Tavian as well. He paced the floor with his hands held high in the air, tears streaming down his face. There was a sudden compulsion to return to Barracuda Cove and he knew it was the Holy Spirit impressing upon his heart. The only thing he could mutter in that moment were words of surrender:

*Yes, Lord, I will go, I will do Your bidding. I will confront the evil of Barracuda Cove and the gross sins of my father!*

### ✳✳✳

**Things are about to get even more heated in the second half of this riveting saga, 'Married to the Devil 2'. You will discover all the answers to your questions, including:**

- Will Magnus survive this treacherous night to follow through with his evil plan against his wife? Or will Erica get the upper hand over her husband?

- Will Netty and her babies survive to expose Magnus?

- Dean and Erica seem to be in the right place, at the right time to end the night in a way that could change their lives forever. Will they give in and risk it all in the name of love?

- Tavian's divine assignment is leading him to establish a church when he gets back home to Barracuda Cove. Will he find acceptance or will he discover that his desire for a holy revolution is rejected by the masses?

- Lily has just found out that Erica was the one who had purchased the bracelet Dean had persistently lied to her about. How will this information affect her relationship with Dean?

- Who is the male accomplice aiding Magnus in his evil plans?

If you have enjoyed the story so far, please let me know by leaving a review. I truly appreciate you taking a few minutes to do so. You can subscribe to my list HERE, if you haven't already done so, so that you can get an automatic email to be informed of the release of "Married to the Devil", book 2. Your email address will never be shared, and you can unsubscribe at any time. Much blessings to you and your family!

Made in the USA
Middletown, DE
07 August 2022

70744108R00184